Twi

The Girl Who Uncovered Rumpelstiltskin's Name

CU00894849

Bonnie M Hennessy

Printed by Createspace

An Amazon.com Company

Charleston SC

Bonnie Marie Hennessy

ISBN: 978-1539753421

Dedication Page

I dedicate this book to my husband, Jimmy, and my children, Molly and Seamus, who have given up the computer and their hold on me for more hours than I dare to admit while I reimagined this tale.

Contents

Some day you will be old enough to start reading fairy tales again.

C.S. Lewis

Chapter 1
A Cup of Tea

The morning mist had almost lifted in the village of Stanishire, the farmers and fishermen were readying the market, women were shouting chores to sleepy children, and Aoife was on her way to collect her father from the town brothel, where the painted ladies entertained men's nocturnal needs.

When she reached the main street, she dismounted and tied her horse to a hitching post. She walked around the corner of the brothel where no one could see her, adjusted her skirt, and ran her fingers through her hair. Practice had taught her how to jiggle the finicky latch so its reluctant grip released and granted her entrance. The back hallway was dark and quiet. Maggie, the young girl who helped cook and clean, was opening windows to release the sweat and perfume-laced air. Broken glass littered the floor, and cards from unfinished games lay scattered on tables.

"Maggie," Aoife whispered.

Maggie turned into the dust motes in a sliver of daylight. Over the years, Aoife had learned to call her gently and not to sneak up on her lest she startle the young girl as she had done the first time they met here when Aoife was eleven and Maggie just nine.

"Eeeeef-uh!" Maggie's eyes lit up as she called Aoife's name. She had always over-enunciated each syllable in what sounded like a sigh of relief.

She took hold of Aoife's hand, pulling her around the corner and into the kitchen, one of the only places in the residence that passed for a respectable room.

"Wait here," Maggie said, kissing Aoife on the cheek. "I'll be right back."

Aoife looked around at the pots hanging on the wall that Maggie kept so shiny. A rolling pin on the counter was coated with flour and the smell of bread baking in the oven filled the dimly lit room. In the corner was Maggie's chair with a basket of women's stockings waiting to be darned. Aoife turned her back to the parlor door and everything that happened there, pretending her visits with Maggie by the fire were no different than visits with the other village girls. The sight of Maggie humming as she patched up stockings always made Aoife think of her younger sister, Tara, lying under her heavy blankets, sewing away at some pattern their mother had her working on. Aoife felt that Tara and Maggie would have enjoyed chatting over their sewing, if only Tara were not stuck in bed with a perpetual cough and Maggie the progeny of a brothel.

"Aoife. You look quite bright and alive considering the early hour."

2

Aoife jumped as Maeve strolled over and pulled a leaf from Aoife's hair.

"I see you've been busy with your studies," Maeve added.

Aoife touched her hair, searching for more debris. Maeve's dressing gown exposed her cleavage and her long, dark curls draped over her bare shoulders without apology. Aoife had seen her dressed, powdered, and painted since she was a girl, and she admired the way her gaze, so piercing, seemed to command respect from everyone. But what had captivated Aoife the most was something more powerful and more impressive than Maeve's beauty. Although crow's feet now punctuated her eyes, and her waistline had thickened, the most powerful men deferred to her, bowing their heads in her direction when she traveled through the streets.

"I couldn't resist the path through the woods," Aoife replied, knowing she could hide nothing from her.

Maeve stared at her. The affection in her appraisal was always slightly distant, stopping just short of motherly.

"Seamus is taking care of things," Maeve said with her usual calm.

Aoife nodded and looked again at the shiny pots, trying to focus on anything but Seamus' highly embarrassing ritual of waking her father, the fairly infamous Finnegan, from wherever he had ended his evening and saddling him on his horse. Maggie pulled a loaf of steaming bread from the oven and set out plates, knives, and a bowl of fresh butter. Each of them took their place around the table as Maggie generously portioned out the bread. Maeve let her shawl fall over the back of her chair and straightened up her shoulders, exposing even more of herself. Aoife flushed and bit quietly into her bread, savoring the flavor and the moment.

There was an honesty and warmth in this kitchen that she never felt in the presence of her own mother. Conversation and warm bread were what made coming to get her father for all these years worth the lashings she used to receive from her mother when she returned home.

"I hear that your latest suitor was seen heading out of town yesterday," Maeve said. "I gather his hasty departure means that there will be no nuptials?"

Aoife shook her head and cast a quick smile at Maggie.

"I can't imagine why you didn't want to marry that one," Maeve said. "Lots of gold, a manor house to the east with more land than you and your horse could ever discover, and handsome, too. What more could a girl want than a man with piles of gold and a good set of teeth?"

"A man who is blind and deaf and preferably feeble – with deep pockets, of course. Then I can live my life in peace and never have to worry about his teeth – or mine for that matter."

Maggie giggled, and Maeve raised an appreciative eyebrow, offering her signature half-smile, half-smirk. Aoife grinned and took another bite of the steaming bread.

"And what do your parents say?" Maeve asked. Her features had softened, but her thoughts remained inscrutable. "I can't imagine they find your refusals as entertaining as we do."

Aoife fell silent. This was an unexpected detour in the script. They avoided direct references to Aoife's family. It made breaking bread between them possible, since the money Maeve took from Aoife's father by night was one of the greatest strains on her family's resources, reputation, and love. The medicine that Tara often went without after her father's reckless trips was reason enough for Aoife to despise Maeve, but she had learned to avoid dwelling on these realities. She needed Maeve enough to tolerate her father's indiscretions, since rescuing him had now become a means of escaping her life. Discussing her family jeopardized everything.

"Well, no, they are not exactly pleased," Aoife replied, her brashness fading.

Maeve wiped the corner of her mouth and cleared her throat. Something in the air had changed.

"You know, at some point, perhaps sooner than you might expect, they will stop coming. First, the young ones with stacks of gold and good teeth. They have the most fragile egos and will seek out friendlier pastures. Then eventually, even the wrinkly ones, with and without gold, will find calling on you not worth the effort," Maeve paused. "The tales of your beauty will be replaced by tales of new faces with more welcoming smiles. The choices left to you will be slim."

The bread balled up in Aoife's throat. She could have had breakfast in her own home if she wanted this type of talk. She suddenly felt incensed that Madame Maeve dared to criticize her.

"My mother mires me in these traps daily," Aoife dusted the crumbs from her hands. "She appreciates neither the risk to my reputation I take coming here nor the fact that I am the one who has run the farm for years now."

"This is true. Your family would be in the poor house and your sister probably with God if not for your courage and your brains," Maeve said. "But I'm not talking about them. I'm talking about you and your future. You must understand that there are consequences for you, whether you say yes or no to the suitors who come your way."

She raised an eyebrow, which seemed loaded with a warning left to Aoife to decipher. It had a familiar ring to it, like the warnings her mother made so often about the consequences of Aoife's trips to Maeve's house.

"No respectable man will ever want to marry a girl who consorts with vile women, not when he thinks he can pay a few coins for her instead," her mother would say.

Her mother lived in such a dream world she did not recognize that Aoife was trying to protect the family's reputation and as much of their finances as was possible. Her mother worried more about Aoife's reputation than the food on the table and Tara's medicine. And because of that, a chasm had grown between them too deep to ever cross.

"My choices are just as narrow as every other girl's. I know that," Aoife said standing up abruptly. Her shawl dropped to the floor, its power to protect her no match for the storm brewing in the kitchen. "But I'd never compromise myself – or give men control over my body for money like you do. Of that you can be sure."

"I wasn't suggesting that," Maeve replied,

completely unruffled. "But it's interesting that you did. And, Aoife, no matter what choice you make – your husband's house, my house, or the nunnery – you are exchanging control over your body for money. Of that you can be sure."

"I have given half my life already to protecting my family. Everyday, whether I'm seeing that fields are reseeded and sheep are sheared or carting my father home from here, I am picking up the pieces of my family's fortune that my father has broken apart," Aoife said with less command of her voice than she would have liked. "And now, after I've done everything I can to save this family, they – and you – expect me to sell myself off to the next buyer, supposedly to protect them? I can't do it."

Aoife knew there was no way for a woman to survive in the world without the protection of a man, yet the security they offered was never guaranteed. Her father's choices still chipped away at the pieces of what was once her mother, Bronagh. Still bedecked in the jewels of their courtship, she found her only solace and comfort in embroidering ornate and regal designs and patterns by the night fire, awaiting his return from Maeve's as if her delicate hands could somehow stitch back together the girl he had unraveled and the lives he had torn apart at the seams. Bronagh would not even consider selling her tapestries or needlework to help support her family, for that would have been beneath a woman of her status. Aoife, however, was not built to sit and sew while their fortune and Tara's health deteriorated at the hands of her father. She needed to be on her feet fixing the problem, not decorating the home they were sure to lose if no one intervened.

Bronagh had traded away her soul for a broken promise of safety and love, and she expected Aoife to do the same. But now Maeve, too? Her advice was nothing less than a betrayal.

"For women not made to curtsey obediently through life, there is no easy choice." A subtle urgency belied Maeve's calm. "However, refusing every suitor is not a means of controlling your life, but rather giving over control to whatever or whomever is left over."

"So I should marry the next man who comes along or end up in a whore house like you?" Aoife said, wincing at her angry words.

She was angry that Maeve had taken her mother's side, but she did not relish wounding the one person who had always been a source of strength and understanding. Despite her words, Maeve's features revealed not even the slightest hint of hurt.

"What I am saying is that you ought to turn away any option which would leave you without hope of peace and contentment," Maeve replied. "But do not fool yourself into waiting for a perfect choice to present itself, because it never will."

Aoife felt her stomach lurch. She needed to get away from this house, this woman, and the truth. Turning around, she marched outside where her father was standing. She walked to her horse and looked to see if he needed assistance. The legacy of too much mead weighed on his haggard figure as Seamus helped him to his horse.

"I'm so sorry to have inconvenienced you this morning, my sweet Aoife," her father's worn voice eschewed sadly.

"I know, father," she replied. "You're always sorry."

He swayed precariously in either direction and then took Aoife's hand suddenly.

"You're too good to me, Aoife," he whispered. "You should be reaching for the–"

"Stars," she finished. "I know, Father."

He closed his eyes and pressed her hand between his.

"My hand's grown since we spent our nights stargazing."

He nodded and Aoife felt a pang of nostalgia sweep over her. She missed the way he used to pick her up from her mother's side by the fire and take her out of doors to look at the moon and stars. The memory of the polished scent of him from her childhood came back over the stench of mead that clung to him now. He had been a good father once upon a time. She looked up, searching for any fragment of the man who tossed her high in the air as a little girl. The sparkle of a tear danced at the corner of his eye. There he was. She kissed his forehead tenderly and he sighed with the soft smile reserved only for Aoife. His favorite.

Seamus helped him into his saddle. Just as she reached her own horse, Maeve walked out the backdoor, holding Aoife's shawl in her arms like a peace offering. Aoife refused to acknowledge her. She was about to mount her horse when Maeve moved closer to her. She wrapped the shawl around Aoife and pressed her hands gently but firmly upon her shoulders, which softened at the touch. She could not remain angry with Maeve. The precipice upon which Aoife lived her life was not entirely Maeve's fault, although Aoife wished Maeve had not encouraged her to jump. With a light pat to relieve the levity of the moment, Maeve helped her onto her horse.

Aoife heeled her horse and rode away with her father following unsteadily behind. She could feel Maeve watching her ride through the village, like a mother might watch her child ride off on a difficult expedition.

Aoife was treading through Maeve's advice when she felt a change in the air. The eyes of someone in the village were bearing down on her, ignoring the privacy usually afforded her during these trips. She tried to ignore the weight of this peeping Tom's gaze, but its persistence made it impossible. She turned her head and caught sight of the offender; a stranger leaning out the window of a gilded coach stared at her. She locked her eyes upon him, seething with hostility toward him and the whole world for casting her in this role. For a split second, he looked embarrassed, as if caught spying through a keyhole. However, whereas most people would have averted their eyes under Aoife's reproachful glare, this dark eyed man held her gaze. But she had no time for games. She heeled her horse and rode away, leaving her father, the village, and this rude stranger behind.

***

Maeve watched Aoife and her father fade away down the road.

"Madame," the man from the coach called to her. "Could you spare a few moments for the son of Bradyn, the late Duke of Stanishire?"

He wore a thick smile and hung his arm over the side of the carriage. His jeweled fingers and embroidered sleeve glittered in the sunlight against the backdrop of the carriage. She straightened and walked at her own leisurely pace across the square, swishing her hips. Nodding politely to several vendors on her way, she finally arrived at his side, tipping her ample cleavage close to the carriage.

"Good morning, sir," she curtsied. "I would like to welcome you home to Stanishire after what must be almost a decade abroad, but the passing of your father hardly makes this a happy return."

"Yes, his passing was quite a shock, especially since I was too far away to bury him myself," he said.

"That is truly a shame."

He drifted away with his thoughts, then seemed to remember himself and turned on his smile.

"My apologies for my poor manners," he said. "I don't think we have been properly acquainted. And what is your name?"

His brown eyes gleamed with golden flecks. They held the power to tempt even the most schooled young lady to sneak away into the shadows with him. The way he flashed his smile showed he knew the power that came with his good looks and wealth.

"Madame Maeve," she replied with a polite curtsy.

"It is a pleasure to make your acquaintance."

"And what think you of our quaint little village?"

Maeve said, scanning the streets. "I doubt it can be half as impressive as all the lands to which you have traveled during your absence."

"It is true that the provincial countryside is far quieter and lacking in the grandeur of the palaces and courts I've visited. But there is an unrefined, unrestrained beauty here that I think will do me good. Like the fine young woman you sent away this morning. While she may not be as schooled or polished as the courtesans of the palaces, she has an allure that makes me think I may possibly feel quite satisfied back home. I have so many affairs to attend to with my father's passing still so new, but if I were to crave company, she appears capable of helping me pass the time."

Maeve straightened up and adjusted her shawl.

"I have a great many girls capable of helping you pass the time in any manner you see fit," Maeve replied with a smile perched on her lips. "I promise you they have been schooled beyond the expectations you might have of such a rustic outpost."

"I would be very interested in determining the veracity of your claims, if the young woman you spoke with earlier might be available this evening."

Deflecting his interest away from Aoife was going to be no easy matter.

"While I would welcome you to challenge my claims with any of my girls, I have no rights over that young lady," Maeve paused. "You would have to speak with her father at their home in the valley over the hills to the east, if it is courtship that you wish to entertain."

He leaned back in his seat.

"And her father was the man riding behind her?"

Maeve nodded.

"Her family allows her to enter your establishment and fetch him rather than a hired hand?"

"A hired hand has rarely ever managed to get him home," Maeve replied.

He leaned further back into his seat, his imagination heading off in a direction that worried her.

"So I will need to negotiate her price with her father."

Maeve did not answer.

"And when might I find him in your parlor next?"

She hesitated.

"Any night is possible, tonight, tomorrow or the next, one never knows. But her father and mother may be found at their home any time you might see fit to call upon them for a visit."

"The kind of wager I am willing to make over a girl with a family like that need not be made inside the walls of their home," he grinned. "I might as well meet him where he is most comfortable and most amenable. I'll expect word from you when he pays your establishment another visit."

His tone was a command, not a request.

"A certain amount of anonymity is part of what my customers pay for," Maeve said. She had never taken kindly to orders. "I provide the space, the darkness and, of course, the entertainment. But plotting is not part of my business. My doors open when the sun goes down."

She nodded her goodbye and turned away. She had been too brash with the Duke, but he was not her gravest concern. As she looked off into the distance toward Aoife's home, her heart pounded.

Chapter 2
Cornered

After she passed her father over to her mother and the servant who he berated as if his headache were somehow their fault, Aoife took her sanctuary in the hills and the woods. She had done her part by bringing him home; now he was her mother's concern. She avoided imagining Tara imprisoned in her room, a witness to every harsh word that was to come. But her escapes into the forest were part of what protected her from becoming as bitter as her mother. As she rode away, memories of the early days when she started carting her father home would inevitably crowd her thoughts.

"You precocious little wretch!" Bronagh would say. "If it's your father's immorality you've inherited, then I will beat it out of you! No daughter of mine will grow up to be a harlot!"

Aoife had cried out for her mother's mercy and her father's protection, neither of which ever materialized to save her. A servant would eventually shuttle Aoife to her chamber where her bruises were tended. The next day, no one, not even her father, would speak of the prior evening's events or Aoife's split lip.

Her mother's sole concern was the shame of her daughter entering a brothel. She would rather Aoife have sat by the fire embroidering intricate tapestries with her, which would do no more than decorate the walls of their home, than confront the problem. The lashings had finally stopped several years ago when Aoife refused to give her mother anymore tears, but her mother's words still cut like glass in her memory.

But as she rode between the trees, whose dark shadows frightened everyone else, she felt their curtain close behind her. She shook her hair, loving the way it rippled behind her. Away went those painful words, slipping and tumbling amidst the rocky path. The remnants of the morning mist, which always lingered a bit longer in this safe haven, cooled and dampened her skin. She slowed her pace, letting the peace of the trees soften the memories, until they dissolved and disappeared. First her heart slowed, then her eyes and mouth relaxed, and, finally, her shoulders let go as the weight she carried slipped to the forest floor.

Over the fallen Oak tree to her left and through a long obstacle course of toadstools and moss covered stones, Aoife and her horse rode toward the crescendo of the river's edge. Down a steep embankment, worn smooth after thousands of years of the river's journey, Aoife's horse sidestepped stones and saplings until she hit the shore. They turned to the left and made their way upstream. The rush of the water and the cacophony of birds filled her ears. She dismounted and tied her horse to a tree and made her way toward a human-sized fern, whose fronds unfolded and stretched in a deep morning yawn. When her practiced hand dipped beneath its lower fronds and lifted gently, it opened like an imperial gate as she bowed reverently and passed underneath and to the other side.

She reached for the ties on her dress and loosened them, her ribs expanding and blossoming. Her outer dress slipped from her shoulders and landed in a puddle at her feet. She picked it up and hung it over a fallen limb and slipped off her linen chemise. The crashing of the falls and the thick mist that instantly coated her skin rinsed away the scent of the brothel.

Alone and far from the world, she stepped into the cool water. The hard stones along the shore gave way to the river's soft, murky bottom. She lay back in the water and surrendered to the swirls and eddies of the swimming hole at the base of the falls. They carried her body with strength and assuredness.

Opening her eyes, she watched as the limbs and leaves of the highest trees swayed and bowed, as the energy in the air condensed and collected itself into a powerful wind. Wispy shadows reached and stretched like long, dark ribbons all around her that would have frightened anyone else. But she knew not to fear the energy behind the enchanted wind and shadows.

Since she was a young girl, she loved giving up control to the mysterious forces of nature that resided here by the falls. As the rock of her family, surrender was off limits to her, except here where she encountered a mystical presence. She floated with her eyes closed, knowing that the magical force that inhabited the air and water here would inevitably carry her safely to shore, as it always did. The wind and shadows washed over her until their pulsing energy evened out and their agitated undercurrent washed downstream along with Aoife's worries.

It was during one of her earliest visits to the falls when she learned she was safer beneath the shadows of this mysterious force than with her own parents. She had snuck away from home and was diving for her sapphire necklace, the one her father had given her because he said it sparkled as bright and pure as her eyes and her soul. After jumping from the top of the falls and losing it, she was frantic to find it. While returning to the surface, her foot became lodged among the tangled roots of the river trees. She wiggled and wrestled with her captor, and then began to kick and thrash and wave her hands, desperate to free herself. Her mind grew dizzy until she could hold her breath no longer. She choked on water, mourning all the breaths she would never catch again until the world grew dark and far away.

Minutes or hours later, she could not be sure, she awoke at the water's edge, somehow alive. She looked around her for a person or an explanation, but the only answer was the shuffle of the leaves and the ducking of a strange shadow. As she lifted her body up, she felt the heavy weight of the sapphire pendant against her chest. It gleamed cheerfully in the light, as though it had never left her, except for a small chip. She held it tight, grateful not only for her life, but for the return of the one irrefutable sign of her father's love and devotion. Now it became a talisman, a reminder that there was something in the woods more dependable than her father and powerful enough to keep her safe from even death.

She had always been told the forest was to be feared. It was supposed to contain dark magic. But Aoife had never believed those fairy tales. That day, however, she realized that at least the part of the tales about the magic might be true. As the grip of death had reached up and tried to drown her, a mysterious, powerful force had rescued her. Since she had not grown up enough to stop believing in magic, the nature of this presence mattered less to her young mind than its apparent affection and devotion to her.

So today, as always, she closed her eyes and slipped below the water's surface, listening to the falls and the rush of the water around her. She opened her eyes and looked through the surface of the water. The rippling edges of the world above moved so quickly and smoothly it was as if there were no hard edges, no separation between tree, sky or bird that could be defined or recognized. She swam toward the shore and climbed up on the large boulder that overlooked the falls and caught enough of the sun's rays through the trees to warm and dry her body.

She had almost fallen asleep, when a cold wind swept over her, snapping her from her trance with a wave of goosebumps. Throaty chortles of nocturnal frogs sounded what seemed like an alarm. She scrambled up to her feet and climbed down the rocky side of the falls to where her clothes were draped. She pulled on her chemise and then her outer dress, cinching and tying herself back into place as she looked around and tried to discern the cause of the forest's warning.

18

Something was wrong. That much was clear. She ran toward the exit by the rocky outcrop.

The wind gave a howl and all of a sudden the shrubs ahead of her rustled and a man stood up from behind them. Aoife froze when she saw him, her eyes frightened, but unmistakably fierce. She recognized him, but could not remember how.

"Who are you, and how dare you follow me here?"

He halted, as if surprised by her hostility.

"I followed you here," he began. "From my saddle far up the hill on my land, I saw you crossing my fields."

Aoife stepped back, taking in his fine clothing and his reference to his land. She knew there was only one man who owned the hills that sloped down to the woods. He might have been the Duke, but men with good intentions did not follow women into the woods. He took a few steps forward, and she pressed her body deeper into the rock behind her. She was trapped.

"I saw you earlier and was hoping for an opportunity to make your acquaintance."

"This is hardly the place for a proper introduction," Aoife shot back, her heart pounding. "Any gentleman would know and respect that."

The force of her chastisement stopped him.

"You might be right," he replied. "As the Duke of Stanishire, I should know better than to approach a lady without introducing myself first to her parents. However, your father did not seem ready for an introduction when I saw you riding home together this morning."

Aoife gasped and her footing slipped. No one besides her mother and Maeve ever spoke out loud about this part of her life. She remembered the eyes that followed her as she escorted her father home from Maeve's. He continued walking toward her, the tread of his boots ominous and foreboding.

"If you have any decency then you will let me take my leave," she tried to inject more confidence in her voice than she felt. "Only a spoiled son with an inherited title would think he could threaten a woman's dignity simply because she wandered onto his lands."

He stopped for a moment, turning his palms up.

"You make so many assumptions about me," he said stepping slowly over the mossy terrain and stopping just inches from her. "What if I were to make the same kinds of assumptions about you? I saw you at the brothel, which I hear is your habit, and I assumed you would be a woman who wouldn't mind an untraditional meeting."

His words made her feel like the whore her mother always said she was destined to become. She had always sworn to her mother and herself that walking among the morally corrupt of Madame Maeve's did not make her one of them. But now as this stranger stared at her like one of Maeve's girls, she felt all her courage slipping.

"I may not be a traditional young lady in every sense, Sir," Aoife said, summoning her strength, "but I am not a woman to be taken in such a manner as this."

He stepped back and looked at her carefully, reevaluating the situation.

"Could you then consider that perhaps I am not just a spoiled Duke seeking to steal your virtue?"

The words of this stranger meant nothing to her.

The only thing that mattered was extricating herself from the situation. She did not trust his intentions. She closed her eyes for a moment, pushing away her fears while she tried to think of a plan. Perhaps mistaking the tremble of her lips for an invitation, he leaned in and kissed her. Instinctively, she slapped him harder than even she knew she could. He stumbled back, stunned. The burn in her hand woke her from her paralysis, and the rush of adrenaline reminded her how strong she was. She seized the moment to make her escape, but was no more than a few steps away when he grabbed her hand.

"Don't go!"

She screamed and felt the echo reverberate through the forest. As if in response, a sudden gust of wind sent leaves from the shore upward into a small tornado around them. Her hair stood up from the current in the air. The Duke jumped back, poised to fight the strange presence all around him. The birds squealed and flew in strange patterns just above his head and the trees shook with a force that cast wrathful shadows in every direction.

"We are not alone," Aoife said, her voice stronger now.

On cue, the wind swirled around them and the shadows grew more pronounced and dark. The Duke dipped his head as the kind of fear that haunts young children at night seemed to settle upon him. He stepped away from Aoife, looking around as if a ghost or something more frightful might materialize. She took strength from his vulnerability and the magical protection afforded her and walked to the edge of the storm.

"You have no right to come upon me this way or to pass judgement on me because of my father," she said. "I walk through the dark places people go, but never has a trace of filth stained the hem of my dress or my soul. Remember that and do not ever underestimate me."

She relished his terror and turned back to the walls of dirt and leaves blowing all around them. She reached out her finger, toward the tornado's edge and sliced through, sending the debris flying outward as the forest's protective spell broke in an instant. As the dust settled, she gasped, admiring the powerful presence hovering all around her. She turned back to the Duke.

"Don't ever try to take something that isn't yours."

She sauntered away, picking up her shoes one at a time without the slightest rush, knowing that he posed no threat to her. She had the support of something stronger, more reliable, and more devoted than her father, mother, Tara, or even Maeve. She was safe. For the moment.

Chapter 3
Dangerous Games

"**A**nother round for the house from the deep pockets of the very generous and very worst card player in history: Finnegan!"

Maeve smiled as cheers and applause rumbled through the air. She noted with an accountant's zeal for detail every turn of the card and trick. She counted as each cracked goblet was refilled and raised in crooked toasts to Finnegan, who grinned through slitted eyes and reddened cheeks. He guzzled his drink and slammed his goblet down on the table. After her argument with Aoife, Maeve had been finding it more difficult to ignore the fact that the deep pockets everyone dipped into had, in fact, been filled by Aoife herself. But Maeve pushed these thoughts away; she would never stay in business if she grew a conscience.

Out of the corner of her eye, Maeve saw Rosaline, one of her newest girls and Finnegan's company for the night, pull his face to her chest. The night, his sobriety, and his purse were more than half gone, so when Rosaline whispered promises in his ear to get him upstairs before he spent the last of his coins at cards, Maeve made a mental note to compliment her timing later. Finnegan gave himself over to Rosaline's talents, and Maeve moved her attention elsewhere. But then the door flew open with a burst of cool air.

All heads turned toward the late arrivals as the cold rush of wind sent cards flying and blew out the candle at Finnegan's table. Ladies not yet employed puffed their chests up and spread their legs wider as the Duke stepped inside. The rich hue of his tunic, the polished leather of his boots, and his glittering jewels, combined with his chiseled jaw and youthful glow contrasted greatly with the graying, balding men the women usually bedded. Rosaline and those whose limbs were already entangled with the regulars cursed their misfortune.

No one noticed the unfamiliar hitch in Maeve's chest or the way her eyes widened. The knot that had formed in her chest weeks ago when the Duke settled his crosshairs on Aoife tightened, threatening to choke her usual ease. Hiding behind a thin layer of calm, she raised her glass to her latest guest and his entourage. He taunted her with a wicked smile.

"Welcome, Duke," Maeve said. "Please make yourself comfortable."

The patrons may have consumed too many rounds to count, but Maeve could tell by the way they sat up straighter and wrapped their hands around their glasses and their women that they were not unaware of the

24

discrepancy between their inebriation and the perfectly coiffed, composed, and sober Duke. Just enough of Finnegan's sobriety remained for Maeve to feel his discomfort. The Duke of Stanishire's manor and the rolling hills of his estate that were stitched into every fiber of his sleeves overshadowed by far Finnegan's status as the patron with the most coins to throw around. She held her breath, wondering how her old friend would handle having his authority usurped.

"Welcome to this evening's fair festivities," Finnegan bellowed, clearly trying to control his slurred speech. He stood and continued, "My name is Finnegan and as the unofficial leader of these honorable gentlemen, I would like to extend to you our deepest sympathies for the loss of your father, a good man who will be sorely missed. May I persuade you to join my party, so we may give you as proper a welcome as befits Madame Maeve's fine establishment?"

Maeve felt her heart pounding at the thought of the Duke taking a seat so close to Aoife's drunken father. She may have been the indifferent harbinger of a host of secret plots over the years, but at the moment, Maeve felt a wave of motherly protection rise within her. Painfully unaware of the trap set for him, Finnegan winked at Maeve, who always permitted him to take the role of leader, as long as he deferred to her as the ultimate authority. Suppressing her fears, she offered him only a reluctant nod, rather than her usual wink and smile. But he was far too invested in impressing the Duke to notice any of the changes in the air around him.

The Duke slipped his thumbs into his thick belt and tipped his head back, letting Finnegan feel the power of his hesitation.

"My father was a great man and I appreciate your condolences and respect," he replied. "I accept your invitation, only if the lady so approves and can manage to arrange it."

His authority kept her candles burning, so she nodded her assent with cool eyes. Seamus, all efficiency, rearranged the tables and chairs so that Finnegan's party and the Duke's were seated together.

Finnegan raised his goblet and toasted, "To Bradyn, the late Duke, and his son's recent return. May you stay and get to know these lands and the people who your father so enjoyed. I think I speak for us all when I say that we look forward to deepening the bonds between our families and yours."

The Duke raised his glass and replied, "To deepening the bond between our families."

As everyone tipped back their drinks, two of the girls made their way to either side of the Duke, linking their arms through his. He was the rare customer who they could afford to share. Finnegan grinned at the Duke. He may have lost his role as leader, but he was clearly in awe of the Duke's power. Maeve felt an unexpected urge to beat him over the head with a stick.

"Please don't let my late arrival interrupt the fun," the Duke said. "I believe there was a card game in progress when my entrance scattered the deck to the winds. Shall we procure another, Finnegan?"

"By all means, yes," Finnegan replied.

He snapped his fingers, with uncharacteristic gruffness at Seamus, who he usually tipped extra for ensuring that no one robbed him while he was indisposed.

Seamus produced a deck, but hesitated over whom to give the cards. Finnegan usually dealt the first hand, but with the Duke present, the pecking order had changed.

"I respectfully defer to you," Finnegan said. "Please, choose the game that suits you. I must warn you, though, we have a pack of skilled players who are only too happy and willing to steal the coins right out from under a man's nose. They don't take it easy on me. It remains to be seen whether or not they'll take it easy on you."

A burst of laughter broke out from all around the room.

"Well, it would be a shame to upset custom. I respectfully offer you the cards to deal," the Duke replied.

Finnegan put his hands up, refusing the Duke's proffer.

"The cards are yours tonight."

"Only if you insist," the Duke gave a loaded smile.

He made eye contact briefly with Maeve, silently bragging to the only person in the room who knew the direction the game was headed.

"I absolutely insist," Finnegan replied. "My fate's probably better off in your hands than mine from the way things have gone tonight!"

He threw his head back with hilarity that proved contagious to all but Maeve.

"As you wish," the Duke nodded and began dealing the cards with a practiced hand.

Under different circumstances, it might have impressed Maeve the way he eyed each man carefully as he rounded the table, sizing up the coins in front of them, their level of intoxication, and probable skill level. Maeve knew that by the time the cards were dealt, he had read the fate of every man at the table.

After each hand, another round of drinks was bought, all of them by the Duke. Everyone was so eager to accept his generosity, Finnegan included, that they hardly seemed to mind losing.

"You are too good a player for this country gentleman," Finnegan said. "I shall be left with nothing but my breeches by night's end."

He downed his drink and missed the table when he slammed down his empty goblet, sending it clattering across the floor.

One of the other men remarked, "Be careful Finnegan or it will take more than Aoife to cart you home tomorrow!"

Finnegan laughed hardily for a few moments, lost in the playful banter.

"Don't speak so commonly of my daughter," Finnegan replied with mock indignation. "She has more dignity and smarts in her tiny finger than any of us here!"

The crowd laughed and raised their glasses in her name.

"I see your daughter owns her father's heart," the Duke said. "I suppose that does indeed make her wise."

"Ah, that she is, my fair Aoife," Finnegan smiled into the new goblet that had been placed before him.

"In my travels I have come across a great many

ladies, many of whom were skilled at music, dancing and hospitality. But smartest of them all were the ones who learned how to weave their way around their fathers' hearts."

"Well I'm sure the women you've kept company with might be dressed in the latest fashions and have mastered a host of instruments, but none of them, not a one, could ever compete with Aoife's wit and resourcefulness. It's a good thing we're not playing cards with her or we'd be left without even a cart to take a one of us home by morning!"

Another round of laughter broke out, grating on Maeve's frayed nerves and driving her from her seat and into action. She walked up to the girls accompanying the Duke and dangled a key with a heart-shaped handle on it. All the girls knew this key led to the most luxurious bedroom reserved for their wealthiest guests. Their eyes lit up and one of them leaned in and whispered to the Duke. He looked up at Maeve and shook his head, not at all deterred.

"Ah, now, Finnegan," the Duke spoke, "You've got me curious. You make her sound famous in these parts. And just what are these unique abilities that extend beyond mere feminine wiles."

"Don't get him started or we'll never get him to stop," the gentleman beside Finnegan said, rolling his eyes.

"Just because she turned down your nephew's proposal doesn't mean you have to be so bitter," Finnegan laughed.

"Ah, so she's a heartbreaker," the Duke said.

"Oh she's more than a heartbreaker," Finnegan

shot back. "She does it with style; a style that has won her fame all in these parts."

"Infamy is more like it," added his neighbor, which sent them all into another fit of laughter.

"But it hasn't stopped the suitors from coming," Finnegan pointed out. "Her beauty is legendary, but her ability to turn everything she touches to gold has made her more than just an attractive marriage prospect, but a business partner that men would rather own than compete with."

"So she has the Midas touch?" the Duke said. "Well, judging by the looks of your losses tonight, she's got her job cut out for her tomorrow."

"Right you are," Finnegan said and raised the new glass that had been placed before him. "But don't worry for me, my friends. With Aoife's penchant for profits, I'll find the means to finance more fun another night… and another… and another and —"

"Now you've intrigued me, dear friend," said the Duke. "Just what is this golden touch that your daughter has?"

"Ah, now you are asking me to reveal my secret weapon and that I cannot do." After a slight pause he continued, "She sees the world differently. With a surgeon's eye – or a prophet's even – she sees the things men like us can't. Cattle. Barley. Men. She sees not what is in front of her but what's behind the façade. She sees potential. I tell you there's magic in her fingertips. A something I can't explain. A something which has saved this poor man's heart and purse strings again and again as any person in town can attest to."

Finnegan was too lost in his ruminations to see the

way his words left the Duke transfixed for a moment, far away in thoughts that had nothing to do with mead, women, or cards.

"Then you won't worry about what you wager on the next round."

Finnegan woke from his daydream, hearing the challenge in his voice. There was an urgency in the Duke's voice that Finnegan did not understand. The Duke tossed his entire purse into the pot, sending gold clattering everywhere. Finnegan looked at his nearly empty purse.

"Don't worry, Finnegan," the Duke's voice was tinged with condescension. "I wouldn't want your daughter to work too hard tomorrow refilling your coffers. It is, of course, the Sabbath. Let's end it here tonight with a toast to her 'talents.'"

The sting was real and a new kind for Finnegan. His tall tales were sources of entertainment for everyone; no one had ever taken him seriously enough to question them. But suddenly, his honor and that of his daughter had been questioned.

Finnegan reached for his purse, but Maeve placed her hand over his.

"Let's trade in this needless sparring for something a great deal more fun," Maeve said, trying to inject a playfulness into her voice to hide her fear. "Ladies, let's have a little entertainment – "

"You're right, Maeve," the Duke said. "This game has grown tiresome."

As the Duke reached for his purse, a flurry of coins rained down on his hand. Finnegan had dumped the rest of his fortune on the table, along with his cards, face up.

The Duke perused Finnegan's hand and he shook his head.

"I'm sorry my friend," he said as he laid his winning cards out on the table.

Finnegan laughed, but it was hollow and unconvincing. He rubbed his head, trying to figure out where the evening had gone wrong when he spied Rosaline slinking up alongside the Duke. She caressed his hair, ignoring the scathing eyes of Maeve, who never permitted the girls to arouse jealousy amongst the patrons. The Duke grinned at Finnegan, whose face had surpassed red and was headed for a consternated shade of purple.

"Who said the game was over?" Finnegan shouted.

"No one said it was over," Maeve interjected. "I think the night is directing some of us to other games. That's all."

She rubbed his shoulders sensually, offering him the kind of attention she gave no one anymore. He seemed to soften under her touch, and Maeve's fingers pressed deeper inside his shirt, drawing him away from the Duke's machinations.

"I've got more game in me if you do," Finnegan said, shrugging Maeve's hands away. The challenge in his voice was a clear appeal to salvage what was left of his pride.

He slipped out from under Maeve's touch.

"I'm sure you've got more game, my friend, but I'm afraid you've got no more gold."

"I've got my good name and my family fortune in

fields, which are worth a lot more than a few careless coins."

"Now Finnegan," Maeve said with barely veiled desperation. "They are worth far too much to throw away over a card game. The game is finished for tonight."

"Maeve, you set the rules for this house, but not for me."

Finnegan shook her off completely and, thus, his last chance to slip out of the Duke's scheme.

"Finnegan," the Duke replied, his voice laden with mock sincerity, "I think the woman is right. The wagering is done for the evening."

"A gentleman would not take all that's mine in just a few hands without giving me the chance to take it back. You are a gentleman, are you not?"

"I suppose if another hand is what you want, another hand is what you must have."

The girls at his side settled back down and pouted.

"I'll give you the chance to win back your purse and everything in the pot. But what do you have left to wager? Surely you wouldn't risk your house, land, or livestock to reclaim so small a pile of gold? Surely even Aoife can't weave gold from thin air."

"She won't need to worry when we are done with this round. I'll wager my livestock, a season's crops, even my lands if there's a competing wager of equal value. Put something on the table I can't resist and let's make things interesting," Finnegan said.

He pulled a long swig of mead.

The Duke leaned back, his gaze resting on Maeve for a moment.

"Well, the offer of your lands is quite impressive. I ought to at least be willing to meet your wager." He rubbed his chin, deliberating. "Perhaps the fertile acreage that adjoins our property and flows all the way down to the river's edge would make the wager fair. I've not farmed it in years and I'm sure that your daughter could do more with it than I have."

There was a collective gasp in the room.

"Enough of this," Maeve said shrilly. "I'll not have lives and families destroyed by the turn of a card in my house."

"Take your leave, Maeve, if you are so bothered," Finnegan shouted. "Ruin is what we come here for and what keeps you in business. On top is where I always end up. I think there's more than a few here who can attest to that."

Finnegan had found his humor and his second wind. The ladies laughed and broke the spell of tension.

"Come now, Madam Maeve," the Duke said. "Let Finnegan do what men do best, lay down wagers and women. Finnegan, I'll give you what you asked for."

The cards were dealt, and moments later as the cards fell in the Duke's favor, a hush fell over the entire room. Finnegan sighed and the floor seemed to fall out from beneath him. He had lost countless rounds in his life. Never the entire game, never his entire fortune.

"I guess your luck has finally run out," the Duke said. "Hopefully your daughter's hasn't."

The Duke rose, ignoring the silence of the room. No one, not even the women, knew what to do next. Never before had they seen a man lose everything in one fell swoop.

"Surely, a gentleman like yourself would not take a family's fortune over a bad round of cards," Maeve said, her near panic evident in the high pitch of her voice. "This has all been in jest, and you will leave tonight satisfied with your pile of gold and your women."

"All this talk of honorable behavior has me weary," replied the Duke.

"But you wouldn't leave a family destitute? Fear is not the kind of rule we've been accustomed to under your father."

"A little fear never hurt anyone," the Duke quipped. "Benevolence was my father's hallmark, but a trait I never owned." He turned to Finnegan and sighed with annoyance. "I suppose I could practice it for fun. I tell you what, Finnegan. I think we've seen enough of your luck tonight to believe you when you say that it is your daughter, not you, who has the golden touch. Perhaps I could give her a chance to prove her skill and produce a little gold for me. If she is as capable as you say, then you can have all of your land and tonight's pot of gold."

"But Finnegan's nothing more to wager against you? What if she can't produce as you see fit?" Maeve interrupted. "What will you will strip him of next?"

"His freedom. That's what most people lose when they can't pay their debts, or the last ten years' taxes."

All the money Aoife had made from the estate had never come close to paying off the family's backlog of taxes. Finnegan's eyes widened, realizing his desperate situation. Refusing the offer meant taking his family directly to the poor house in the morning. Accepting the offer meant thrusting the responsibility of protecting the dwindling family estate and his own personal freedom upon Aoife. He wavered, but only for a second.

"I accept."

"Finnegan, you can't do this!" Maeve exclaimed.

"Hold your tongue," Finnegan scolded her. "I may have foolishly wagered away my fortune over the fickle nature of cards. But this time I'm putting my faith in Aoife. And Aoife has never let me down."

"You say she has the golden touch," the Duke said. "She can find the worth in anything and… anyone. The barn stalls on my lands are filled with hay meant for the upcoming winter. If she can make gold of it, then your life is yours again to ruin. If she cannot, then your life as you know it is over."

"But how is she to turn straw into gold? That is an impossible request!" Maeve protested.

"Not according to her father," the Duke replied.

He stood and marched toward the door, the rest of his company in tow. When he reached the door he turned back and pointed at Finnegan.

"I will expect her by noontime tomorrow. And she won't leave until she's proven her worth."

Finnegan sank into his chair and felt the weight of all his sins on his shoulders, or, rather, on Aoife's shoulders.

Chapter 4
Wits, an Ax, and a Little Magic

I will not wait for the Duke in his chamber," Aoife told the servant. "The Duke wants me to make gold of straw, and that I will, but not inside his private chamber."

Aoife made no effort to remove her cape or gloves. She was more concerned with removing the memory of Tara weeping into her covers as she bid Aoife goodbye that morning. The tears had only exacerbated her cough. Everything Aoife did was to protect Tara and pay for the doctor and medicine she so badly needed. Her mother and father had offered weak embraces as they followed her out to her horse. Despite his recklessness and her mother's habitual disapproval, they needed her too, and she could not erase the family ties that bound her to them. Now that her father had promised to officially hand over the title of the estate to Aoife if she saved the family from ruin, she finally felt a real hope that her life, and Tara's, would change for the better. No more would he be allowed to take the profits she made to spend at Maeve's. No longer would her work be for nothing.

The Duke's laughter echoed unexpectedly around the stone entryway. Startled, she looked around. He stood with his arms crossed looking down over the second floor railing. His expression was bemused as he began to walk toward the stairs. She resented the way he had caught her by surprise again.

"You're so strong willed and determined, Aoife."

"Determined to prove that what my father so rashly bragged about during your party last night is actually true. I'll wait out front for your groundsman to show me the land, crops, and livestock. After he gives me an account of your stores, I can make a plan."

Aoife maintained a stoic countenance. The smallest hint of vulnerability was a liability she could not risk.

A hurried looking man rushed in from a side room. He looked from Aoife to the Duke.

"My Lord, I was summoned to be of assistance to – your guest – in perusing your lands and assets."

"Yes, Cashel. I witnessed the order," the Duke said. "Aoife, your father claimed that you could turn mere straw into gold. So what, may I ask, do my lands, cattle and sheep have to do with straw?"

Aoife watched the way he eyed her curiously. His interest in her did not just seem rooted simply in lust or even ego – things she had seen in the men at Maeve's. She could not discern what exactly he wanted from her, which made her uneasy.

"Had you spent more time here, you would know

just how often I have turned a profit from livestock, fields, as well as straw. If it is proof you want of my skill, then stand back and let me show you." Aoife turned to Cashel. "My horse is saddled and ready to ride. I expect an account of crop and livestock earnings." She turned back to the Duke. "I shall return later in the day to make my calculations and lay my plans."

She mounted her horse, surveying his gardens and the lands beyond. Her fingers ticked away along the reins, as she counted off the acres. When she pulled out a leather bound notebook and a sharpened piece of coal from her satchel and began scrawling notes, the Duke chuckled.

"A young lady who roams the woods and local brothel of Stanishire unaccompanied and who may possibly be able to manage the affairs of my estate as well as a man. Perhaps I have finally met my match," he said. "Cashel, have my horse brought about immediately. I will accompany my guest."

"There's no need," Aoife countered, "unless you can keep up."

***

"So the head of cattle has yet to return anywhere near its numbers prior to the illness that plagued the area three years ago?" Aoife asked.

"Well, no," Cashel replied. "It will take some time before the herd is fully recovered, which has been the case for everyone affected."

Aoife nodded and continued to pour over the records. The barn was cold, but the sun shined in from the open door where Aoife had pulled over a table and stool. She took off her cape and flipped through the ledger pages, formulating various possible plans.

"What confuses me," she continued, "is why you are still, three years after the destruction of the herd – "

"I don't know that I would call it the destruction of the herd – "

"That is generally what we would call the loss of almost a third of its numbers. That aside, what I am curious about is why you are still planting and harvesting the same amount of hay and grain. There must be a rather large and unnecessary surplus. That would mean a wasted investment of money, time, and manpower, unless you were selling it off for a profit. But I see no indication of any such reallocation of the surplus. Am I missing a page in the log?"

Cashel took a breath and fumbled through an explanation that made no sense. The Duke leaned against the doorway, making no move to interfere.

"So what exactly has become of this three year surplus?" Aoife asked, wondering if the man might actually have been siphoning off the excess for his own benefit.

"I tried to speak to the late Duke about it, but he was rather ill and could not be bothered, so it was ultimately decided to do nothing with it."

"It's been accumulating for three years?"

"Well," Cashel's eyes danced nervously to the Duke, "yes."

When Aoife demanded to see the stores of grain, Cashel all but crumbled. He reluctantly lead the way and spilled out excuses about the bad weather over the last few years and the infestation of rodents that had consequently moved out of the fields and into the barns and outbuildings.

What she found was startling. Two new buildings had been erected to house the growing excess, but they had not been lifted the proper height off the ground to keep the vermin from turning it into their own private pantry. They had bore holes on every side and grain spilled around the buildings in a manner which, had it not been such a waste, would have been comical. All the while, the Duke followed a few paces behind, listening quietly as Aoife made mincemeat of Cashel's logic. She thought of the people in the village breaking meager loaves of bread that never proved enough, while for three years the late Duke's grain had been wasting away and fattening the rats.

"I suppose if I were to ask to see the surplus hay, I would find much the same degradation and waste?"

"I could bring you to see it, but – "

Cashel's unfinished sentence answered her question. She turned and walked back to her seat in the barn and poured over the manor's books. She tried to block out the Duke, who walked around the barn, toying with tools she assumed he had never used. After several trips back and forth to the granary and then to the stalls where the straw was kept, Aoife estimated some numbers, sealed her inkhorn and lay down her quill.

"Although the condition of the surplus grain and straw has been compromised, there is still a hefty amount that can be salvaged," she stated. "While I personally would prefer to see the people of the village benefit from an excess that is clearly of no use to you, I do feel that turning a profit from this accidental find is possible. There is a rich farmer, Niall, over the hills to the north, nestled in a valley, who has suffered greatly from the rains that your groundsman spoke of. He keeps a full purse for just such emergencies. If we act quickly, I believe we might reach him before he makes multiple bids on the smaller excesses of his neighbors. It would be in his best interests to deal with us."

She handed the Duke her notebook, showing him the price he could expect. It was more than seemed fair or compassionate, given the farmer's plight, but she knew he would pay it, and there was no price too steep for her family's safety. Her family's estate was one step closer to becoming hers. He took the book, surveying her calculations and the final gain for him. His expression betrayed his surprise as he handed it back to her.

"Impressive work," he said after a moment. "I can't say that you magically turned my straw to gold, but I cannot deny that you worked a magic so simple that it frightens me my own man could not do the same."

Cashel shifted his weight from side to side.

"Well then that is it," Aoife said, trying to keep the momentum moving in her favor. "I have proven my father's claim and fattened your coffers. I hope you enjoy the small fortune I have made you in a mere matter of hours. And should you have a new, more effective granary built, this surplus, which is sure to continue for a few more years until the herd is fully recovered, will go on to supply an annual return. I'd say you gained quite a treasure today."

She hoped she had let him feel like he had won. If

he felt any humiliation or besting, she knew she would remain at his mercy.

"Cashel," the Duke said, "Go back to the manor and have a contract drawn up and ready for my signature. You may find all the numbers you need in Aoife's ledger."

"I am only too happy to accompany him in order to make sure – "

"That will not be necessary," he interrupted. "I doubt Cashel will make any mistakes, knowing that your eyes will review his work."

"Then I will prepare to deliver the contract," Aoife replied.

"We can let that wait until morning," the Duke replied. "The day has been long and we could all no doubt use a meal and some rest."

As he dismissed Cashel she watched apprehensively as he disappeared around the grain stores. The Duke stepped closer to her and she moved back, searching the periphery of her vision for all possible routes of escape.

"Come now," he said. "Why do you move away from me? Does my presence really frighten you so much?"

"The boundaries of propriety between us are quite blurred and would make any woman reticent," she replied calmly.

"But you blur the boundaries of respectability by the very people you count as your family and friends," he said. "Your father. Maeve."

"You've no right to look down on people you don't know. There's more goodness in them than you."

The Duke's lips hardened and he took another step toward her.

Her eyes widened, realizing too late the power of the rash temper she inherited from her father. The deal, the estate, and her family's future were slipping through her fingers.

"I don't understand you. From the moment you met me you have seen nothing but evil intentions and shallowness in my every move," his voice sounded wounded and exasperated underneath. "Yet you hold your father's hand outside the brothel and converse with its proprietor. Why are you so intent on judging me so harshly?"

"I have walked where the dark sides of men and women play since I was a little girl," Aoife shot back, unable to censor herself. "I have looked deep into those people you think so low. Maeve is a harlot and my father a drunkard, but they are filled with as much goodness as anyone else. At least they wear their darkness out in the open for all to see, which shows more courage and honesty than those who put on fancy clothes and try to fool the world into thinking they are as magnificent on the inside as they appear on the outside."

"And so that is what you see in me?" he pressed. The urgency in his voice surprised her. "You see the darkness in me that I cannot hide. And tell me, is it so terrifying, so awful, so disgusting to look upon that not even a compassionate soul reader such as you can bear to look upon me?"

She was beginning to understand. He wanted the acceptance, love, and implicit absolution he had seen Aoife give her father and Maeve. Underneath his finery he seemed more broken than her father, but she had neither the interest nor the time to mend another man. Tara needed her and taking care of her father was a difficult enough task. But if she was going to rescue her family from this mess, she had to do so very carefully so as not to rouse any more of his thorny anger.

"If you want to be seen," Aoife said in as gentle a tone as she could muster, "you can't force it. You can't trap me by the falls or in a barn against my will and then expect me to want to know you. You've given me little reason to see any good in you."

He turned from her and paced the barn, thinking over her words.

"Warming women with my charms has always come easily," he said turning toward her. "Which is why I find you so alluring and incredibly frustrating."

He ran his fingers through his hair and walked away from Aoife. When he reached the table where Aoife had been working, he picked up a large glass jar filled with grain and turned it round in his hand, watching the light bounce and refract around the room.

"Most women are not interested in getting to know anything about me beyond my title and my riches, and I have never minded that at all. But you are the first person who I have ever wanted to see more of me. And I'm used to getting what I want."

He grimaced and mulled over something in his mind. After an unsatisfied grunt, he threw the jar against the wall. Aoife winced and stepped back as the shattered glass and grain flew through the air. She darted toward the wall to try to escape the barn, but it was impossible to sneak out unseen since he was stationed near the entrance.

"Don't leave!" he called as he caught sight of her.

In an awkward move he reached for her and missed her hand but managed to grab the front of her dress before she got away. The front of her bodice ripped and his grip slipped, sending Aoife stumbling until she fell flat on her back with a shriek. She was dizzy from having the wind knocked out of her, and her head throbbed where it had struck the ground. She looked down at her torn dress. In a panic she turned over and tried to crawl away. Her hand fumbled around and felt something stone cold and heavy lying on the barn floor. Her vision came back to her just enough to recognize the long handle of a rusty axe in her grip. As the Duke reached for her arm, she did not hear the apologies pouring from him. All she knew was that his hands were on her, and hers were wrapped around the handle of an axe.

A sudden blast of wind blew through the barn and sent hay and animal feed flying up in the air. The Duke released her and watched with a haunted expression as the mysterious wind and hay swirled around them like an angry tornado, its circumference expanding and contracting with far more force and substance than it had by the river's edge yesterday. At first, Aoife blocked her eyes with her arms from the flying debris, but she slowly dropped them, realizing that it was flowing around her without touching her. She looked about with growing amazement.

Her skin prickled as the forest presence she knew so well placed itself between them. The spinning torrent of straw grew faster and throbbed louder with each second until it reached an unbearable intensity. All at once there was a burst of energy and wind as the tornado of hay shattered into infinitesimal particles. The torrent of dust billowed up to the top of the barn and then cascaded down in a soft rain upon the barn floor, coating everything in a fine, yellow dust.

For a moment, all was silent, like the hush of snowfall, as the dust floated down upon them.

The Duke stood up and looked around the barn.

"I'll not run from shadows or the temper tantrums of monsters!" he shouted.

He spoke to the air as if the creature he addressed might appear. He turned and looked down at Aoife, with the axe dangling from one hand. He looked offended and even wounded as he took in the sight of it.

"Am *I* monstrous enough to require deadly force?" He looked emotionally spent and raw.

"Your actions give little evidence to the contrary," Aoife replied, her breath still unsteady.

"If it is a monster you believe me to be, then I suppose it's a monster I must be. But that's no matter. I am done with you, for now," he said and stumbled toward the door. "I will leave you to make good on your father's deal."

"Arrange for the papers and I'll have the gold for you by tomorrow," she said, her voice a confused tumble of terror and business.

"No papers," he shook his head. "There will be no papers or deals. Your father claims you are gifted with the golden touch. You have until sunrise to turn this barn of hay into gold!"

"You can't possibly be serious!" Aoife cried. "I

have already fulfilled your deal, and the paper is being drawn up now. This is ridiculous. No one takes literally my father's poor metaphors!"

"I deal not in metaphors but in facts. Your father said that you can spin straw into gold. Succeed, and you shall win your family's freedom and a great deal of my lands. Fail and all the evil you see in me will most certainly fall upon your family."

He slammed the doors and locked the darkness upon her.

Chapter 5
The Guardian

"**B**oy," Aoife heard the Duke bark. "Come this way and keep watch here tonight. No one is to enter or leave. You are to open these doors under no circumstances until I return tomorrow."

She had been so close. The deal was nearly done, and yet she had still lost.

All was ruined.

All was gone.

Aoife dropped to the floor and wept into her arms. The tears came freely now that she was alone.

"Surely you are not crying over the Duke?"

The gravelly voice that came from the darkness was full of a strange merriment.

"Who are you? Where are you hiding?" Aoife tightened her grip on the axe as she looked further into the darkness.

"Why, I am the one who sent the wild-eyed Duke

fleeing and kept you safe from your own murderous rage. That's a deadly piece of metal. I'd better not turn my back on you."

An uneven ruckus of footsteps moved from one side of the barn to the other all too quickly.

"I'll do what I need to protect myself. I advise you to show yourself if you have nothing to hide."

In the silence that followed, a candle sitting on the table where Aoife had been pouring over the Duke's books sparked, seemingly by itself, and Aoife watched as its glow grew brighter. Aoife made her way to the workbench where the candle illuminated a small portion of the barn. She picked it up carefully at first, in case there was some hidden danger. When it proved harmless, she held it just ahead of her as she looked around.

"I've no intentions of harming you," the voice said gently from the other side of the barn.

"Then if you mean no harm, stop hiding in the shadows. Step into the light and introduce yourself."

"So you think an introduction will make friends of us? That we will then sit and commiserate over the fine weather we're having, the Duke's poor hygiene, and the chip in your sapphire pendant? Is that what you think?"

She stopped. No one knew about the day she almost drowned or the chip. No person that is. Only the mysterious shadows in the woods who saved her knew. But this voice was all too human.

"You think your unearthly courage and inherent ability to look past people's flaws have prepared you to share tea with a being that most believe is best left to live in the darkness?"

"How do you know about my necklace?"

Aoife had barely noticed the heightened pitch of the voice as it began to pick up speed.

"The one you almost lost all those years ago in the river?"

"Not to mention my life."

"Oh yes, and your life," the voice sighed. "What a pity that would have been."

"So it was you who freed me from the water?"

Aoife stepped over a fallen broom towards the voice.

"I couldn't let you die." A flurry of footsteps echoed nearby and she turned to try to follow them. "I've grown too used to your visits, clever girl. Let's see how many more pieces of the puzzle you can sort out."

Aoife moved with uneven steps toward the corner of the barn where the hay was piled high. Could the magic she experienced in the forest be more human than she ever imagined? Scary stories her father used to tell her and Tara by the fire of witches and fairies came back to her faster than she could sift through them.

"And it was you who swirled the hay and dust up that frightened the Duke away."

"And shall I grant you a wish for your genius? What will I ever do if you figure it all out?"

His voice had skipped again to the other side of the barn, this time up high in the loft.

"That day in the woods," Aoife began.

She rushed over to catch a glimpse before he skipped away again, but tripped over a loose board in the floor. She tumbled to the ground with a thump and the light went out.

There were hands at her side, righting her up so

quickly that she was not even sure she felt them. She reached through the darkness, but the form evaporated faster than an apparition.

"Thank you."

"You're welcome."

The voice was just a few feet away. Aoife's eyes adjusted slowly to the darkness. She thought back on all the days she spent floating in the creek's current, watching the trees dancing with supernatural grace overhead and the leaves rustling in chorus. Was it possible that this abstract presence – this presence that tended to her – was personified in the shadowy figure that seemed human and stood now just feet away from her? She reached out to touch him in order to verify his existence, but that seemed impolite in light of his sudden and unexpected humanity. Her hand dropped to the floor where she sat.

He cleared his throat and the sound of boots clipped at a more human pace across the floor.

"It seems that trouble finds you no matter where you go."

"I would say that my father's trouble finds me no matter where I go."

"Now some might agree, and it might be true. But when most people would run the other way, you're running toward his trouble, no matter where it takes you. You are afraid of nothing."

"My sister would no longer be with us, and my parents and I would have been destitute and living off the charity of others if it were not for my efforts to manage our lands and fortune."

"Efforts? I'd say it's more your courage to go

wherever and do whatever is necessary to save those you love."

"My mother calls it my reckless attraction to debauchery and all that is filthy."

"Don't listen to her," he replied dismissively. "She does not appreciate how she has benefited from your unbiased, extremely forgiving nature. She fears your brazen audacity because she knows it is more powerful than her own ineffectual whine."

Aoife laughed softly and folded her hands in her lap. Strangely, the rocky, squeally edged voice calmed her as much as the graceful rocking of the forest.

"You know so much about me," Aoife spoke into the void around her. His admiration of her tenacity fueled the flutter in her chest. "And you speak of my – audacity – " she lingered over the word, "as if it were something to cherish. As if it were not shameful."

"Shameful? Your mother should be ashamed for not valuing the way you see everything and everyone in this world for who and what they are without becoming bitter and angry. You walk right into the doors of Madame Maeve's and drag your drunken father out with little more than the twist of your brow, and you hold his hand the whole way home. Instead of running away into the woods after he told you about the bet, you rode your horse through the center of town today and straight up to the Duke's front door. You schooled him and his landsman in wit. And if we lived in a world with fair rules, you would have already won – despite the losing hand you were dealt. And when all of hell's fury descended upon you, you were prepared to take his life." He paused and sighed. "When I saw you grip that ax I knew…"

The room fell silent. Aoife leaned forward.

"You knew what?"

"I knew that if someone had to kill him, I didn't want it to be you. I need to know that there is one person in this world who is pure and unsullied."

She flushed. No one had ever spoken to her like this.

"I don't know how to thank you for all you have done for me."

"Well, I wouldn't thank me just yet," the voice replied. "I haven't rescued you from tragedy tonight. My cowardliness has only delayed the inevitable."

"I do not know what is to become of me tomorrow. But I sense that he wants something from me that goes beyond – physical. It's as if he wants something from my soul."

"I know something about having your soul ripped out."

Aoife took a breath to ask what he meant and then thought better of it. She turned her gaze toward the moonlight spilling through the gaps in the barn.

"May I ask your name?"

"Ask, you may, but there is none to give," he replied evenly.

"I hope I have not offended you in some way that has made you – "

"The offense belongs not to you, but to the mother who never saw fit to name me."

"That is an offense, one I can't imagine living with," she said.

"Be glad you can't," he replied. "To be regarded

as too insignificant to deserve a name is perhaps the most painful degradation a human can suffer."

The silence that followed hung heavy in the air.

"I am so grateful to you and have so many questions, but I don't know how to address you properly and respectfully."

"Properly?" he replied. "Respectfully? Those are social considerations no one has ever given me. The closest thing to a proper address for me is the one I was given in the absence of a real name. By those who have known me, I am called simply, the little man."

"Little man," she whispered, considering what it revealed about his humanity.

She wanted to ask more, but the warble in his voice told her it was a subject best left alone.

"I might as well prepare for the poor house at sunrise," Aoife said, remembering her plight.

"So that's it?" he sounded disappointed. "Where's the girl who was ready to take off Satan's head just moments ago?"

"I think that perhaps my 'audacity' is not enough to fight the Duke's power."

Aoife rubbed her head with exhaustion.

"Ah, don't disappoint me, Aoife," there was an edge of irritation in his voice. "It's not such a hopeless situation. Surely you're not going to let his brute strength render you a helpless damsel in distress! That's not the Aoife I know."

"If you knew me, you would know I am not a sorceress with endless stores of wit and magic. I know it's hard to believe, but I do not actually own the Midas touch."

Aoife put her head in her hands and wept silently, her tears more hopeless than angry. The darkness gave her the privacy to let them out.

After a moment he said, "You know, even audacious people have been known to accept help from time to time. That is, when they find themselves in need and when they find a certain someone who knows how to fulfill that need."

"And are you magical enough to beat the Duke at his own game?"

"Making gold of straw is mere child's play for me," he sounded incensed by the question. "And coincidentally, beating the Duke happens to be my life's sole purpose."

"Before I say yes, I would like to meet the person who keeps rescuing me when I need it most."

"Oh, that. First my name, then the meeting. Of course you would eventually want to see me. But before it comes to that, what have you to offer me in return for my help?"

"Oh," Aoife blinked. "I suppose that's only fair. I suppose if your promise is real and my family's estate is to become mine, I would owe you my freedom in every sense of the word. I would be willing to give you gold or land – "

"I'm about to spin straw into gold for you, so how is gold an attractive reward for my services? And land? The forest is my home. What need have I of fields?"

Aoife winced at the agitation in his voice and the sense that she had offended and disappointed him. Nothing had ever felt as important to her as retaining his affection. She clasped her hands and thought hard about her next words.

"You're right. Money is not a proper reward for all you've done for me. But without knowing your name or having met you, I'm not sure what to offer."

"If you could figure out my name, that would be the greatest payment of all!" he replied sarcastically. "Knowing who I am would solve a great many of my problems. But I can't give you my name. And you think that seeing me will somehow grant you more insight into who I really am?"

"Well," Aoife stammered. "I have never known anyone who I had not met, so it only seems sensical to — "

"Sensical. Obvious. Necessary," his voice was flat. Aoife stepped back a little as the click of his heels drew nearer. "Well then know me by my face and form you will, for if you are like everyone else, then that is all you will forever after know me by!"

A tiny flame grew from the candle which had been righted and its flicker grew and danced, softly at first and then with growing agitation, as its light sparked in longer fiery fingers around the room. An unnatural glow began to fill the barn, and Aoife grasped the torn seams of her bodice. A figure a little shorter than Aoife stepped slowly into the light. Draped from head to toe in a dark cloak, only his bulky outline was visible.

"So if seeing me is knowing me," his whisper had turned slightly fiendish, "Then know me!"

His silhouette was too crooked to be real. The twist of his spine made it seem as though his arms were very different lengths. The glow of his cataracted eyes, somewhere between a murky blue and dun, bore into her. She fought the paralysis that infected her and tried to move away from his garish form. She tried to turn around, to scream, but her cries only fueled his laughter. Fear and panic overwhelmed her. No matter which way she moved, she felt darkness descending upon her.

But then a soft whirring began to fill her ears. A malignant amnesia spread across her brain, comforting and quieting her fears. His form, which had terrified her, faded away as the whirring flowed over her like a soft breeze as she slipped further and further away from consciousness.

"Sleep away from this world," he said in a surprisingly soft voice. "Sleep tight while this world is bent and turned upside down – or right side up. And when you awaken you will stand amazed and thank the heavens for the miracle that has rescued you. But as the minutes turn to hours and then days, you will dismiss this event as strange and unusual, but ultimately something to put on a shelf while you continue on with your life as if everything that you have known of the world is exactly as you have always thought it was before this nameless little man appeared. Or will you prove yourself able to wake from the nightmare of this existence? Will you see the walls of this world as flimsy, arbitrary and breakable? Will you see behind it to the Truth? Will you have the power to see the real me underneath this broken frame?"

Chapter 6
Never Enough

A light too bright for her to ignore invaded her consciousness. She fluttered her lids and felt the sun pouring in through a crack in the barn wall upon her. She covered her eyes against the blinding morning sun, the ache of her head reminding her of all that happened last night.

She pressed her hands beside herself and felt her cloak tucked snuggly around her body, shielding her from the damp morning air. She rose up slowly, testing the throb of her head. Voices in the distance reminded her of the gravity of the situation. She opened her eyes and struggled to her feet, wondering how she had been moved onto the bed of straw and who had wrapped her cape around her like a blanket.

When she stepped out of the hay stall, all around her from floor to ceiling were endless piles of gold coins. Some were stacked into neat, tidy towers, while much of it lay in glittering heaps. There was more gold in the barn than Aoife imagined existed in any King's coffers. She reached out hesitantly, afraid to touch a single piece for fear it would crumble into dust like an unfulfilled wish. Her trembling fingers finally touched the cool edge of a coin sitting high atop a pile that stood taller than any childish structure she had ever constructed. She gasped, her heart overwhelmed by the reality of the moment as the tower of gold clattered to the floor. Aoife sank to the ground and ran her fingers through the mess with tears streaming down her cheeks. Her wish had been granted. The force that had protected her all her life, the little man, had done so once again. He had rescued her, despite her unforgivable reaction to his misshapen form.

In the middle of the barn amidst the heaps of gold sat a tired looking spinning wheel and a stool set low to the ground. Aoife vaguely remembered seeing it covered in cobwebs in a corner along with some unused farming equipment.

"Was this how he had done it," she wondered.

She walked over and sat upon it – the seat and the wheel long since cooled, but a few pieces of hay entwined together in a long strand remained wound around the wheel. She pumped her foot against the pedal and it tugged the remaining strand round and round. A last gold coin slipped out beneath the wheel, a clue to the miracle he had created all around her.

"Thank you, wherever you are," Aoife pressed her hands together in a sort of prayer, wondering if he was somewhere in the air and able to hear her gratitude, to hear her silent apology. With head bent, Aoife noticed that her sapphire pendant was missing.

She looked about her and in the folds of her cape only to realize it must have served as payment for his magical deed. The man who could spin gold into straw saw a fractured jewel as payment enough? The image of his face surfaced and she shuddered, instantly overwhelmed by remorse. She wished she could have offered the nameless little man a payment that would have given him more comfort and solace than a cracked necklace. She tried to hold the memory of him in her mind to steel herself and deaden the chill that prickled her skin. But her efforts were interrupted by the sound of voices drawing nearer. She stood and admired the sight of her luck piled high all around her.

There was the sound of throats clearing and the scuffle of feet in front of the barn.

"I still don't see what part I have in your deal with Finnegan," Father John whispered outside the barn.

He was a priest at the local church, whose belly seemed too round for one devoted to a life of poverty.

"I already told you, Father," the Duke replied. "It is only your presence here as a witness that I need along with all these townsfolk to avoid a dispute from any of the parties involved."

Aoife surveyed the glittering gold all around her and lifted her chin victoriously.

"Let's open this door and see how powerful your daughter's touch is."

Finnegan coughed loudly and Aoife smiled. The latch gave way, and the sun poured in, lighting up the room like a prism of wonder.

"Holy Mary mother of… How has this…"

Father John's voice floated away from him.

The Duke, Finnegan, Father John, and a handful of townsfolk stood frozen on the threshold.

"Why do you look so shocked, Father?" Aoife said coolly, intent on savoring the moment. "This is what you told everyone I could do. Come in, everyone, and admire it for yourselves."

The Duke squinted at Aoife, accepting her invitation. He stepped inside and walked toward the pile nearest him.

"I promise you it is real," she said. "I think this might be the first time that losing a bet will actually profit you."

The Duke picked up a coin and turned it over in his hand. He pivoted and tossed it back to Father John. The whisper of voices began to grow behind him as the shock let go its hold on their tongues.

Aoife caught sight of an older woman dressed in the neat clothing of a house servant. Her thick frame spoke of a lifetime's service inside the manor where the meals were more generous and more frequent than those given to servants who worked outside. Her dark eyes were wide and locked on Aoife. She searched Aoife's eyes, her gaze far too intrusive for a well-trained servant. Though it did not appear to be laced with anything sinister, the weight behind it was enough to make Aoife look away first.

"So your father's tales have proven true."

Finnegan had dropped to the floor and was running his fingers through the gold like it was water, no doubt slipping as much of it as he could into his pockets when no one was looking.

"I have fulfilled my end of the bargain," Aoife said.

She wanted to get out of the barn and away from the Duke in order to collect her reward, her family's estate, which, despite its past struggles, was more valuable to her than all the gold before her.

"I trust that you are pleased with what you see and that I am free to go."

The Duke walked toward her with a deliberate clip in his step.

"And just how, might I ask, did you manage this feat of wonder?"

"The 'how' has no bearing on this situation. Sharing my secret was not a part of the bargain."

"Aoife, how you spun this gold is not just of importance in regards to the rules of our bet, but in regards to your very soul and the lives of all those who might touch this gold. Show or explain to us how you managed this feat without the help of some other source. Surely you would have been living much more comfortably all these years if in fact you had known all along how to turn straw into gold. So reveal who taught you this art? Who was it that crept in here by night, and what offering did you make him?"

There was a collective shuffle and clatter as the townspeople turned abruptly and dropped any gold they might have been quietly pilfering. A hush overcame them all and several made the sign of the cross.

"Witchcraft and dealings with dark spirits is not permitted, is it, Father John?"

"Now I will not have you tossing those ideas around my daughter!" Finnegan interrupted. "She – "

"I am simply pointing out the obvious. This is not humanly possible without the aid of dark magic. If you could display the process, offer an explanation, then maybe we could all understand just how it is – humanly – possible. Or if you could even manage to do it again right now and show us all."

Aoife narrowed her eyes, enraged. If she could not prove the absence of dark magic, then the pyre and its flames awaited her. Her body, her family's fortune – none of it would ever appease the Duke and his wounded ego now. What kind of a man would let it all go so far? She was not sure how to stop him, but she refused to give in so easily to his games. Her hands went to clasp her sapphire pendant, as she often did in moments when her nervousness got the better of her, but as she touched her throat she remembered it was gone. Its absence and the piles of gold shimmering all around suddenly lit her up with confidence. The little man had protected her in every moment of need so far. There was no reason to fear that he would not do so now.

"I do not perform tricks on command; that has never been my way. But I will prove myself – tonight after I have rested and when the audience has retired. Lock me up – again – wherever you please. Let Father John accompany me if you want someone of Godly authority to ensure that no one but me is responsible for all that you see before you. No tower is too high or too secure. And in the morning after a night's long work in a place where no one could help me in my endeavor, you shall find more piles of gold than you see here before you now. That should satisfy you. But I will only do so after you have made a promise before Father John, the people of Stanishire, and God that when I do as you have asked, you shall question me no further nor threaten my family's fortune or safety."

The Duke nodded and clasped his hands behind his back, mulling over his next move. Aoife knew he was up to something, although she wasn't sure what.

"The round tower is high, with not more than a sliver of a window that you can barely put your hand through. Father John is loyal to me. I would not agree to this endeavor unless you were sure of your own abilities. For if you prove unable to replicate your golden touch tonight in the Godly presence of Father John, then it will be clear to all that it was only by courting dark magic that you succeeded, and you shall therefore pay the appropriate mortal price. But if you are able to show Father John your skills, not only will I refrain from questioning you any further, I will blot out any doubt about your mortal soul by making you my wife."

A bevy of gasps erupted around the barn. The house servant clapped a hand over her mouth and looked from Aoife to the Duke.

"I have already won. Why should I fear beating you again? It is obvious that you have offered to marry me only to use my talent for your own personal gain. You wish only to make me your slave!"

"Now Aoife," her father chimed in, "let's not cast accusations so recklessly."

He pulled her aside and whispered, "My child, I worry now for the safety of us all. We are in an impossible position; let's not put our lives at stake by angering him any further."

"But Father – "

"Quiet now, my dear Aoife," the Duke interrupted. He nudged Finnegan out of the way and whispered in her ear. "It is not the gold you've produced that I'm interested in or even how you made it. And I certainly don't want to send you to the pyre."

"Then why on earth have you even brought up the possibility of dark magic?"

"Because you've slipped through my fingers again like you did by the river. You beat me and – well – no one ever beats me," he said, sounding flustered. "If only you would let go of your stubborn view of me – your mistaken view – then maybe you would understand what it is I want from you."

"It will be hard for me to figure that out if you continue with this threat of sending me to the pyre!"

"Then end the threat," he said looking into her eyes. "Let's stop trying to beat each other."

"I'm all for that. I never wanted this – "

"Then marry me."

Chapter 7
Another Cup of Tea

As Aoife looked through the westward tower window, the sun slipped away too quickly. The glow of twilight promised to hang on until well into the short summer night. She closed her eyes, worrying over the precious few hours of absolute darkness she would have for her plan, if her reliance on the little man could be called a plan.

Aoife refused to think about the engraved box laying open on the table. The Duke's last minute visit that evening with the ring that still sparkled in the candlelight had been startling. He had seemed desperate to convince her that they could forgo the challenge if she accepted his proposal. Perhaps, he thought twice about the death threat he had imposed upon her, but forcing her into marriage did not make him any less monstrous.

A breeze ruffled through the room, flickering the candle's light. Father John was too sleepy and drunk from the libations he kept hidden in his robes to notice the subtle changes in the atmosphere. With her eyes still closed, Aoife smiled with relief. Despite her reaction to his appearance, he had come. Ever so slowly, she heard Father John yawn and slink down fast asleep upon his bed of hay. The air pulsed and whirled gently throughout the tiny turret and Aoife slowly opened her eyes, determined not to faint this time.

"So you've managed to get yourself locked up in a tower now," he said and began to pace, his face hidden by the hood of his long cloak. "Your life and death circumstances leave me little time to sleep."

"I wish I could say I wanted only your company, but I need your help again."

"And why should I care about anything that happens to you?" His voice was acidic, and Aoife could feel him twisting the very air.

"Because for some reason you do care," Aoife's voice was calm as she worked harder than ever to suppress her fears. "You have rescued me more times than I am probably even aware of. You have followed my restless wanderings through the woods and my trips to collect my father. You have bent the edges of nature for my amusement. And all this because you care."

"It's not true," his voice was rough, but its anger had broken. "How can I avoid seeing you when you run freely through my woods as if you owned them? It's impossible to ignore your trips and swims!"

"About those swims," she crinkled her eyes playfully, sensing that his bite was more pretense than real. She knew how to break the last vestige of his resistance. "Of every dive I have ever made into that swimming hole, I have never once worn a stitch of clothing."

He stopped his pacing and stood still. For the first time since she had met him in the flesh, he was at a loss for words. His form suddenly looked not fearsome, but lonely, lost, and fragile. And his stolen moments with her had been what? A sort of secret indulgence? An infatuation? Perhaps something more? Aoife felt a blush rise to her cheeks.

"I'm not embarrassed," Aoife said, despite the strange feeling of vulnerability that had crept up on her. "You probably know me better than anyone. You have seen me, all of me. And I haven't scared you away."

Aoife walked slowly toward him, wanting to make him feel as safe with her as she felt with him. She needed to regain his trust. His defiant stance before her revealed that he was not as small as Aoife remembered. She reached up to the edges of his hood. He cringed. She waited a moment, leaving her hand suspended in the air.

"Let me see you."

She gently took hold of his hood and lifted it off his head. He turned and hid his face from her. The murky eyes and the sagging flesh looked as ghoulish as she remembered, yet less frightening without the element of surprise. She cupped her right hand under his chin and gently turned his face toward her, noting that he was less than a head shorter than she was. He obeyed, but curled his lip. She held his gaze steady. His growl was like a wounded animal, fighting the hand trying to offer healing. She cupped his face with both hands. She felt the thick folds of his flesh and the uneven stubble of hair. His gnarled lips looked more like a protective shield than a threat. And his eyes. Their hazy film and the heavy fog upon them seemed like a painful curse of birth, not a reflection of his soul.

He narrowed his eyes, but Aoife found his efforts to push her away actually drawing her closer. The cloudiness of his eyes hid none of the pain of his alienation or the crushing burdens life had given him. Neither did it hide the beauty locked beneath. Her heart pounded and her face burned, knowing that here before her – twisted features and all – was a man who understood her and had shown her more love and loyalty than she had ever known. That was what mattered to her.

"You are seen."

His eyes welled with tears and he angled his head to the side, wilting into her palms. He looked away first. He turned and wiped his tears in his cloak, leaving Aoife's hands suspended in the air.

"I should have let you drown all those years ago. None of this will end well. I feel it," he said.

"What do you mean?" Aoife asked.

"I mean all of this," he waved his hand dismissively through the air without looking at her. "You think you can cure me by looking upon my face without fainting. You think that this means we are somehow connected in a way that goes beyond the boundaries of the woods and the night. But I know that's not true. I am the worthless, nameless man with a face not meant to be seen in the light. And for that, I will pay dearly."

"Have I offended you? Please, that cannot be. You are the only person who has ever done things *for* me instead of *to* me."

"Don't worry, Aoife," he said wearily. "I will not let any harm come to you, no matter what the ultimate cost to me. If I died, they wouldn't even have a name to etch on my stone, if anyone even found my corpse."

The defeat in his voice made Aoife wince with remorse. She wished she needed nothing from him but his company, or that she knew some way to assuage his sorrow.

"I would do anything to give you a moment's peace from this world."

He straightened as if a thought had come to him. He turned toward her.

"What?" Aoife asked. "What is it? If there is a way for me to repay your kindness, tell me."

"Come back to my home," he said. "Share one cup of tea and then I will return you to the tower and spin your gold."

Aoife looked from the slumbering priest, to the locked door, and back to him. The thought that he wanted nothing from her but her company was intoxicating. She could see the way he leaned back, bracing himself for rejection as she so often braced herself for disappointment. She took his hand and nodded.

Without warning he swung his cape over her body and a current of air blew over her with the force of a March wind, but the temperature of a summer breeze. Darkness shrouded her for a moment before the sparkle of the stars burst forth in the sky all around her. She was riding the night wind high in the atmosphere, the world below her far away, her drama a mere speck on the map. Her arms stretched out wide like the wings of a bird and she felt his arms extended below them, buoying them up and guiding her flight. Her heart and her arms opened wide to the universe with an unparalleled sense of freedom. Up she flew, faster than any creature on earth, until she thought her heart would burst and then down they dove until they reached the edge of the forest.

They soared just above the treetops circling right and left in a rhythmic dance. Then with the ethereal grace of a fairy, they came to a gentle stop above the tree line deep in the forest's core. With arms outstretched and still uplifted by his, Aoife felt their bodies pivot and descend in a slow magical spiral as first her toes, her knees, and then the rest of her body dipped below the treetops and toward the forest floor. Just before she reached the ground, Aoife felt him hesitate, holding onto the moment for a few seconds longer, before setting her down.

His arms slipped from her body, and he shied away into the shadows. Aoife touched the windswept cool of her skin and hugged herself as she stepped forward, her mind and body still descending from the heights to which she had soared.

"That was incredible!" she said. "I've never felt anything like it."

She turned to him, but he was standing far away. His cloak caught a hint of moonlight. She walked over to him and paused. After a moment she took his hand and tugged him into the light, happy that he did not resist.

"How do you do it?"

"I was showing off a bit," he laughed and shrugged his shoulders. "I can do it whenever I want. But most often, I just dissolve into the air and find my way around. That way there are no eyes to behold me, no fainting ladies to catch."

Aoife halted, then reached up and stroked his cheek in apology. But when she spied an inviting little cottage over his shoulder at the other end of the clearing, she forgot her guilt.

"Is that where you live? It's so beautiful. Let's go inside. You promised tea."

She was already off with his hand in hers. From the corner of her eye, she spied a smile on his face that lifted some of the weight of his sagging skin.

Underneath the full moon's light, the cottage's whitewashed walls stood bright against the forest greenery, and the steep pitch of the roof yawned longingly toward the sky. Hanging from each window was a box of flowers, their colors bright reds, blues and purples – strangely vibrant considering the sun's arduous journey through the trees.

Aoife reached for the latch on the front door and then seemed to remember her manners. His hand trembled as he reached for the handle. Aoife laid her hand over his and they released it together. He closed his eyes for a moment and then pushed the door open. Aoife touched his cheek and stepped across the threshold.

He stepped behind her and lit a candle on a long wooden table. He walked from corner to corner, from table to ledge, using the first candle to light all the rest until more than a dozen illuminated the room with their ethereal flames.

The furnishings were all simple, but artfully crafted. Beyond the cozy furnishings, the walls were covered with paintings of everything human. A large canvas of maidens washing laundry at the river's edge with their skirts and sleeves rolled up under a warm summer sun. A peasant family breaking bread at a table. Two lovers walking through a field, their fingers entwined, their expressions full of longing. A mother bent over a child's cradle, smiling and cooing a soothing lullaby to his outstretched hands. In one after another, the darkness of the background stood in stark contrast to the illuminated glow of their skin, the vivid colors of their clothing. They were everyday rituals and rites of passage.

Near a window facing the clearing where light poured in, stood an easel speckled with paints and surrounded by bowls and brushes stained from heavy use. All around him he had created the life she guessed he longed for.

Hanging from the ceiling were strings of sparkling gems and gold coins like the ones he had spun for Aoife. The largest rubies, emeralds, diamonds, and gemstones that she had ever seen dangled just above her head. She reached up to touch one, looking to him for permission. He nodded and she grazed her fingers against them, sending them fluttering and tinkling like fairy chatter. Prisms of light danced all around the cottage.

"Where did all these jewels come from? Can you make them as well as gold?"

His mouth trembled nervously as he stepped toward her.

"A deer drinking by the side of the river, throaty chirping from a bird's nest, a girl dancing barefoot in the forest – they are all beautiful things that I can see, but only from a distance," he said. "Yet I have the ability to

74

hold on to their images."

He put one hand out with his palm facing upwards like an offering. Closing his eyes he laid his other palm on top and began to move it in slow circles. His hands began to circle faster until a spark of light caught like a candle. As its glow spread and grew into a bright golden light, his hands separated and in a flash of light there stood a brilliant, sapphire colored stone. The room was filled with a momentary burst of light and then the magic of the moment collapsed inward into the stone in his hand.

He gestured for Aoife's hand, and she tentatively placed hers on top of the gem. A burst of heat and then an immediate pulse of energy filled her body as the image of her riding through the forest the day she met the Duke rose up all around her. She could smell the forest, hear the birds above, and see the ripple of her own hair. She was there, outside of herself looking on from his eyes.

"They're all memories I can keep and revisit any time I wish with the touch of my fingers."

He stepped away and reached up to the ceiling. With the flick of his wrist, the jewel found its home, strung above their heads with all the other memories the little man collected and watched. He ran his fingers over a few, smiling as the mysterious images brushed his fingertips and senses.

"I've never seen anything like it."

"You should see it in the morning when the sun lights up the east windows. It's like," he pulled back the excitement in his voice. "If you ever saw it, you would never forget it."

Aoife wondered if she might get the chance some day. She walked toward the hearth, large enough for warmth as well as cooking, and rested her hand upon the mantle. A breeze fluttered across the room and ruffled her skirts softly before rising up beneath the embers and coaxing the waning flames. A long tendril of dying smoke separated into two and then three and then more as the embers glowed brighter and then hotter until flames licked the sides of the hearth and stretched into a blazing fire.

Aoife turned toward him and opened her mouth to say something and then saw in his hands a dainty porcelain cup of steaming tea. She smiled graciously, accepting his offering. He motioned beside her to a chair that sat facing the fire, its fabric a rich tapestry of vines and flowers, and she sat down. He sat across from her in a matching chair. He reached between them to a small table and offered her cream and sugar, both of which she silently accepted and he wordlessly poured and scooped. She leaned back into her chair and he did the same, the only sounds the crackle of the fire before them.

Was it a spell, Aoife wondered as she sipped her tea, or was this what real peace and security felt like? She closed her eyes and breathed deeply, feeling her shoulders soften and drop for the first time since she was a little girl, before she awoke to the nightmare her father had made of her life. Slowly she opened her eyes and found him looking tremulously at her, his tea steaming and untouched. She smiled and watched the way he luxuriated in the warmth of her happiness. Never had anyone given her so much and asked so little in return. Never before had she been able to fill someone else up so completely just by sharing a cup of tea. In this light, the folds of his skin seemed less defined.

A feeling was growing within Aoife that she did not recognize and did not know how to contain. She had spent too much of her young life protecting herself to understand what it meant to be cared for and appreciated. The combination was addicting and she found to her own surprise that in this moment she cared little about his looks.

She rose and placed her empty cup on the table. She stepped over and took his teacup and placed it beside her own. Taking his hands in hers, she pulled him up before her. His eyes welled with tears as she raised her hand to his cheek again. He seemed taller than he appeared back in the tower. She leaned down and kissed a tear, feeling him tremble to the core. She looked deep into his eyes before pressing her lips to his, the pull more powerful than any of the reservations inside her. It was not the gnarled limbs she felt as they touched her skin, but his love as he wrapped his arms around her. He hugged her closer and she felt the last shiver of his fears dissolve.

At last, he stepped away and gripped the mantle, trying to contain his emotions.

"You've finished your tea," he swallowed hard. "I'll take you back now. You have more than fulfilled your end of the bargain."

"The bargain? You think I kissed you as part of a bargain?" Aoife was too drunk from their embrace to comprehend his cool response.

"Bargains and deals," he replied trying to inject some of his impish front back into his voice. "That's what we do. I'll get you back to the tower and your miserable life."

"But I don't want to go," Aoife replied.

"Oh, so you want to stay? Here with me?" He quipped. "You want to stay and be mistress of my house and serve me tea and darn my socks? You can look beyond a lot of faults in people, but I doubt this is the face you'd choose to wake up to every morning."

"Why do you doubt me? And why do you think I'm so awful that I couldn't – "

"Keep from fainting in my presence? Look past what this world gave me for a face?"

"I doubt you have followed and protected me all these years because you think I am an ordinary girl. So why would it surprise you to find that I might…"

Her sentence hung unfinished. All she knew was that she felt more for him than she expected to feel, and she was not ready to leave with him degrading their connection.

"Finish the sentence, Aoife! Or can't you? You can't finish it because we both know that love is not a feeling you or anyone else could ever have for me."

"That's not true!"

"Then say it," his words were an icy challenge. "Say that you will stay here with me until the morning. Say that you will give up your family, your latest crisis, your whole life and remain right here to wake up to jeweled sunrises. I've room enough, sustenance enough, and magic enough for us both to live happily ever after. I could give you all that your heart desires, including your freedom. I could give you everything. But do you want it if it comes with this face?"

Images of all she would leave behind if she left sprung up in her mind. The Duke would take everything from her family. She saw her mother and father left homeless, working with their hands to survive, and Tara lying in a bed of squalor with no fire to warm her as she coughed herself into a premature death. Or worse yet, the fires of the pyre might claim them for their ties to the mysterious Aoife and the dark powers with which she turned straw to gold and then vanished from the tower. She saw the flames consuming them, sending their screams high above the smoke and ash while she sipped tea with her protector.

Their lives.

His heart.

His ultimatum meant that someone would suffer, and she realized how right he had been. It would be him. She had to return to protect her family, which meant that she would decline his offer. She did not have to know his life story to know that she would not be the first one to walk away from him or to make him feel rejected.

"I want to stay with you very much, but my family is counting on me." Aoife closed her eyes for a moment before opening them to his icy glare. "Their lives depend upon my return. I cannot stay no matter how I feel about you."

He leapt up and circled behind his chair.

"Let me go home, and I will return to you after their lives are safe!"

"Promises! Empty promises!" He yelled. "I've heard enough of them in my life. Go home to your tower, your family, and your miserable life."

"I don't want the life I had!" she pleaded. "If you

can help me turn that straw into gold one more time, then I can save my family. Then I can come to you, freely and of my own will."

"And exactly what will that freedom mean when the Duke's ring is wrapped tightly around your finger?"

"I will never marry him!" she shouted.

"Silly girl," he shot back. "Have you learned nothing of the world? If you tried to refuse him, he would only pose a new threat and then another upon your family until you inevitably said yes. For whatever selfish reason, he wants you, and he is a man who stops at nothing to get what he wants."

She turned away from him and sat back in her chair. Despite the agreement she made with the Duke, he did not seem ready to let her go. On the other hand, the little man's offer was so much more authentic – even with all its magic – than any offer awaiting her at home.

"I cannot risk my family's lives to protect my own," she cried. "Please understand. No matter what my parents have done, they are still my family. And my sister, I would never leave her behind to die. Ever. Can you not just give me a few more hours? Let me finish this business and then fly me away before the Duke can make a wife of me. Surely you can give me a few hours more."

His chest heaved as he considered Aoife's counter-proposal. While he wore out a path in front of the fire, she prayed that he would grant her this one last wish. He stopped and looked out the window. Finally, his body straightened with an unnatural rigidity, and he shook his head.

"You're hardly the first woman to break a vow of

loyalty to me. I'll not be left alone this time. I'll not wait alone while you warm your feet before a fire with people less deserving and less devoted to you than I am." His voice was resolute. "I'll not be the one cast aside again. Not this time."

He left her by the fire and walked outside into the night. She followed him to where he stood under the starlight. The wind roared, forcing him to yell louder above its fury. She dropped to her knees, frightened by the storm brewing around them.

"Your choice remains simple. It's me or your family. Choose me and you may stay here under my protection and enjoy as much freedom as you please. Choose your family and I will take you back to the tower and spin your gold. But my services will cost you more this time than a chipped necklace. You will have to marry the Duke, and when the time comes, hand over to me his greatest treasure."

"Why do you have to reduce this to an ultimatum? And why would you punish me by forcing me to marry the Duke? What has he to do with any of this?"

"There is no compromise when you must choose between those you care about. Someone is going to get hurt. And as to the price, he has everything to do with this. I have my reasons, none of which I have to share with you," his voice was uneven and strained. "So let's not delay the inevitable. With the price in mind, who will you choose? Your family. Or me?"

His words were harsh, but the silent plea, the barely hidden hope that he would be chosen, hung heavy in his every breath. Aoife shook her head slowly from side to side.

"I have to go back for them," she whispered. "I can't leave them like this."

"But you have no problem leaving me," he said defeated. "I should have known better than to think you could see past my face. You can see past the sins of whores and gamblers, but not my face," he looked at her with a pained expression. "I will take you back. I will spin your gold. And when you rise in the morning you will agree to marry the Duke. You'll not see me again for a little while. I'll go far away from here. But your job, when next I appear to collect my payment, will be to hand over the Duke's greatest treasure."

"And what does that mean?"

"Nothing you need to concern yourself with right now," he said, his thoughts shrouded in mystery. "Do we have a deal?"

"You've left me no other choice."

"No, no," he waved his crooked finger at her. "You had your choice, and you chose a life with people you despise over a life with me. Never forget that. I know I never will."

She wanted to argue, but his angry glare left little room for debate. She nodded in agreement, her shoulders dropping with regret. He whirled his cape around and she felt herself born up into the night air again. The wind whipped and tossed her body around the sky like a leaf in a tempest. She reached out for his hands, but their reassuring touch was nowhere. Had she a voice she would have been heard all through the forest screaming for her life.

Chapter 8
Shackled

A clatter of laughter and cascading clank of metal pierced the thick fog that hung heavily over Aoife's mind. Father John laughed softly as he crammed his pockets with gold. Towers of coins loomed far above Aoife's head and their precarious leanings once again defied explanation.

As Aoife rubbed her forehead, an unfamiliar weight on her hand caught her attention. She glanced down, her thoughts still slow and thick, but in a sudden startling moment of clarity she saw the Duke's ring shackled upon her finger. She froze as the amnesia of the prior night instantly evaporated. She grabbed the ring and tried to pry it off. But as she struggled, the ring tightened its magical hold like a vice, throbbing and threatening to strangle the life out of her finger. Despite its mysterious grasp, Aoife twisted and tore, the fate of her finger far less important than that of her independence.

She sighed and wept softly, the loss of her freedom hanging heavy upon her. She looked down at the stone and her future, noticing that it looked different than it had when the Duke showed it to her the night before. He had left the box open by the candle, hoping perhaps that the ring's sparkle would convince her to forget the tower and his challenge and marry him instead. But something unnatural marred its reflection this morning. The blue topaz's lucid, liquid glow and its transparent sparkle were gone. A greenish haze coated its once dazzling surface. She rubbed it with her skirt, but her efforts proved useless. Within the large stone a storm was brewing; swirls of darkness moved in a twisted torrent that promised only misery. She looked away, feeling the cataracted eyes of the little man staring back at her through the mottled muck that clouded the ring. Whatever spell he had cast on the ring the Duke gave her had left its mark on its surface.

The sound of approaching footsteps startled Father John. He pocketed a last few handfuls of gold and straightened his robes, seeming to notice Aoife for the first time.

If he said anything to her, she didn't hear it. If the voices that filled the tower were directed at her, she did not listen. Nothing seemed able to reach the bottom of the deep well into which Aoife had fallen. Out of all the curious witnesses who had entered, only the anxious servant who had stared so strangely at her the day before caught her attention.

The Duke looked around at the towers of gold, swallowing hard and barely containing his shock. He picked up a piece of gold and turned in over in his hand.

"I have heard tell of some who are capable of such feats as this. Tell me, Father John, was there a visitor last night who made this miracle possible?" he said turning toward Father John.

The Duke's expression, devoid of his easy arrogance, appeared hesitant and almost frightened.

"I held vigil all night, and nowhere in this tower did I see or hear any visitor, my Lord," he replied.

"You are certain that there was no man here?"

"I saw no one."

He looked relieved, slightly. Aoife wondered if he had perhaps been telling the truth when he said he did not mean to put her life in jeopardy.

"Then you stand by Aoife and her claims that she alone is responsible for the gold in the barn and this tower as well."

"On my honor," Father John said swallowing hard, "I saw no other soul here accompanying the young lady in her task."

A seam in his cloak gave way and a cascade of some thirty pieces of gold tumbled to the floor. The Duke's eyebrow twitched wryly as he eyed the gold. He stepped toward Aoife.

"Then the next question is did you witness her producing the gold and if so how did she – "

The Duke halted in his step, his gaze locked on the ring on Aoife's hand. He looked up at her, and a sense of elation melted his features into a childlike smile, the likes of which Aoife had never seen him wear. He took her hand in his, and she tried not to shiver at his touch.

"Aoife," he said at a loss for words. "You won. You filled this room with riches and could have happily walked down those stairs and back to your home. But you have accepted my proposal to become my wife."

Aoife remained stoic as he kissed her hand. He seemed moved near tears, but they moved her not at all. He saw the ring on her finger as a choice made of her own free will. As a result of that assumption, he felt more triumph than if she had demurred and placed the ring on her finger in lieu of last night's bet.

He kissed her on the lips, and searched her vacant eyes for a sign of love.

"I see you are as overwhelmed as I am," he said. "You can find the words to explain your change of heart later."

He put his arm around her turned them both toward the small group of people behind them.

"I present to you with the greatest of happiness, my future bride," he said.

Finnegan shouted his approval, and the witnesses began to cheer. Everyone looked thankful that the morning had ended with a marriage announcement rather than a burning.

Aoife felt the Duke swelling with pride beside her and witnessed the small assembly including her father clapping before her. How could no one notice her sadness and the forlorn expression she wore? Here she stood in the moment of her greatest despair, and everyone around her was ready to celebrate. Or was the transparent charade of her acceptance simply a detail about which no one cared?

No one except the older servant woman. She

didn't appear sold on Aoife's acceptance, but she didn't seem concerned, as much as she seemed suspicious.

On the other hand, her father's face, hung heavy with last night's drink, was now puffed up with this morning's gloating. It was so different from the glow of the little man's gracious smile beside last night's whispering fire – the glow of simple gratitude for her presence and nothing more.

"To my daughter," he cheered with his hand raised, as if he held a glass of mead and was speaking to his friends at Maeve's. "The most beautiful and talented girl a man could hope for. I give her proudly to you, my Lord, yet with a heavy heart, knowing that she shall no longer be mine. She is a rare gem, my daughter. The kind that is not easy to part with, except when a man knows he shall gain a son of such honor and might as you, my Lord."

Her father was far from perfect, but he had always held her in the crook of his arm like his favorite little girl. Yet now, in the presence of all this gold and the royal titles near at hand, he could not see or would not acknowledge that there was no way she wanted to marry this man. Aoife felt betrayed, wondering how he did not realize how unhappy his little girl was.

Chapter 9
Something Red

The opalescent pearls and the sparkling emerald that hung around the woman's throat housed more life than her empty eyes and mouth. Her cool, ivory skin looked as frozen and immovable as marble. Aoife thought she looked like a drowned mermaid ripped from the water's current and propped up like a fisherman's trophy. She stood with arms outstretched on her pedestal for all to admire and gaze upon, the lifelessness of her body an irrelevant and inconsequential footnote.

Bronagh's smile mocked the corpselike reflection that stared hauntingly back at Aoife from the mirror. The tendrils of her hair that usually hung so freely were twisted and tied into a complicated braid. Her hands stretched out in either direction as needle and thread sewed her limbs snugly into her wedding gown. Its heavy beading and embroidery weighed her down even as the boning sewn into every seam propped her up, giving the appearance that she still lived.

A morbid sense of relief had filled Aoife when she heard that Tara was too ill this morning to join them. She laid upstairs sweating and shivering with fever and chills, waiting for the apothecary's herbs to take effect. Aoife would never have been able to remain so remote with Tara in the room. Tara would have seen through it all, and Aoife would have had to explain. And how could she explain any of this? Tara was the only one who truly deserved Aoife's sacrifice, but there was no way for her to tell this to her without burdening her with guilt. So for once, Tara's illness and consequent absence felt like a temporary blessing.

It was safer to swim far beneath the surface of her countenance, far away from the sting of the nightmare that her life was becoming right before her very eyes.

From the corner of her consciousness, Aoife pitied the seamstresses sent to her home by the Duke to sew her into her dress, knowing that her mother's needlework was far superior and that she was overseeing their work with biting criticism.

The sting.

Aoife looked down at her hand and noticed a bead of ruby red blood that had bubbled up on her fingertip. The seamstress must have pricked her when she finished the lace seam by her wrist. She turned over her hand and watched as the bead grew and ballooned bigger until it finally spilled upon the floor. Aoife admired the perfect circumference of the droplet while the women continued stitching and her mother's voice echoed at the edges of her attention. She wondered if, like a doll filled with sawdust, this tiny puncture might prove large enough for her blood to spill out completely upon the floor and release her from her prison.

"You've pricked her!" Bronagh yelled. "Did you bloody the dress?"

Bronagh pressed her handkerchief against the wound and pushed Aoife's skirt away from the droplet of blood on the floor. Aoife knew her mother held her hand very tight and it should throb, but she felt nothing, like when her mother used to whip her for bringing her father home. She had become very good at receding inside herself and hiding from her mother's ire.

"Aoife, what's wrong with you? Step down," she said and then turned to the seamstress. "You. Clean this up."

Her mother's order sounded eerily similar to the one she gave the servants after she beat Aoife.

"Yes, Mother," Aoife replied blankly. "We wouldn't want anyone to see your daughter's blood all over the floor. That would be very inappropriate."

Her mother turned toward Aoife and pursed her lips.

"Aoife, I will not have you playing games today. Marrying the Duke will provide us more riches and wealth than your father or even your manish penchant for profits ever could."

"The wealth of which you speak is far greater now that I added two rooms full of gold to it."

Her mother's features cooled uncomfortably and she looked away.

"Yes, we are all aware of that," she replied.

Aoife knew her mother would never ask questions about how she turned straw into gold. Bronagh never asked questions whose answers she did not want to know.

"Just remember," Bronagh said, "you must play the part of the happy bride. You are to make your future husband feel he is your sun and all the warmth in your day."

"Dress me up, hand me the script and I will do as I am told. I am like the little doll you always wanted me to be, Mother. But do not expect me to look lively, since I have never heard of a doll that lived."

Bronagh's features hardened over. Aoife gazed at her mother indifferently and then stepped back up on her pedestal and stretched her arms out wide.

"Stitch me up."

Chapter 10
of Whores and Mothers

Aoife stepped into the gilded coach while the maids
sent by the Duke held the hem of her wedding gown
above the dusty ground. She sat carefully while they
arranged her dress within the coach. Her father stepped
forward to sit beside her on the trip from their home to
the church, but Aoife held up her hand.

"If my freedom will be sacrificed on the altar for
your purse, then I will go there unaccompanied. I want
to taste these last moments of freedom alone."

He looked like he might argue, but Aoife's icy
stare silenced him. He nodded and walked back to the
smaller carriage with Bronagh. Aoife looked up to
Tara's window and was surprised to catch a last glimpse
of her out of bed. She stood in her nightgown with one
hand pressed to the glass and a handkerchief over her
mouth. She traced a heart in the moisture like she did
when Aoife was gathering flowers from the garden to

bring up to her room when they were little. Aoife waved, the sight of her sister a reminder of why she was giving up her freedom.

Both coaches lurched forward and made their way to the church in town. The dirt kicked up and Aoife wanted to turn and take one last look at the only home she had ever known. She had trampled these fields barefoot and climbed every tree in sight. She had snuck secret sweet treats from the kitchen and eaten them behind the stone wall. But she eyed the road ahead, refusing to let her parents mistake her nostalgia for her childhood for sorrow over the loss of either of them. She knew her anger would soften and relent eventually, as it always had in the past, but for now she lingered in her resentment.

The coach slowed as it approached the edge of the town. The people of Stanishire were out shopping and visiting as if today were no different than any other. The world's indifference to her plight seemed merciless. Aoife spotted Maeve in the middle of the onlookers. With her shoulders pressed back and her eyes locked on the carriage, she stood out amidst the steadily moving crowd. The deep purple gown she wore appeared almost royal. Aoife wondered if Maeve had ever known what it was like to blend in. As the coach drew nearer, Aoife ordered the driver to stop.

Aoife nodded to Maeve, silently beckoning her to the coach. Maeve's gaze flickered for a moment to the coach behind carrying Aoife's parents, but then moved toward Aoife with her habitual grace and ease. Aoife could see the deliberate swish of her hips and the calculated cool with which she frosted her movements.

When she reached the coach, Aoife spied the subtle, uneven rise and fall of her chest.

"You told me once to make my choice carefully so that I did not end up left in the dust, and now here I am – dust kicking up all around me – heading toward a future with a man I detest," Aoife's words were soft and sad.

The lace edging of Maeve's bodice shuddered at the defeated ring in Aoife's voice. Maeve blinked hard, and Aoife wondered if it might actually be tears she pushed back. Aoife's fate suddenly seemed all the more tragic. She gripped the side of the coach, as if it might offer her the strength she needed.

"You don't seem the type to marry for money, so I'm not sure why you have chosen to marry this one," Maeve said, waiting for an explanation that Aoife was not free to offer her. When Aoife's silence proved that none would come, Maeve continued. "I am hardly one to fabricate silver linings in impossible situations," her words were plain and honest. "But you will decide what this choice does to you. Will it bend your neck? Will it break you? Or will it make you more of who you already are."

Aoife furrowed her brows. Maeve pulled her soft lavender shawl closer about her.

"You've a gift for finding your way through impossible situations, Aoife. Why would this new life be any different? You may lose your way for a time, but do not lose your *self*. I trust that you can find ways to still be yourself within those stone walls."

"But I've already lost myself," Aoife said. "I do not see how I'll ever find a way to be me again."

"You will," Maeve's urged. "Bat your lashes. Share your smiles. Let him enjoy your midnight sighs, and learn to make him sigh as well. I promise that you will be surprised how much he will grant you when he thinks he has sway over your heart. Letting him *think* he has won does not mean you have lost."

Aoife laughed, hadn't her mother told her something similar about making her future husband feel like the center of her world? What would her mother think if she knew how much she and Maeve apparently agreed upon? How similar was the training of wives and whores.

Maeve laid a perfumed hand upon Aoife's. Maeve's strength and wisdom poured into Aoife, and she laid her other hand on top of Maeve's. Maeve nodded to her definitively and laid her other hand on the pile. Maybe she could do this. Just maybe there was enough of her self and enough of a future left to live for.

"Let's get moving!" Finnegan shouted.

They nodded to each other, silently generating as much strength as they could for the path that lay before Aoife. As the coach lurched back into motion, their hands held tight for a second and then slipped apart. Aoife lifted her chin and nodded goodbye.

Chapter 11
Playing the Part

She sat before her mirror while her servant finished combing her hair. Fiona, the servant who had surveyed the scene so completely in both the tower and the barn, appeared more collected and reserved today. She gazed only indirectly at Aoife and up until now had spoken only as necessary.

"You made a beautiful bride," Fiona said.

Aoife cringed, preferring silence.

"I was a servant to the Duke's mother and had quite a hand in raising your new husband, especially after his mother passed. There was something in his smile today that I have not seen since he was a boy. Maybe being in love will do him some good."

"I doubt his smile had much to do with love," Aoife replied coolly.

"Ah, do not discount his feelings for you," Fiona said. "He left home at the young age of seventeen, and until he met you, he had not spent more than a night under this roof before leaving again for other places. He may not have courted you in a traditional fashion, but his love for you may prove more powerful than the things that ail him."

Aoife looked at Fiona in the reflection, her silver-streaked hair tucked and pinned back tightly so that the huge swell of hope in her eyes was impossible not to notice.

"If you have any thoughts that I can spin magic or heal old wounds, you can put that right out of your head. This is no fairy tale wedding, and I have no secret powers or strength, despite what that gold in the tower might have led you to believe."

Fiona ran her fingers through the thick waves of Aoife's chestnut hair, loosening a tangle with a hand as careful as Nell, the nurse who had helped raise Aoife and Tara. Fiona had the same tender touch, despite the thick knuckles and papery skin of her aged hands.

"Spinning straw into gold is not the only measure of magic," Fiona said. "That's not what I was talking about. Your magic is more real and more powerful than a pile of gold. You have bent the knees of more than one haunted man. I suppose what thrills me is also what frightens me, for if you cannot undo what has been done, I don't suppose anyone can."

Her words were a quiet plea Aoife did not want hear. Aoife had little interest in solving mysteries or mending any more broken people.

The click of her chamber door as it opened sent her heart pounding. Fiona's hands involuntarily squeezed Aoife's shoulders ever so gently, sending a shiver down her spine. Fiona curtseyed in her bulky servant's attire and left, but not before Aoife caught her loaded gaze wandering from the Duke to Aoife.

Even before the Duke came to her room, Aoife knew what was to come. The loss of her virginity was imminent and would thus have to be deemed inconsequential in order for her to survive. From what Aoife had seen of men's desires at Maeve's, sex would strip away the last vestige of what separated her from the painted ladies. She had bartered her body along with her freedom for her family's security. Aoife looked at her reflection, wondering who she would see the next time she looked.

She watched stoically in the mirror as he leaned down and kissed her hair and then her cheek. After a moment he took her by the hand and she stood up to face him. Aoife sensed that he was waiting for her to kiss him or give some sign that she wanted him the way he wanted her.

Maeve's advice to learn to play her part in order to win the game came back to her. He kissed her softly, trying to melt the hardness he must have felt in her, but his desire and his yearning for her only pushed her further away. She pressed her hand against his chest and then stepped away. She turned her back to him so that he might undo the pearled buttons that bound her body within her gown.

As he kissed the back of her neck and then slowly released one button at a time, Aoife closed her eyes and drew down the curtain upon her soul. She needed a safe distance between them. She let her attachment to her skin, then her limbs, and then her body slip slowly away from her like reeds floating down river, so that what happened to her body would not happen to her. She slipped away under her skin like a child hiding from monsters under her blanket. Her thoughts blended into the pulsing of her blood, the current carrying her away from the darkened room and his touch. She slipped deeper within, into the nearly invisible pores of her bones, the places only death, decay, and the apothecary's magnifying glass could reveal. As she poured herself into each and every space, her self dissolved into fluidity. Like the birth of the universe, a thousand tiny pieces of her self burst from her body, which no longer held her soul hostage. Her spirit expanded and shimmered through the air like diamond confetti floating through space.

As his lips neared her waist, her eyes opened slowly, the character of Aoife, the dutiful wife, had risen to the surface and was playing her part like an obedient automaton. Then and only then, did she turn toward him and press her body to his, coaxing him gently but firmly to the bed. He obeyed the swish of her hips but stared into her vacant eyes with a hint of disappointment. He raised his hand to her cheek but she caught it before it made contact. She kissed the back of his hand and then fastened it to her waist. She pushed him down on the bed, and any questions he might have had drifted away as Aoife bathed him in a sea of pleasure.

He was gentle and passionate, nothing like the manipulative force that had cornered her in the woods or into their marriage. Although she was grateful for the shift in his personality, she was not ready to forget how she had ended up in this marriage. He stayed with her all night with his arms around her while he slept. The feel of his body pressed against hers was a reminder of all the freedom and privacy she had lost, the very things that had always defined her. As she lay awake all night, she replayed Maeve's advice and reassurances about how to find her own private freedom within the marriage, which was the only thing that kept Aoife from losing her mind under the weight of his arms.

Chapter 12
Caught

It had been a long day and Aoife rode back to the manor house, exhausted and starving. Earlier than the servants and, more importantly, her husband, Aoife rose, as had become her custom throughout the first month of their marriage, and headed outdoors. Her early morning strolls and rides had started out as escapes from her husband's attentions. Over time, they had become nearly all day expeditions in which she managed to tour every corner of the estate until the herding patterns of every animal and the rotation of every field were as familiar to her as the woods. She could not stop from criticizing Cashel's decisions and imagining all the improvements she would have loved to make. Every time he saw her roaming the fields or the barns, he scurried off before she had a chance to tell him exactly what she thought about the way he ran the estate.

The Duke was content with her outings and

seemed happy to be able to spend his days overseeing the business of his lands, the needs of the people over which he ruled, and of course his bachelor habits of hunting, riding his horses into the ground, and whatever else it was he did when Aoife was not present.

She had given up trying to talk to the Duke about her ideas for the manor. She had approached him several times with her ideas for updating the plans for the fields and livestock. He listened patiently, his eyes entranced by her, and then he would put his arms around her and tell her not to worry about such things as animals and land anymore.

"You have more wealth than your father could ever take from you," he would say. "With me by your side there is no need for you to worry about these things any longer."

She would walk away fuming. Since leaving home, she had become painfully aware of just how important overseeing and working her family's estate had been to her. It had started out as a necessity, a means of keeping her family from financial ruin. But over time, it had become so much more. When she planned the crops for a season, turned over the soil, or was present for the birth of a spring lamb, she was the architect of her life. She was willing her future to grow literally and figuratively all around her. She didn't see mud; she saw the seeds she planted below the surface that would spindle their way out of their shells, twist their way to the surface, and burst forth with an explosion of life and beauty and possibility.

And now all that possibility had been taken away from her and exchanged for pretty dresses and sparkly baubles. The Duke had thought himself so kind for having used the gold she had supposedly spun to hire a man to oversee her father's estate and provide him with enough gold to squander to excess at Madame Maeve's. As she walked circuitously around the grounds of the manor, she mourned the lack of purpose and direction that had become her life and found herself despising Caleb, the man who had taken her role at home. Like Cashel, Caleb, too, ran from Aoife's tough questioning when he saw her coach approaching for a visit.

She also mourned the sanctuary of the forest she had lost along with the little man's protection. Often on impulse Aoife ran toward the woods and her secret refuge by the falls only to remember that these woods were the little man's domain. She had ridden her horse to see him about three or four times in her first month at the manor. Each time she brought what she hoped was the Duke's greatest treasure. And each time he had laughed at her offering, reminding her that he would seek her out when the time was right.

She was angry with him for making her marry the Duke and for waving this mystery of his greatest treasure over her head, but angrier with herself when she thought about how her life would have been different had she chosen to stay with the little man. She remembered the warmth of the fire and his smile and the safety of the woods. But there was no release to be found there anymore and no safety that she could count on since she had hurt him.

When she reached the manor, she used the servants' entrance by the kitchen.

"Good afternoon, my Lady," the cook greeted her.

"The bread and stew is warming over the coals and there's a cool pitcher of cider upstairs waiting for you in your chamber."

"Thank you kindly," Aoife said, taking the steaming plate.

She headed up the back staircase and tiptoed down the hall to her room. She rounded a corner and reached for the latch on her door when it opened suddenly, revealing Fiona exiting with a dress that needed mending.

"My Lady," Fiona said with surprise. "Let me help you with that."

Aoife tightened her lips, but handed Fiona the plate. She had learned that there was little point in refusing Fiona's assistance. Aoife walked over to the table by the window with the view of the woods. Fiona set down the plate and poured the cider.

"I trust you enjoyed your ride today?" Fiona said.

Aoife replied with the usual quick nod, trying to avoid conversation. Aoife felt Fiona eyeing her closely as was her habit. Aoife's survival here was predicated on keeping her relationships cool and removed, but underneath Fiona's polite words was a desire to open up something between them.

Aoife was ready to dismiss her so that she could finish her meal in privacy and then fall asleep for a few hours before the evening meal in the dining hall with the Duke. Her all day excursions were exhausting, but so too were her nights with the Duke. She never denied him any of his passions. When he knocked at her door, Aoife rose to meet his embrace and never feigned a headache or any of the other ailments employed by dispassionate wives. Always a quick learner with an eye for gaining her freedom, she realized that the more pleasure she provided him by night, the more pleasure he desired to give her by day, which in Aoife's case meant freedom.

"I see your husband has left you another gift, my Lady," Fiona said before Aoife could dismiss her.

Aoife buttered her bread without looking up. After her excursions, it was not unusual for her to return to her room and find the Duke's fingerprint somewhere in her space. Propped up on her vanity was almost always a gift of some sort. A jeweled bracelet of sapphires and diamonds. A golden locket. A gown of emerald silk spilling over her chair. She eyed it all with disdain, evidence of the price he put on her love and affection. Indifferent and immune to their power, Aoife walked past them and flopped on her bed to. She could not deny the change in him and the way he treated her, but it did not matter. Why he had changed or how he felt for her meant nothing after the way he had trapped her and threatened her family. And why did he even want to marry her? Was it out of spite because she had rejected him by the falls? Or was it simply greed that drove him to want to own the woman who could spin gold? But he had never asked her to replicate her golden touch. And why was that? She had saved up a store of reasons why she couldn't do it again if he asked, but he never did, which seemed odd. Wouldn't anyone else have asked her to continue spinning wealth?

She shook her head, refusing to let questions about the Duke take up too much space in her mind. Kind words and sparkly gifts could not erase her knowledge of his calculating scheme to ensnare her.

So when he gave her his gifts, she would see him later at dinner and say, "Thank you for your thoughtful gift. Your tokens always show the finest taste."

"I'm glad to see how happy they make you," he would reply. "I know I didn't court you the way I should have, and I regret the way things began between us, but I wish to please you and spoil you now as you deserve."

"Your attentions are noted."

He would lean back in his chair and watch her silently while she ate. But always in the air was a sense of expectation, a sense that he was waiting for something from her that she had yet to give. She was polite, but she would never give him her genuine affection, which had become both her source of power over him and her revenge for all that he had done.

Later that night after an unusually long evening meal, Aoife was in her chamber rubbing her neck and removing the pearled choker he had given her when he entered unnoticed by Aoife and Fiona. She scratched at the back of her neck where the clasp had irritated her skin and tossed it into a drawer.

"So I see my gift pleases you less than I had hoped."

Aoife jumped. Fiona, curtseyed stiffly but deeply before heading toward the door.

"I am so sorry," Aoife stumbled, "to have seemed so…. unappreciative of your efforts to …"

She straightened her skirt and cleared her throat, trying to jump back into character in order to finish her sentence. His heels clicked slowly across the room. He looked down in the drawer where his gifts lay in a heap, like tangled seaweed and shells coughed up on the distant shores far away from the manor. He picked up yesterday's bracelet, only to find it entwined with several other chains and jewels. Snarled as they were, they looked cheap and meaningless. Aoife instantly wished she had not said no when Fiona asked to organize them.

"So it *is* an empty gratitude that rings in your voice when you thank me."

"No, no," Aoife replied. "My apologies for my carelessness. I should have stowed your gifts away with greater care."

Her secret ingratitude might get her in trouble.

"There is no need to apologize. I can see what is in you heart, or not," he said disconsolately. "I only hope that I can find what feeds your heart, so I might reap the rewards of fulfilling your desires."

He kissed her on the cheek and left her to herself that night. She should have welcomed the peace. Instead she found herself wide awake replaying his words.

Chapter 13
Visitors

"**Y**es, Mother," Aoife nodded. "I will consider having the drapes embroidered."

"It is your duty to make this your home," Bronagh said, "a place which the Duke will be happy to return."

Aoife walked passed her mother, pretending to heed her latest lesson on wifely responsibilities, and sat next to Tara, whose usually pale skin was glowing with warmth and life. Since her marriage, the Duke had granted Aoife's request to seek out the best care for Tara. He sent the doctor who had cared for his father to Tara and asked for regular updates on her health, which had surprised Aoife. The doctor made his recommendations, which proved more effective than any of the doctors Aoife and her family had procured for her over the years. Her cough was so much improved that she had been able to leave their family home for walks and visits to see Aoife regularly.

The last time Tara came, they had enjoyed a picnic under the trees. Tara told a story about the tricks she had begun playing on their father. Most recently she had taken to using her needle against him. He had complained that the reason he was running out of money so quickly was because of the holes in the fitchets in his tunic where he kept his coins. As to why he was keeping coins there instead of his purse he did not answer. Tara rifled through the laundry and found the tunics he had complained about. She filled them with coins and then sewed up the seams so that he could not reach inside the fitchets to get them. Tara stood up and paraded around the blanket, mimicking the way their father had angrily dug into his pockets and ripped at the seams with futility to get those coins. She had a feisty side that no one had ever seen because she spent so much time in bed. Her drastically improved health was Aoife's only consolation when she thought too hard about how strange her life had ended up.

While their mother continued to inspect the drapes and furnishings, Aoife took her sister's hand and leaned her head on her shoulder, remembering the way Tara used to call to Aoife when she was cold. Aoife would sneak out of bed and crawl in beside Tara and rub her hands and feet. Before long they would settle into a warm sisterly embrace and fall asleep.

In the midst of Aoife's nostalgia, something in the adjoining room fell to the floor with a loud bang. Aoife coughed hardily as she stood up and tugged her mother away from the door of her private chamber.

"Mother," Aoife said ignoring her mother's

backward glances, "while unexpected visits are lovely, I must ask for some privacy. If you don't mind, I need to rest before dinner."

She nodded with a cheerful smile and motioned for Tara to follow. Her mother looked quizzically back toward her chamber for a moment but then smiled at Aoife.

"You are such a smart wife," Bronagh said, beaming with pride. "It is important to look your best for your husband, especially in the evenings."

Tara rolled her eyes.

"It is so wonderful to see you looking so well, Tara," Aoife said. "Next time I will come see you, and we will sit under the trees all day and maybe even go for a ride if you are well enough."

"I will be well, or as well as I can be with my sister gone and married." Tara hugged Aoife and whispered, "Are you sure you're happy here?"

"As I tell you every time you ask, as long as you are well then I am happy."

"You act as though this marriage is exactly what you always wanted," Tara replied. "But I know you too well to believe that."

They held each other before pulling apart. Tara eyed her suspiciously, seemingly aware that her sister had been hiding things from her. But she did not push. Their mother was present, which left very little time for honest talk.

Tara grabbed one last embrace from Aoife before Bronagh ushered her toward the door.

"Now do not forget to have those curtains replaced," Bronagh reminded Aoife. "It won't be long before you are receiving guests, and you would not want them to see moth holes any more than you would want them to see you without your hair fixed."

"You're right, Mother," Aoife replied.

"I never thought I'd hear those words from my older daughter," Bronagh said. She scooted Tara through the door and turned back to Aoife. Her sweet smile revealed her long ago girlish beauty. "I'm so proud of you, Aoife." She reached out awkwardly and patted Aoife's shoulder. "You have grown into a fine young lady."

Bronagh's compliment was sincere, which made Aoife cringe from the tip of her carefully braided hair down to her satin slippered feet. She tried to cast off the feeling that only after she had surrendered the parts of herself she loved the most did her mother finally approve of her. She would probably begin suggesting tapestry designs for the two of them to work on together during their visits. Aoife tried to shake the image of them stitching side by side as she headed to her private chamber.

When she opened the door, Maeve was reclining as comfortable as ever on the settee by the window. Aoife looked forward to Maeve's visits, which had become more regular than her family's. Maeve looked just as at home and at ease meeting Aoife in the manor house as she did when they used to meet at the brothel. Nothing ever ruffled her sense of calm and control.

"I've been meaning to speak to you about those curtains," Maeve smiled. "I am not going to return until they have been replaced."

Her laughter was contagious, and Aoife shook her

head.

"My mother and sister surprise me sometimes," she said. "I'm so sorry to have left you prisoner."

"You owe me quite the apology. The scraps of food they serve here are hardly edible," Maeve gestured around her with sarcasm. "Thank God you'll be free of this prison soon enough."

"The gold plated finery of this manor makes it no less restrictive than a dungeon," Aoife said, sensitive to criticism.

"Even still, are you sure that you want to go ahead with the plan you've hatched?"

"Absolutely," Aoife said emphatically. "There's no other way." She took a deep breath. "You were just about to show me how to hide this away in my skirts."

Aoife pulled out a leather purse from the drawer where she had dropped it an hour before. Maeve rose and crossed the room to Aoife. She took the purse and the belt it was attached to in her hands with a mischievous smile.

"And where are the coins you've been hoarding?"

"Right here."

Aoife dug through a chest of jewelry for a large wooden box at the bottom. It was nothing to look at, but it had a heavy lock.

"Too big," Maeve shook her head. "Much too big and hard to get to. Remember, you need a pile of gold on you at all times that can sustain you until Seamus can get to you. He will bring the rest of the gold I am secretly holding for you, which I have to say has grown quite large in the two months you have been here. Thank goodness you spun too much gold for anyone to count, let alone notice you've been siphoning off. I don't suppose you will ever get around to explaining how you managed to 'spin' all that gold in the first place?"

Her wedding ring began to emanate heat and contract ever so slightly around her finger. Every time Aoife considered talking about her deal with the little man, it tightened, reminding her that their relationship and deal were a secret she was not allowed to reveal.

As if she could forget his hold over her after the way he mocked her efforts to bring him the Duke's greatest treasure during their secret meetings in the forest. As if she could forget the day she tried to run away and had nearly been killed. While riding her horse just days after the wedding, she began to feel a panic rise in her as she thought of spending the rest of her life married to a man she despised. She sped through the forest, not caring if she offended the little man as she tried to outrun the scream building inside her. She and her horse were covered in sweat as they rode through the forest and neared the far edge, the boundary between everything her life had become and everything it could become if she just let go of her devotion to Tara, her family and the deal she had made with the little man.

Just as she was about to leap over a fallen limb and into the glen on the other side, the horse bucked and halted, throwing Aoife head first to the ground. The little man's laughter rang through the air. At the edge of the forest a translucent wall appeared before her, stretching from the earth to the sky. Its surface warbled like the springy-rainbow like substance of a soapy bubble. She reached out to touch its filmy substance and felt a fiery heat sting her fingers, warning her that the little man would not let her leave, not until their bargain was complete.

She could explain none of this to Maeve.

"There are some secrets that are better left unknown," Aoife replied.

Maeve shook her head as she always did when Aoife made such replies.

"Whether you can spin gold or not anymore, I don't imagine you'll need much more to keep you financially free for many years to come."

"I am not quite ready yet," Aoife replied without looking up. Maeve cinched the purse.

"Do not wait too long," Maeve looked at Aoife with concern.

Aoife fell silent. She wanted to leave. She had been searching the manor and subtly interviewing the servants as best she could to try to discern what the Duke owned that was of great value. But nothing she had brought the little man had satisfied him.

Maeve sighed and shrugged her shoulders.

"Lift up your dress," she said.

The segue was so instantaneous that it could have only come from Madame Maeve. Aoife tried to hide the blush in her cheeks. Lifting her skirts before Maeve paled in comparison to the advice Maeve had been giving Aoife about pleasuring the Duke to gain her freedom. She hiked her skirt over her knees and then up above her waist so that her under slip was exposed. Without hesitation, Maeve knelt before her. She searched through the folds and Aoife asked Maeve if she wanted more tea as a distraction from this intimacy.

"Right here," Maeve said as she tied the belt

around a loop in between the two layers of her dress. "Even if he decides to take you without a moment's notice, the purse will remain hidden."

Whenever they discussed her escape plan, Maeve's expression changed. She was more serious, and devoid of humor.

"See," Maeve said. She threw Aoife's skirt around, demonstrating how hidden the purse was. "If something happens, and you have to leave before you plan, you'll be ready."

"If everyone thinks I am dead, then I will not have to worry about anyone looking for me."

"True," Maeve said. "If they find your clothes by the river, they will search for a time, but then assume you were accidentally washed away."

Aoife turned from Maeve and walked toward the window, looking across the grounds to the woods. The plan was ready and she had saved nearly enough funds already. Now she just had to wait for the little man to tell her what he wanted. She imagined the day their deal was complete, and she would finally escape. She would wait for a rain storm to come upon her while out on a ride. The servants would wonder why she did not return as the clouds poured down. They would whisper to Fiona that someone ought to inform the Duke. Dutiful Fiona would continue on with her chores, one eye watching the storm. Only when the storm was at its height and Aoife's riderless horse returned to the manor would she realize her mistake in waiting. The Duke would be informed, but what would he do? What would he say when her rain soaked clothes were found lying in a muddy, rumpled heap?

By then she would be gone. A woman with money could start a new life with whatever identity she made up for herself. And when she was settled and was sure she had the means to care for Tara, she would send for her. Aoife touched her head where it ached when she thought too far ahead.

"It's ok to be frightened," Maeve said calmly. "Women's choices are never easy, no matter how much gold we carry hidden in our skirts. We can form attachments in the most unlikely places that can make even the most necessary separations difficult."

Aoife stood speechless, wondering if Maeve thought she was delaying her escape because she was developing feelings for the Duke, which was completely ludicrous. Completely.

Chapter 14
Faith

Aoife flung the satchel across the room, feeling nothing but frustration as the jewels scattered all around the floor. She had had enough of men and their orders. If all the jewels that the Duke had given Aoife did not amount to his greatest treasure, then what could the little man want? She had lost her temper with him during their meeting in the woods that morning, asking if he expected her to deliver the entire manor to him as payment. After three months and endless searches for this mysterious treasure, Aoife was beginning to wonder if the little man even knew what he wanted. He kept saying that he would reveal what it was when the time was right, but perhaps that was a lie, and this was a way to punish her and keep her in his debt indefinitely.

And the Duke was just as frustrating. He spent his days hunting and riding his horses and listening occasionally to her ideas about the estate like he was entertaining the wild stories of a child.

"Now leave that to Cashel," he said to her repeatedly. "You don't need to worry yourself over money or cattle or hay any longer. You and the rest of your family are well taken care of now. You are free to enjoy your life instead of working to save it."

She had won their bet, proving that she was a woman passionate about her freedom and more capable than his own landsman at running the affairs of the manor. Yet all he seemed to want from Aoife was to see her dressed and beautiful every night for dinner, showcasing all the finery he assumed she enjoyed.

She walked over and picked up the stray jewels and the satchel. She poured them in a drawer and slammed it shut, pitching over a vase of flowers onto the floor. Gathering them up, she cursed the Duke and his efforts to woo her. In addition to jewels, he had started leaving flowers in her room. It was sweet, but it changed little. It only proved that he knew nothing about her. During the walks they took together around the manor, all she saw were the plans and changes she wished she could make. But instead of listening to her, he gave her flowers.

Despite the little man's manipulations, at least he knew her. Had she run away with him from the beginning, he never would have handed her trinkets or tried to put her on display like another object in his collection. That was the life her mother wanted, not Aoife.

The thought of her mother led to thoughts of home and Tara. She reminisced about all the times they shared meat pies that Aoife smuggled up to Tara's room in the afternoons while they were supposed to be resting and napping. She missed her sister's wild stories about the mermaids that lived in the far away sea they had visited once as small children. She remembered Tara's detailed descriptions of their seaweed beds that drifted with the tides and their siren songs that made men their slaves. With nothing to do but read, Tara had immersed herself in books about places she would probably never see. Aoife wondered if the shell they had brought home from their long ago trip, which brought the sound of the sea to their ears, was still beside Tara's bed. Homesick for her sister, she ran out of her room and down the stairs with her riding hat in hand. She needed to go home, throw open the front door of her house, run up the creaky stairs, jump into bed with Tara, and pull the covers over her head.

When she got to the front door of the manor, her stomach dropped. The clouds which had been rolling overhead in thick waves had coalesced and rain began pouring down. She would have to wait out the storm. A noise caught her attention, and she saw Cashel sitting near the door, probably also waiting out the storm. He cleared his throat and offered up a weak greeting. Taking out all her frustrations on the poor brainless fool whose authority she resented, she immediately engaged him in a battle over the estate.

"I don't suppose you've given anymore consideration to my ideas."

"Yes, my Lady, I have," he replied with a quavering voice.

"'Yes, my Lady, I have,'" she mocked him. "I'm so tired of being called my Lady and then being ignored.

I know for a fact that those fields have been fallow for longer than eight years. They are more than ready for new planting. They have rested longer than my grandmother's ghost!"

"It could be brought back into the rotation, but we would need to bring in extra labor to prepare it in time for the planting," Cashel said, his voice a nervous flutter.

"That should not be much of a problem considering the number of people willing to work themselves to the bone for little more than a pittance. We would need to start the planting season less than a month earlier than usual to ready the new fields. That's hardly an obstacle worth losing the income sure to be generated by reinvigorating that land."

"Well, I would need the Duke's approval for any changes to the – "

"Then it is a good thing that I am right here," the Duke's voice rang out from the top of the staircase above them.

Aoife and Cashel turned. She had become so contrived and guarded with her emotions around the Duke that she resented having been caught arguing and yelling at Cashel. She straightened her dress and cleared her throat.

"As you know, over the last several months that I have been here, I have been making inquiries about your estate," Aoife said. "And I was simply advising your landsman, as I have advised you, that it is time to revisit the plans made almost a decade ago about the proceedings of the estate. But rather than argue pointlessly, I will take my leave when the rain lets up and visit my sister."

She turned toward the back hall to the kitchen, ignoring the Duke's stoic features and the way his hands pressed into the banister.

"This means a great deal to you, Aoife," he said. "Making profits."

"No," she replied with irritation. "Profits have been a mere necessity for survival for my family and me. But finding a field, a barn, a farm that everyone else has given up on and uncovering the potential that's been hiding there in the dirt waiting to be discovered." Her voice softened with nostalgia. "Going where others see nothing and planting a seed and watching it reach toward the light and produce – that's what I live for."

"Finding worth in that which makes others turn away. I suppose that is what I brought you here for," he said, more to himself than to her.

Aoife froze, sensing something thoughtful in the way he gazed at her.

"Cashel, I've no real patience for these matters and now that I listen to my Lady, I see that she makes a lot of sense," he said. "It seems we would be wise to follow her advice."

Aoife stood speechless.

"If she does as well by our fields as she has by the excess grain, I shudder to think of the riches we may expect to see her produce," the Duke said as he walked down the stairs. "And in regards to all future decisions, you are to defer to her commands."

"But – "

"That is all," the Duke interrupted Cashel. "You have your orders."

The Duke's gaze never wavered from Aoife's. He

lingered quietly for a moment, and it seemed to Aoife that he enjoyed her surprise.

"I appreciate your faith in me," Aoife said.

This was the first gift given solely for the sake of pleasing her, rather than just as a means of buying her affection.

"I have always had faith in you," he said, searching her eyes. "Judging from your reaction, faith in your talents means more to you than emeralds and flowers. I had no idea it could be so simple. If faith in you is what you need, then I will give proof of it everyday. And maybe one day you will mine something more valuable than my estate and make us both richer in happiness for it."

He kissed her gently on the cheek and walked past her and out the front door.

***

The rainstorm kept her from running off to see Tara. Instead, she sat up in her room putting together her goals for the Duke's estate. The next morning Aoife rose early to put into motion her plan for the expansion of the fields. She was pulling on her mud stained boots reserved for her outdoor walks when there was a bang at her door. Aoife opened it to find Fiona struggling with a large roll of paper, a leather bound book, and an inkhorn that was about to fall to the ground.

"Your husband asked that I bring these things to you," Fiona said, slightly out of breath. "He said he found them in his father's things and thought they might be of use."

"What are they?" Aoife asked as she untied the string around the rolled up paper.

She and Fiona unrolled the parchment, revealing the late Duke's detailed map of all the lands surrounding the estate. There were notes about elevation, drainage, and even markers differentiating various fields.

"I knew a great deal more land had been farmed in the past," Aoife said. "If I can locate these markers between the fields that used to exist, I can resurrect these walls."

"That seems very helpful," Fiona said as she squinted at the words Aoife guessed she had never been taught to read.

Next Aoife opened a dusty ledger that was likely as old as she was and began to pour over the pages.

"That's Bradyn's handwriting, I mean, the late Duke's," Fiona said. "I could spot it anywhere, although I can't say I know what it says."

"It looks like a detailed account of the planting schedule and harvest yields for the past – " Aoife paused as she flipped the pages forward to see where they ended, "twenty or so years. It stops about two years ago."

"Oh," Fiona straightened up. "That would be about the time the late Duke fell ill. He tried unsuccessfully during his last few years to get his son to return home. The gossip around the kitchen was that he had no choice but to put his estate in Cashel's hands because of his health. I think he always hoped his son would return home and take charge. But he never did," Fiona said. "Not until it was too late."

Aoife ran her fingers over the letters, touched that

the Duke entrusted his father's most private papers to her. She flipped through the yellowed empty pages at the back.

"I think this last gift will prove even more helpful than the others," Fiona said as she turned Aoife's hand over. She patted playfully at the ink stains on Aoife's hand. "The mouth of your inkhorn is a bit faulty. Maybe this one will be more reliable."

Aoife picked up the inkhorn, aware that it was her careless hand and not a faulty inkhorn that accounted for her stained fingers. The rain had stopped outside, and Aoife could see out the window that her horse had been brought round the front of the house as she had requested earlier. She grabbed the new inkhorn and put it in her satchel along with the ledger. She slung it over her shoulder and headed for the door with the map under her arm.

"Wait," Fiona called after her, "I haven't secured your hair! And your cape! You need your cape!"

Aoife barely heard Fiona's pleas as she headed down the hall for the stairs. Her mind was racing. The Duke had given her his family's map and ink to create a new vision for his estate and her own future. She imagined the fields she wanted to have sewn, the granaries she wanted built and more. She had a chance now to do everything she always wished she could do at home, without the interference of her mother's wrathful eye and her father's wasteful ways. Having a tower and a barn full of gold at her disposal was not such a bad thing either. As she ran out the front door and to her horse, she tried to avoid thinking about how the Duke had treated her yesterday, because these new pieces of him did not fit together with her image of him as a cruel, manipulative man with only selfish motives. She leapt up onto her horse and headed out to the fields. She held tight to her reins, but felt her grip on her anger loosening a little.

Chapter 15
Mending Fences

As the days turned into weeks, Aoife dirtied more than one dress riding around the fields of the Stanishire estate and making plans for the harvest. She marched through the mud and scaled the fences and stone walls separating livestock and fields for planting until one day she tore the back of her skirt so badly that she had to hold it together to keep the wind from creating a scandalous scene. She barked orders to the field hands who were trenching a field as she walked backwards toward the barn. They pretended not to notice her torn dress or the boulder she stumbled over.

She tried unsuccessfully to knot her dress together so she could continue working without going back to the manor to change. She was about to stomp her foot when she spied a washtub down by the stream with clothing hanging out to dry on the trees and bushes. Right in the middle was a pair of men's breeches. Without a moment's hesitation, Aoife bolted for the stream and tore the pants off the line as two washerwomen scolded her for her thievery.

When Aoife rejoined the field hands, they could hardly contain their shock at the sight of a woman clad in breeches, breeches that one of them probably recognized as his own.

"I'm heading off to repair the area of the stone wall that's fallen apart at the edge of the field," she said, breaking their stunned silence. "I don't want to bother planting only to have the cattle stampede through that gaping hole before its time to harvest."

She turned and walked away, taking large strides and reveling in the freedom of her breeches. She had just pulled off a stalk of high grass to chew on, when she saw the Duke on his horse watching her from the other side of the stone wall. She stopped and felt her stomach lurch, waiting for a castigating tongue. The field hands could say little to her, but the Duke, her husband, could condemn her choice of apparel.

"It's a beautiful day for mending fences," Aoife said acidically.

He gazed down at her, a hint of bemusement curling the side of his mouth. She walked over to the wall where the stones had fallen askew and began to lift them back into place, glaring at him and waiting for a sarcastic remark. He watched her, his crooked smile stretching until she was ready to throw a rock at him. She did not want to be chastised, but she definitely did not want to be laughed at either.

"Hold on," he said as he dismounted.

Aoife leaned forward, perched and ready for a

battle of words. He walked over to the wall and removed his gloves and coat. He leaned over and began to dig the dirt away from a large boulder that had probably fallen years ago and had been partially buried. Her shoulders softened and her anger relented at the sight of his dirt caked hands prying the boulder free, revealing how much of the stone was hidden beneath the earth. It was a big job, and before she knew it, she was leaning over the wall and helping to remove the earth.

Aoife stole glances in his direction, taking in the beads of sweat on his neck and the large heaps of dirt he tossed aside. When he began to pry the last of it free, Aoife stepped back as he rocked it back and forth until he was able to lift the oversized stone out of its cavity and place it back onto the wall where it had once lay. He stepped back, and Aoife took in his ruddy complexion and the flecks of dirt on his face. He leaned down to pick up other stones that had fallen on his side. Not to be outdone, Aoife picked up those on her side and together they fit them all back into place until the wall stood complete and whole again.

"Thank you," she said.

He nodded to her as he brushed his hands off and walked back to his horse. He climbed into the saddle. Aoife was searching for something more to say when she noticed his jacket and gloves sitting on the wall. She scooped them up and hopped over the wall; he looked surprised as she handed them to him.

"You've done impressive work," he said.

His eyes swept the landscape, marveling over the vast changes she was making. The weeds of several fields had been cleared, and dark soil, rich with promise lay before them. A tremble of pride rose within her.

"I guess I have a gift for building walls," Aoife said.

He turned from the landscape and ran his hand across her cheek.

"Walls are important," he replied, "but I hope you don't build this one too high."

"I think this wall is just right," Aoife replied.

"That's good to know," he said thoughtfully. "Let me know the next time you need any boulders moved."

He looked down at her breeches and seemed on the verge of saying something but held his tongue. As he turned and rode off, Aoife looked down at herself and stifled a laugh before getting back to work.

In just such a scandalous manner, Aoife continued working the estate wearing the pants she had stolen from the clothing line. After a few days, she found several pairs of breeches made to fit her figure lying on her bed. Fiona could barely stifle her shock that the Duke was allowing Aoife to dress like a man. Aoife continued to wear them, and as days turned into weeks and then into a month, Fiona stopped huffing as she collected Aoife's soiled trousers and tunics off the ground.

One evening when she returned home after the sun had gone down, she found a letter on her table. She grabbed it, wondering if the Duke had missed her at dinner. She regretted being out so late, as she wanted to tell him about how Cashel had been chased by an angry goat while she gave him his daily orders. Over the last month since they rebuilt the wall together, the Duke had begun to ask Aoife more about her plans and her daily work. A kind of comfortable conversation had grown between them in the evenings. She discovered that she had a gift for making him laugh with stories about how she bested Cashel with her logic, knowledge, and even her physical abilities. She was convinced Cashel would have been out of a job weeks ago had not the Duke laughed so hardily over Aoife's retelling of their battles. He listened to every detail of her day and watched with interest as she showed him on the maps how she was reconfiguring the fields.

While she leaned over the map just the day before, he brushed her hair behind her ear. She had smiled despite herself, but he had pulled back, almost apologetically. He had not visited Aoife's chamber since before they built the stone wall together. She normally would have been relieved by his absence, but found herself more dissatisfied than she cared to admit.

The letter she opened revealed that she had been missed, but by Maeve, not the Duke. Underneath her sarcasm, Aoife could hear Maeve's disappointment at having missed their afternoon talks over the last month.

"I wonder if you have neglected your duties to your husband as much as you have our afternoon tea. And did I actually see you wearing a man's breeches in the fields? Do not let your mother catch you. I don't think she would survive it."

Aoife snickered. Her mother had not caught her in pants yet, but the thought of her expression was motivation enough to keep it up in the hopes that she would one day see Aoife.

"Please let me know when we can meet. There are plans to be finalized and details to attend to."

Aoife felt her stomach drop. She had been so hard

at work, she had barely thought about her escape plan. Now she was sewing seeds of promise, envisioning a future lusher and greener than anything she had known, and she felt more invigorated than ever before. At home with her family, she had run things, but always with limited resources and always with her father gambling the profits away. Here at the manor she was creating a vision all on her own without any constraints, and the success of this season would fuel even more bounty in the future – if she did not run away. Truthfully, she had avoided thinking about her escape plan. And perhaps more importantly she had had no time and a lot less interest in discovering the Duke's greatest treasure. Up until recently, nothing had been more important to her than turning it over to the little man in order to end her imprisonment.

She sat down at her chair and imagined herself riding through the woods and over the more than twenty miles beyond Stanishire with her pilfered fortune. She pictured the little farm she would purchase and the life she would start as a wealthy widow. These dreams used to bring a swell of excitement, but now she found herself afraid to admit that she might be considering a different life.

She wanted to see the fields expanded and the new granaries completed.

She wanted to see her handwriting in the manor's ledger.

And then there was the Duke. She had felt a loosening in her heart, but was that wise? Was it advisable to trust him or any man? Aoife scratched her head, unable to make sense of her emotions and loyalties.

None of this mattered, she reminded herself. The little man was waiting to extract his price. She ripped the letter in two and tossed it in the fire. She did not know how to face Maeve when she could explain none of this to her. The little man had built a wall around her that she was powerless to tear down. She could not change the path of her life until he was satisfied. Only now, there seemed to be more than one path to consider.

***

About a week later, after a grueling day of work in a steady downpour, Aoife had returned to the manor too tired for her afternoon bath. She let Fiona help her out of her rain-soaked clothing, and then crawled right under her covers.

She must have slept through the rest of the day, for when she next opened her eyes, it was dark. Sitting on the bed beside her was the Duke, caressing her cheek. It was his first visit to her chamber in over a month. Startled, Aoife began to rise up, but he eased her gently back against her pillow. He brushed her damp hair off of her face and sat quietly while she adjusted her eyes to the room and stretched her aching muscles. He lifted a warm cloth and wiped her cheek. His touch was careful as he wiped away speckles of mud.

"I'm not much of a lady right now, am I," she said a little embarrassed.

"From the looks of you, I'm starting to think being a lady might not be as important as most people think," he replied.

Aoife reached up to touch her tangled hair and sticky skin. As his dark eyes rested on her, she felt a flutter run through her. The respect and admiration he had shown her and his growing attentiveness had worn down the animosity she used to feel for him. The morning before, she woke up and found a note with just two words, "Miss you." She imagined him slipping into her room for the first time in over a month only to find her snoring from exhaustion.

"I ordered a fresh bath," he said.

She looked over at the bath and tugged the blanket close to her naked body. He stood and held her robe up just enough to give her the guise of privacy. She felt a shred of disappointment that he did not even try to look. After a moment she rose slowly out of bed, every muscle aching and throbbing, and slipped into her robe. His expression was neutral as he guided her to the steaming bath. Over her shoulder she could see that his eyes remained as stoic and unmoved as Fiona's when she undressed Aoife. His attempt to give Aoife her space was becoming maddening.

They walked to the bath and she took off her robe. He busied himself with moving things around, as if he was trying to avoid staring at her. As her body slipped beneath the water, he hung her robe over the side of a chair. She watched his movements and admired the broad line of his shoulders. The discovery of the strength of his arms and the firmness of his body had surprised her during their first nights together. His entire life seemed run by servants, leaving him little reason to have done anything worthy of hardening his muscles. But she had seen the way his ropy arms heaved the stone back into the wall. There was strength in him beyond what she had assumed. Ever since that day, she had found herself imagining him without his clothes, surprised by the heat that rose in her body.

"I'll leave you to your bath," he said.

"Before you go," Aoife's voice rushed out and then halted. "Could you hand me the sponge – please."

The steam rose between them as he handed her the sponge, which sat just inches from her fingertips. She flushed, feeling precariously vulnerable, and handed him back the sponge and pulled her hair over her shoulder. She leaned forward in the tub and hugged her knees to her chest, letting her body tell him what she wanted.

He seated himself on the stool beside the tub, dipped the sponge in the water, and placed it between her shoulders, letting the hot water drip down her back. She sighed as the tension began to release. He swished the sponge across her neck, her back, and her arms, caressing every inch with a careful reverence that felt close to worship.

"I could wash your hair for you, if you want," he offered.

Aoife turned and searched his eyes. Her veil of protection had not fallen. Emerging from deep within him she saw a layer of admiration for her and a vulnerability that his pride had overshadowed until now.

She let go of her knees and sat up straight, her arms crossed in front of her chest. He dipped a bowl into the water and poured the water over her head. A few streams slipped into her eyes and he gently wiped them away. As he washed her hair and rinsed it clean, her desire for him grew. She leaned back and rested her arms on either side of the tub, willing her fears to dissolve away. She had spent so much of their marriage keeping a veil of protection between them, but after all that had grown between them, she did not want to hide from him anymore. He was no longer a threat to her, but someone she just might be falling in love with.

He breathed deeply, his eyes never straying from hers. For the first time she looked within him and saw the point far behind his hunger for her that was full of sadness and tragedy. Aoife knew darkness and she knew the light that lived hidden in the most unlikely of hearts. The heat of the water, his touch, and the moment made it easier for her to admit how present the light within him was and must have always been in him, too. She could see that he might not be so different from Maeve, whose outer story reflected nothing of her inner landscape.

After he helped dry her off and wrapped her in her robe, he took her hands and walked over to the hearth. Removing a blanket from the seat beside the fire, he flung it into the air like a magician's cape. It floated to the ground and he tugged at the edges until he had made a space for them to sit beside the fire.

"I've never had to use anything besides lavish gifts and my smile to win a woman over, so I hope you won't mock me if I don't say the right thing."

"I appreciate your effort," Aoife replied.

"Appreciate," his spirits sank slightly. "There's that awful word again. That's worse than mocking me. I hope you'll never use that word again."

"Perhaps I won't," Aoife said.

"So help your husband get to know you better," he

said gently. "Tell me what kind of woman you are so that I don't give you any more useless gifts."

No one had ever asked her such a question. She felt that everything that followed between them would hinge upon this moment.

"I am a woman who never wants to be confined by a definition," she replied, searching his eyes.

"I see," he said. "Then how am I to know how to speak and act so as not to offend you?"

Aoife planned her words carefully.

"By continuing to do as you have already begun to do. By talking with me, instead of at me. By listening to me, instead of your own voice. By letting me live, instead of commanding how I live."

Was it possible for her to find happiness with him? There was a long silence, as she awaited his response.

"I think with you, I can do that."

As the night stretched on, he listened as she told him stories of her life before him and her childhood. Aoife was grateful for the freedom to reminisce. She told how her cousin, Liam, had once tried to make a fire with a flint rock. After failing miserably, he had relented and allowed Aoife a turn. To his astonishment Aoife managed a spark and fanned the embers into a flame. In his excitement Liam tripped and sent a pile of hay tumbling too near the fire, which then bloomed up the side of the wooden henhouse. The Duke laughed as she described the hilarity of her mother in one of her finest dresses chasing chickens around the yard with Aoife while the field hands put out the fire.

It felt strange the way her anger toward him had

faded. He had accosted her in the woods, won her over a game of cards, and threatened her family – all horrible, unforgivable things, she knew. But now he was laughing over her childhood and letting her have a kind of freedom she had never known. She leaned on her arm, liking the way her words tumbled out so easily.

He looked at her, longing for her, yet consciously subduing his need, steadfast in his attempt to give her the space he had learned she required. His desire for her and his efforts to please her made for an intoxicating concoction – one Aoife had never tasted before. Her growing affection for him had initially made her feel like a traitor to her own instincts, but these feelings of self-betrayal were losing their grip on her.

She took a breath and committed herself to what was perhaps the most reckless act of rebellion she had ever committed. It was not her mother, father, or her society that she defied tonight, but the very rigid walls she had built around herself. Casting aside the instincts that had preserved her from men like the Duke her entire life, she leaned in and kissed him gently. She felt his body reacting and wrapped her arms around him and kissed him with all the passion that had been building in her these last few months. She had never felt as powerful as she did in that moment expressing her desire for him. She pulled away just enough to look into his eyes.

"Do you 'appreciate' my kiss, my Lord?"

"Appreciate is too weak a word to ever use in connection with you, my dear, Aoife. You've brought my crooked soul to its knees, and I've every hope that through you I will be reborn as something better than I ever thought I could be. But I would like to ask if you could call me, not by my title, but by the name I was given – Ronan."

She slipped open her robe, the heat of the fire on her flesh no match for the heat pulsing through her body. She stood up before him and rolled her shoulders, her robe slipping to the floor in a spill of gleaming satin, along with the last vestige of her restraint. Light from the fire lapped all around her figure, silhouetting her every curve against the wall's canvas.

She pulled him up to her and held his face in her hands. After a moment's paralysis, his arms slipped around her. At the feel of his touch, she lost control and ripped at the buttons of his vest, her touch far rougher than his had ever been. As their bodies pressed together, he looked surprised by the intensity of her desire.

Surrendering no longer felt like an act of capitulation to Aoife, but a powerful means of expressing her passion on her own terms. She watched his surprise as she pulled him to the bed. She pushed him down beneath her and bathed him in a sea of caresses, making love to him with her whole self present. He lay back and watched her love for him bloom in his open hand in way it never had within his iron grip. When they finally tumbled onto the sheets, they both fell silent, catching their breath. After a few moments he tugged Aoife closer to him and she tucked herself into the crook of his arm where she fell under the restful spell of a heavy sleep.

When she awoke, the brightness of the morning light filled the room. Since coming to the manor, she had never awakened after sunrise. She squinted and looked around, surprised by the sight of Ronan still beside her.

She tugged the blanket at the foot of her bed and pulled it around her body.

"Don't go," Ronan pleaded behind closed eyes.

"And where might I go without a stitch of clothing, *Ronan*?" Her voice was playful and brought a boyish smile to his lips.

She lifted her head and kissed him.

"I hope you won't ever feel the need to escape."

He pulled her closer.

She clenched the sheet in her hands, the word 'escape' reminding her of the plan to leave him. She looked at him, his soft lips and closed eyes exuding quiet bliss. She grew hot with guilt and confusion. She had pushed her plan aside and avoided Maeve for some time now. She did not want to leave him anymore, but was that wise? Could she really trust him? She wasn't ready to make up her mind yet. She kicked her blanket off the bed and nestled further into Ronan's arms, all her plans and secret meetings with the little man laying in a confused rumple on the floor.

Chapter 16
Threats

The forest was warmer than usual as Aoife's horse flew over the mossy floor and toward their meeting spot. She no longer counted the mushrooms on the fallen Oak, she never flung her hair free under the forest canopy, and with sadness she stepped around the handicapped fern at the gateway to the falls, which still bore the scar from Ronan's boot during their first meeting. She tried to ignore its presence and the dark origins of their relationship. Such remembrances made it difficult to reconcile her feelings for him.

"I'm here!" Aoife shouted. "You can step out of the wind and show yourself."

The little man's omnipresence required little in the way of greetings, but Aoife preferred to keep their dialogue more human and less mystical. The breeze that swayed the trees grew, its strength building upon itself until all the woods and all the earth, it seemed, were bound in a choreography that loomed over her in a demonstration of strength.

"I have seen too much of your magic to be frightened by a few bent trees," Aoife said.

A darkness, sudden and all encompassing, filled the woods. When Aoife looked up to the sky, a melding pot of gathering clouds that pressed together and coagulated into a stormy mound of ominous black. Lightning flashed, striking one of the larger trees at the river's edge. Aoife screamed as the sound of the tree's base snapping and shattering into millions of splinters echoed throughout the forest. The limbs burst into flames and the whole tree rattled and wobbled for a moment, its fall inevitable. As it tumbled from the opposite bank toward Aoife, she turned and ran. She fell to the ground and covered her head with her arms. The tree crashed with a violence that shook the earth, sending leaves and debris high into the air.

Aoife coughed and wiped off the dirt that covered her skin and littered her hair. Her horse whinnied and bucked, trying to escape the tree he had been safely tethered to. As the dust slowly settled, she saw through the haze the silhouette of the little man standing on top of the fallen log, his hands perched on his hips.

"So happy you could join me for a visit."

Aoife coughed again. His power seemed to have grown in proportion to his resentment. She looked to the fallen tree and wondered if he despised her enough to have let it fall on her.

"So what have you brought this nameless little man today?" he asked with a playful note in his voice.

"I've brought you what I believe may satisfy our

deal," she said.

His increasing agitation made it more important than ever that she settle her debt with him.

"And what is it you are so sure is your sweet husband's dearest treasure," he mocked her.

"It was not any of the jewels he gifted me."

"That's not saying much for his gifts – or his love."

"It was not the golden candelabra or the – "

"All fine things, but none of them his greatest treasure."

"So I realize I must be going about this all wrong. His greatest treasure may not be something of monetary value, but of sentimental value."

The twitch at the edge of his cocky grin revealed that this change in her thinking may have been right. Over the past months, she had been asking Fiona questions about the things that Ronan valued, making sure that her questions were casual and sporadic enough so as to avoid rousing any suspicion.

"To feel sentimental, he would have to care for something besides himself – not that he doesn't love you, his adoring wife."

She looked at him steadily, hoping not to give away everything that had changed between Aoife and Ronan since she had last been to these falls. She did not need to hear him ridicule her feelings for Ronan, feelings she was not yet confident enough about to share with anyone.

"What I have brought you today does carry great monetary value, but its sentimental value is what I believe may make it his greatest treasure."

Aoife unfastened the clasp around her waist to her outer dress. The little man's eyes darted away. Beneath her dress, she unfastened a man's leather belt. From beneath the thick folds of her outer dress, Aoife pulled out a heavy sword. She held it out to him like an offering. The little man stepped toward her. Despite the craftsmanship that made it an effectual weapon of death, its handle was thickly encrusted with a rainbow of jewels. Aoife oscillated her hands so that the gems glittered. The jewels that hung from every possible place in his cottage persuaded her that the sword's majestic gleam would mesmerize him.

His trembling fingers touched the stones and swept the length of the blade hidden safely beneath its engraved, metal sheath. This had to be it, she told herself, or even if it was not Ronan's greatest treasure, maybe it was tempting enough to satisfy the little man.

His fingers began to wrap around the edges of the sword ever so slightly, and then he looked to Aoife for permission to take hold of it. She nodded, willing the pounding of her heart to hold steady. He looked at the sword like it meant more to him than she understood. He stepped back, his gaze and his mind wandering far away from her and the woods. He sat down on the fallen tree.

It hurt to watch the way his chest rose and fell in uneven hefts, and his eyes trembled and glistened at the rims. This sword seemed to resurrect something in him.

"What does this mean to you? Why has it caused you so much pain?"

"What do you know of pain? Of misery that squeezes your heart until it's a bloody mess!"

"I don't know what your life has been," she

143

admitted. "But I can listen."

"Listen?" His shriek was on the edge. "You think listening will undo what has warped my soul beyond the twisted frame of my body?"

"It was not so long ago that you and I talked through the night and the words between us softened the pain in both our hearts," she said brushing her fingers across his hands. "Maybe not everything has been lost between us. Maybe I can help you find some comfort."

She squeezed his hand and he looked up at her.

"Everything in my life is eventually ruined," he said. "Everyone turns their back on me. It is the way it always has been and always will be."

He closed his eyes and she saw in the hardening of his shoulders that he had sealed himself off from her and these feelings. He let go of the sword long enough to wipe his eyes. He admired the carvings on the sheath and then turned his attention back to Aoife, who sat still upon the ground.

"This treasure is of noble heritage and one that no doubt means much to your dear husband," he said, his voice spent and tired. "It's the late Duke of Stanishire's sword, the one he wore at his side for his most serious business. But this is not your husband's greatest treasure, nor is it a treasure that will satisfy our deal."

He handed back the sword. His eyes turned cold and hard again.

"Go and take him to bed," he sneered. "Fawn over him. Whisper sweet words in his ear— "

"And what would you do if I refused to play this game anymore?" Aoife said sharply, cutting him off. "I don't think you know what you want. I think this whole debt is just a means to drive me mad and punish me for not staying with you."

"Aoife," the little man raised one brow. "You are no longer the center of my everything. That changed when you chose your family and the Duke over me. I give little thought any longer as to how to please or punish you. Go back home and wait until the answer is made clear."

He dismissed her and turned to leave. His apathy stung.

"I've done your bidding far too long. Burning all his treasures to the ground would put a quick end to your scheming. Or telling the truth and outing your plan would end the secrecy. Your invisible wall at the edge of the forest cannot stop me from talking. And this ring and its power to strangle my finger at the slightest mention of our deal won't stop me either! I can live a long and happy life with only nine fingers, so go ahead and squeeze, because it's only my dead finger you will get from me now."

She turned her back on him and headed to her horse.

"Don't forget that your family depends upon the support your marriage gives them. If you told your sweet husband that your whole marriage was a means for you to steal his greatest treasure for an evil little man whom you paid to trick him with all that gold, are you sure he would understand and wrap his arms around you? Or might he see you for the lying woman that you are and cast you and your pitiful family out? Are you ready to make that gamble?"

She slowed her steps.

"I seem to recall that when the choice was between your family and me, you said you couldn't bare leaving them to face the consequences of your father's recklessness. You chose them over me. But now that your dear husband might get hurt by our deal, you are willing to risk your family's safety and security to protect him? Your fickle loyalty wreaks of hypocrisy. Or is it just evidence that you'd rather be with a worthless man who won you over a game of cards than me, the nameless little man who has been your savior all your life."

It was not true. He was trying to trap her again with his misshapen logic. He was taking choices she had made and sewing them together like the patches of a quilt. She needed to slit the seams and rip apart the distorted narrative he was creating.

"This is not about who I love or – "

"And how am I to see it any other way? It's the way it's always been and always will be until I break the chain."

The wind began to shake and the little man stepped back for a moment, stumbling over an uneven rock.

"You'll never love me, Aoife," he said. "No matter how much you care for me, you've lived too long in this world to ever look upon me as anything but broken."

"That's not true," Aoife replied.

"No," he continued, as if he were too far away with his thoughts to remember that she was there. "You couldn't. No one raised among your kind ever could."

He looked up at her, searching her eyes as he took

another step back from her.

"How can we end this? I'll do whatever it takes."

"Be careful what you wish for, Aoife."

Chapter 17
Patience

The warmth of the afternoon sun found its way through the thick walls of Aoife's bedroom. As she stretched, Ronan wrapped his arms around her. Sleeping in her bed was becoming a habit for him the past month, one Aoife liked. She turned and kissed his cheeks, his nose, and finally his lips. He opened his eyes and propped himself up on one arm, flushed with an idea.

"Let's go somewhere, Aoife. Let's get far away from this place. I've seen so much of the world but never with you by my side. We can go wherever you want."

Her heart sank. She wanted to say yes more than anything, but she knew that she could not go anywhere until she was done with the little man.

"It sounds so tempting, but I'm not so sure," she said. "I mean, not now at least."

"Why not?" Ronan replied, sitting up. "We have nothing holding us back. I've always hated this place.

When I left, I swore I would never come back; it was only my father's death that dragged me here, and since I returned, it is only you that keeps me."

His honesty only amplified her guilt. She was beholden to two men, and there seemed no way to satisfy them both.

"I never felt happy," Ronan continued, "until now. And I am very afraid of risking what we have by staying here. I am not one to talk about my past, but many memories I would rather remain in the past hover all around me here. I know I sound cryptic, but I do not want them catching up to me or tainting what we have."

His love for her seemed so strong that she felt the truth rising in her throat. They had grown so much closer. She wondered if he might understand how it all happened, forgive her, and help her end the bargain with the little man. But if the truth angered Ronan, she knew the kind of retribution of which he was capable.

"Please say you will leave with me."

"I wish I could make you understand, but I cannot," replied Aoife. "There are things preventing me from leaving right now."

"That's all the more reason we should go."

"No," she replied. "You don't understand. Since the day I agreed to marry you…"

"Yes," he whispered.

"There are things that I have not told you," she said.

All at once, the heat in her ring burned hot, too hot, and its grasp tightened dangerously around her finger. She pulled her hand away from Ronan. The burning and contracting of the ring, and the hurt in his eyes broke her confidence.

"What have you not told me?" Mistrust filled his voice and his gentleness faded.

"I didn't mean that. Just that there are things I need to take care of before we leave," she said, rethinking her honesty in light of the shift she could already see in him. Perhaps he was not ready for the entire story. "You and I are building something I never thought we could, and I don't want to let that go. But I need you to trust me and give me a little time."

He searched her eyes and took a breath to say something, but sighed instead. He leaned down to kiss her hand, but his body suddenly froze.

"This is not the ring I gave you."

They locked eyes.

"This looks like the ring I gave you, except the stone was a light blue Topaz. It was my mother's and I would know it anywhere. This stone — "

"Of course it's the same ring," Aoife interrupted, intent on calming him. The growing mistrust in his voice was more proof that she could not let him know what she had promised the little man.

"But it's not the same color. This looks," his voice wavered. "It looks dark and filmy, like pond scum."

"You must have forgotten the exact color, or perhaps it just needs a cleaning. It's just a ring, nothing to get upset about."

She raised her eyebrow feigning naiveté. He narrowed his eyes suspiciously and grabbed her hand to peer at the ring again. He shook his head.

"It can't be!"

He tried to pull the ring off for a closer look.

Aoife yelped as the ring tightened its hold.

"It does not come off," she barked, rubbing her sore finger. "Don't bother. I don't anymore."

"Where did you get this ring, Aoife? Tell me exactly how it got on your finger!"

The seething mistrust in his eyes rekindled her own mistrust and disdain for him. How could she have ever opened up to him or put her faith in him? If a discolored ring and a wish to delay a trip elicited this type of anger, then he clearly had not changed at all. His actions of late were merely pretense or a failed attempt to truly change his ways. And she had given herself to him, which made her a fool.

"You got exactly what you wanted," she said as she pulled the blanket tighter around her body. "Despite all my resistance, despite the very hand of magic that made straw of gold, I still married you. You ought to smile at your good fortune. It would seem that you have someone very powerful looking over your shoulder."

Ronan shivered at her words and searched her eyes. He shook his head as if in disbelief and backed away from her. He looked from the ring to her eyes and back to the ring.

"This can't be happening... not again."

Chapter 18
Storm Clouds

"**I**'m telling you they're filthy! I can't see my own reflection," Ronan yelled. His voice echoed throughout the house as he chastised a young servant girl. "If you can't get it right this time, you will be sent out into the fields!"

"Yes, my Lord," she replied with a rigid curtsey.

He turned on his heel and stormed away. Aoife hid in the corner. When Ronan walked by her, she could see dark circles under his bloodshot eyes. It had been a month since their argument, and still they were not speaking. As he neared the corner, a shadow leaned out and sent him jumping like a skittish cat. Its long fingers stretched up the walls, and Ronan's hands reached up protectively to his throat. After a moment, the fingers dissolved to Ronan's relief, and he made his way out the front door.

"Don't cry, Lizzy," Aoife heard Fiona whisper to

the servant girl. "He's not himself these days."

"My fingers are worn from trying to wipe away the dirt he insists linger in every mirror," the young girl wept.

"Well it's not the mirrors that are the problem," Fiona said, more to herself than Lizzy. "He's got to stop with the drink. It's making him mad and turning the entire household upside down."

Fiona guided Lizzy toward the kitchen.

Aoife stepped out after they had passed and looked toward the corner where the shadow had lunged toward Ronan. Ronan had not seemed as shocked by the silhouette reaching for his throat as Aoife might have expected. How often was the little man haunting him? And what did Ronan think his presence was?

A dread began to fill her. Her conscience whispered that Ronan's drinking and loosening grip on reality was Aoife's fault. Because of her deal with the little man, he had turned his evil magic on Ronan, too. She felt like a little girl again, blaming herself for the demise of others.

She shook her head and reminded herself that Ronan was far from a victim. He had *forced* her to spin the gold. He had *forced* her to marry him. Had he not tried to own her, then he would not have ended up at the center of the little man's revenge. And now he had put this child inside of her. She had nearly lost her mind when Maeve diagnosed Aoife's growing list of symptoms. Maeve was disappointed. This was precisely what she had been worried about all along. This child complicated everything. Maeve had warned her that she needed to leave soon before Ronan or anyone else realized she was pregnant. It would be impossible to keep this from Fiona much longer.

She marched down the hall, determined to outrun her thoughts. As she neared the foyer, she heard a soft cackle in the shadows.

"Your little tricks do not frighten me," she said aloud.

The laughter continued, undeterred by her show of strength. Dark claws stretched out from the shadows and across the floor toward Aoife, but she stood still and held her ground, despite their sharpness.

"Leave him alone!" Aoife shouted as they nearly reached her. "I promised you his greatest treasure, not his sanity. You can't break the rules any more than I can. If you don't leave him alone, the deal is over."

The shadowy claws gnarled into fists and then stretched and morphed into talons, ready to drag her away and shred her to bits. Aoife raised her foot high in the air and stomped on the sharpened shadows. The echo of her heel reverberated around the hall, and her conviction that she would find a way to beat him and everyone who had forced her into this game grew stronger. Nothing fueled her determination greater than efforts to control and subdue her. She watched as the claws shook, lost their strength, and then dissolved into the light. She stood on the stone floor ready to take back her life. And she knew where to start.

She raced off on her horse alongside the woods, knowing this was Ronan's favorite route. They had ridden these hills many times together while they were falling in love; she knew she would find him on his horse beside the Elm, whose branches stretched higher than any on the property. When she crested the hill, she saw him leaning against the tree, looking out upon the valley below, his horse grazing nearby. The tread of her horse woke him from his daydream, and his features hardened when he saw her. She rode over, and he helped her dismount with jittery hands.

"Good morning," she said.

"Is it a good morning?" he replied.

"I suppose neither of us has had a good morning in some time," she said. He looked away, her honesty unnerving him. "I've been thinking about your desire to leave this place," Aoife continued, wasting no time with small talk. "I think you were right."

His brow pitched high.

"While I would like to go with you," she continued, "I still have some things to attend to."

His expression fell, his disappointment melting some of the frost around her heart. He still cared for her.

"But you were right," she continued. "This place is not good for you. You should go."

"I won't leave," he said.

"But you should," Aoife insisted. "There are affairs that you can attend to away from here, and I can handle those at home."

"Aoife, I don't doubt that you can handle the estate," he said, looking down at the ring on her hand. Neither had dared to return to the subject of her cloudy ring since the night they argued about it. "But there are things here that are mine alone to shoulder, and I love you too much to ever leave you alone here."

What things were his to shoulder? Did Ronan fear that the dark shadow of the little man that had begun to haunt him would come for her if he left? He had no way of knowing that it was she who set the little man loose on him. His sudden vow of love and chivalry clashed with the coldness he had shown her these past weeks. She took his hand in hers, telling herself not to be taken in by his inconstant affection. She only held his hand and feigned kindness to get rid of him and ease any guilt she felt over the little man's scheme against him.

"I can care for myself," Aoife whispered. "I always have. But you should leave."

Under the weight of her rejection, he wilted. It was obvious that she had hurt him. Her next words spilled out of her before she could think them through or stop them.

"If you decide you want me with you, then I will join you when I can."

Did she say that as part of her plan to get rid of him or because she was sad that she may have hurt him? She suddenly was not sure of anything anymore.

"Of course I want you with me," he said. "There's nowhere but by your side I want to be anymore."

It was tempting to believe he was sincere when she remembered their tender moments together. She hated herself for this weakness, believing that no matter how much he might love her, he would never be fully cured of his manipulative, selfish ways.

"I promise that if you leave, I will find a way to make everything right."

The wind began to swirl, fanning her emotions as well as her fears that the little man was nearby shaking his fists and rattling the skies overhead.

"You are so strong, Aoife," he said, ignoring the storm building around them. "Stronger than any person I have ever known and certainly stronger than I am." His voice was filled with a strange kind of guilt. "But I'll not run away this time, not when my nightmare has turned itself on you."

Aoife stepped back in surprise. What was this nightmare? She attempted to speak, but the sky opened up and poured down on them. He pulled her under the tree and she felt the strength of his arms as they held her close. Despite the argument, the weeks of silence between them, and all of her best efforts to keep her distance, she could not deny her feelings for him.

His love for her saturated every breath that escaped his trembling lips. His hands slipped from her waist and cradled her rain-soaked face. After a moment's hesitation, he kissed her and the sound of lightning cracked the atmosphere and shook the earth. Electricity prickled through her hair.

"The baby," Aoife cried out as she instinctively covered her belly.

She looked at Ronan, surprised by her own admission. He watched the maternal way she covered her stomach, and his eyes lit up.

"You're pregnant?"

Aoife looked into his eyes, melting at the sight of his unrestrained joy. She nodded silently, her heart pounding as the wind whipped. Unphased by the fury all around, Ronan kissed her again, her touch and the news of the baby seeming to give him back the sanity and inner strength the little man had been stealing away. If she could tell him everything, then maybe they could fight this thing together. He wrapped his arms around her, and she felt something inside him break apart. He pulled back and looked into her eyes.

"I love you so much," he replied. "And now I have this other person to love, too. I fear that I won't be allowed to keep you both, that something will divide us and I will lose you."

"Why do you worry about losing me?" Aoife asked.

"Since I was a child," he whispered, "there has been — "

Lightning struck close to the tree.

Ronan grabbed Aoife and ran a few steps before throwing her to the ground and covering her body with his. Sparks rained down overhead and the ground shook as a bough from the giant Elm broke.

The limb landed on Ronan's back, knocking the wind out of both of them. Aoife gasped for air under Ronan's limp body. She freed her arms and tried to shake him back to his senses. His head rolled to the side and a thin trickle of blood made its way from his head and down his cheek.

Aoife screamed to the little man. Ronan's life was not a part of the deal. She shuttered as something between a growl and laughter reverberated over the rolling thunder.

Chapter 19
Potions and Promises

"**I** won't drink it," Aoife shook her head at Fiona, "not ever again."

"But it's supposed to be good for you and the baby."

"I don't care what the apothecary says," Aoife shook her head vehemently. "That concoction is disgusting as are all the other herbs they've been forcing the cook to sneak into my food."

Since finding out about the pregnancy, Ronan had become relentless in his devotion to protect her and the baby. There were daily visits from doctors and an apothecary who had now set up residence in the manor. They checked her pulse, measured her belly, mixed potions, and made recommendations about everything from the temperature of her bath to the order of her prayers.

"But don't you want to keep the baby safe and

healthy?"

Aoife gave her a reproachful glare. Under the fiery sparks of lightning that had struck the tree and lit up the darkened sky, the two lives, which had felt like shackles around her wrists, suddenly transformed into her family. The hour she spent under the tree with Ronan waiting for help, the three men it took to free him from under the limb, and the hours he spent unconscious and far away from her washed away all her anger toward him. She did not fight her love for him anymore. And now she had a greater purpose for fulfilling her bargain with the little man. She was no longer fighting for an unappreciative mother or an impossibly weak father; she was fighting for her own husband and child.

"Ah, you must be patient with him, Aoife," Fiona said. "Stories have trickled down to him about the difficulties the Duchess had carrying her babies. I'm sure they weigh heavily on his mind as he thinks of his own child."

Aoife had found some comfort from Ronan's protective instincts. She had always been the protector in her family, so his attentions were a newfound luxury for her.

"Tell me of his parents," Aoife said, pushing the potion aside. "He rarely speaks of them."

Since her pregnancy Aoife was not allowed to do many things for herself as a precaution. Although Tara came by for visits and they enjoyed many meals together in her room, inevitably she would need to return home and Aoife was left alone. And Aoife did not want Maeve to see her confined to a bed by pregnancy. She did not know how to tell her that she had fallen in love with the man who she had been fighting so hard to escape. She feared appearing emotional and weak and so she had not replied to her two last letters. With no one else around, Aoife had been forced to accept Fiona's assistance. She tended to Aoife's every need with a motherly affection that was hard not to love.

Aoife sat up in bed and patted the mattress beside her. Fiona sat in the chair beside Aoife's bed.

"The Duchess, Ashling, did whatever it took to protect her child."

Fiona looked sad for a moment and then laughed softly.

"She was a lot like you. When she decided to do something, no one could stop her or change her mind. After so many miscarriages, when she became pregnant for the sixth time, she decided take matters into her own hands. I can still hear the excitement in her voice, like a young girl with a secret, when she came to me with her plan."

***

"She exists!" Ashling whispered. "The woman in the woods from your father's stories, the one you told me about – I've found her, or the huntsman I hired found her."

"What are you talking about?" Fiona said as Ashling pulled her into a seat in her private chamber.

"The woman in the woods who you said had powers that even the fairies envied," Ashling said. "She exists and, although I don't know if she keeps a cauldron bubbling in her kitchen, it appears that she does have some sort of power."

"Ashling," Fiona whispered, frightened by how far away Ashling had been swept by this tale. "You can't possibly think –"

"That she can solve what the doctors, apothecaries, midwives and all their potions have not been able to?" Ashling said. "Yes, I do."

Fiona did not know what to say.

"The huntsman is waiting in the woods for us and I have two horses saddled and ready to go."

Ashling's eyes were set and so was her will. She heard the word "no" very rarely and obeyed it even less frequently. So without argument, Fiona followed her.

The journey through the woods was as long and arduous as Fiona had feared and just as deep as her father's story had foretold. Never a great rider, Fiona ducked awkwardly under limbs and brushed cobwebs from her eyes. The horses slipped over mossy rocks and roots, the forest floor beneath them a place the sun never reached. There was no path to follow and Fiona feared the huntsman might be kidnapping them for ransom or worse.

After more than two hours, Fiona wasn't even sure they were still in Stanishire territory. Suddenly, he stopped short.

"Her house is in the middle of the clearing just up ahead," he said with an anxious glance at the cottage. "You may leave the horses with me, and I'll feed and water them. Knock loudly and have your purse handy. She's not one for small talk, but she speaks in coin very well."

"I don't like this," Fiona said.

The huntsman's wariness was not comforting.

"Everyone converses in money," Ashling said, her eyes fixed on the cottage. "It doesn't dissuade your belief in doctors, priests, or butchers. Why should she be expected to trade her arts any differently?"

Ashling was already off her horse and walking toward the clearing. The huntsman helped Fiona down and took the reins of the horses. Fiona lifted her skirt and made her way over to Ashling's side. The clearing was filled with high grass that undulated in the breeze. The sun felt warm against Fiona's cool skin as she stepped out of the shade of the trees. A doe and two of her young poked their heads up only a few feet away and froze, catching their scent on the back of the breeze. A rabbit jumped into the brush and sent the deer running for the woods. The high peak of the thatched roof, the sinewy sliver of smoke traveling up from the chimney, and the path that curved from where they stood all the way up to the front door looked far more welcoming than the huntsman had indicated.

Without looking back, Ashling stepped onto the path and walked with a fervent speed all the way up to the front door. Fiona practically ran to keep up and called to Ashling as they approached the door, afraid she might charge right inside. Ashling's knuckles hovered an inch from the door, her breathing heavy. She rapped with more force than courtesy. Fiona held her breath, remembering the stories of dark magic that her father had told about the mysterious woman in the woods. She had potions and cures in abundance, but all of them came with a price, he had said. When the door stood idle and the house silent for several moments, Fiona reached out for Ashling's hand. She swatted it away and rapped angrily again on the door as though it belonged to the God who had stolen five babies from her. She pounded away and then the heavy door opened slightly.

Ashling caught her breath and a stray hair drifted out of her braids and into her eyes. Fiona grasped her arm, afraid of what lurked beyond the door's squeaky hinges. Ashling reached out her hand to push open the door, but Fiona pulled her back.

"Please, my lady," Fiona whispered. "It could be some sort of a trap."

"I've been trapped in a long line of death," Ashling said and shook off Fiona's hands. "There's nothing more she or anyone can do to me that's not already been done."

Her eyes were fierce, and Fiona could only watch with shaking hands as Ashling pushed the door open. A heavily worn broom stood by the front door, leaning against whitewashed walls. After the door's squeally hinge fell silent, Ashling stepped over the threshold. Fiona hesitated for a moment, but her loyalty to the Duchess was stronger than her fears, and she finally drew in enough breath and courage to step over the threshold.

"Hello," Ashling called. "Is anyone home?"

The sweet scent of lavender was confused with the musky smell of shriveled roots unfamiliar to Fiona. The Duchess' eyes took in everything from the hanging herbs on the ceiling down to the cozy chair before the fire where a kettle hung close to the flame. She walked toward the teacup sitting on the small table beside the chair. Fiona's heart pounded as Ashling picked it up and looked inside.

"Please, let's wait outside," Fiona said, the fear in her voice boiling over. "We shouldn't be in her home handling her things without permission."

The door closed behind them. Fiona squeaked like a mouse, and Ashling was so startled that the teacup fell from her hand and crashed upon the floor.

"Well, this is a strange introduction," said a woman with thick, dark hair that hung in spirals down her back.

Her piercing green eyes were set against skin whiter and more perfect than the shattered teacup had once been. The basket she carried was filled with berries.

"I'm so sorry," Ashling fumbled with her words and hands. She knelt down to pick up the pieces. "We, I didn't mean to — "

Her sentence was left as broken and unfinished as the pieces in her hands.

"You didn't mean to what?" the woman asked. "You didn't mean to make your way into my house uninvited? Or you didn't mean to break my cup? I'd like to excuse you, but without a full apology or even an introduction, you can imagine just how difficult that might be for me."

"I'm sorry for everything," Ashling said, trying to resurrect her calm demeanor.

Fiona had never seen her so unsure of herself and so thrown by anyone, not even her husband. Ashling straightened up and stepped toward the dark haired beauty.

"My name is Ashling, the Duchess of these lands and this is my servant, Fiona. Stories of your great talents have persuaded me to travel here to meet you."

"Your lands," she said with a smirk. "So it's my acquaintance and conversation that you've come for?" she tilted her head and locked her emerald eyes on Ashling. "Or is it just a cup of tea you want?"

"I dare say I could use a cup of tea after our long journey, but – "

She held up her hands, which still held the broken cup, and shrugged her shoulders in an apology. The woman crossed the floor with her basket of berries still hanging from one arm and faced Ashling. Although Ashling was known for her golden waves and her high cheeks that still held the rosy bloom of one much younger, her looks were no match for this mysterious beauty. Barefoot and untamed as she was, she stood several inches taller, every curve as perfectly placed as if by artist's careful hand.

"I'm not so poor that I don't have an extra cup, or two, for tired wanderers," she said without betraying any emotion, "especially if those tired travelers have come so far just for my – tea and conversation."

After an uncomfortably long pause, she turned and walked toward her cupboard. She put her basket on a shelf and took out three cups. She arranged slices of bread and butter and bowl of sugar. She made no attempt at conversation and only nodded when Ashling complimented her home. She pulled over two more chairs from what passed as a dining area and arranged them around the fire. She poured and passed the tea around and then finally settled in her customary seat by the fire. She took a long sip and made no attempt to break the silence.

"I must say," Ashling finally attempted, "I've sought out information about you and your talents. While they did make mention of your beauty, their descriptions pale in comparison to the woman before me. They also did not mention your name, which I still do not know."

"Your sudden appearance left little time for a civil introduction. My name is Ena. I ought to warn you to be careful with the illusion of corporeal beauty," she said, placing her empty cup on the tray. "All beauty is temporary."

"While age renders all our facades temporary," Ashling countered, "I doubt there's a woman alive who wouldn't give anything to own your beauty."

"And I'd remind them of the old adage 'be careful what you wish for,'" she smiled sardonically. "So please tell me, why is it that you have traveled hours from your pristine tower without your husband's consent to seek my counsel."

Ena smiled for the first time, but it was far from warm.

"I come to humbly ask you," the tear stained words wavered in Ashling's throat, "to protect my baby. I've conceived and carried so many, but none have survived into this world."

The empty teacup chattered in her hands and a sob slipped out. Ena's home and the hope Ashling felt she offered had turned their introduction into a sorrowful sort of confessional. Ena stood up and paced the room.

"So it's a live birth you need," Ena said.

Ashling nodded, unable to utter another word without being overcome by tears. Fiona wrapped her arm around her. Ena apparently relished the shock of pain, not the soothing of it, for she rolled her eyes and crossed the room. She moved Fiona out of the way and pulled Ashling up to her feet. She settled her hand on Ashling's belly with an intimate caress that hinted of something sinister. She closed her eyes and seemed to be listening.

"This one is destined to be lost as well," she said, now looking into Ashling's eyes. "It's not made to survive your womb. But if what you want is a live birth, then I can make that happen," Ena said.

She released her hand and watched Ashling gasp and clutch her belly. Ashling sat down in the chair, rocking with grief.

"We'll make your womb a fortress that can hold your child," she continued, "even if God and nature wish otherwise. But are you willing to look God in the eye and shake your fist at him? Are you willing to say that you know better and shall carry this child into this world, and thus defy the very hand of God?"

"Yes, yes," Ashling sobbed. "My husband and I, we need this child."

"And you're willing to trust me with your life and the life of this child?" Ena challenged her.

"Yes, I will," Ashling reached up and clutched Ena's hands.

Ena offered almost no response, physical or emotional. She looked at Fiona, who shook with terror in the presence of this woman who until today was nothing more than a fictional character in her father's stories. Ena eyed Fiona from head to toe, a look of private victory lighting up Ena's face.

"You will get what you desire. Your ill-fated child will survive the confines of your faulty womb. You shall produce a male heir for your anxious husband and I shall receive my payment and just reward."

Chapter 20
Preparations

"You have never told me about how Ronan's mother finally managed to carry him into this world," Aoife said to Fiona a few weeks later through closed lids.

The unanticipated dizzy spells had become a part of her every morning and precluded her from her daily walks with Ronan. As Aoife became more ill, having guests of any kind became too difficult. Talking with her mother and even her sister only increased Aoife's nausea. And even tough she longed for Maeve's company and advice, with so many caretakers keeping close watch on her, discreetly sneaking in the proprietor of Stanishire's brothel was nearly impossible. Her health also kept her from meeting with the little man in the woods. He was never far from her thoughts, but for now she was forced to trust his cryptic assurances that he would come to her when he was ready to collect his debt. She had no choice but to close her eyes much of the day and rest. But Fiona was always there as Aoife's caretaker. She expected nothing, not even conversation from Aoife. Instead, she offered stories about Ronan's childhood. Aoife simply laid back on her pillow and listened.

"How did Ena keep the baby safe?"

"I nursed her through the pregnancy at home, following every direction Ena gave me to the final detail. No one knew of Ena or the treatments she had given us. And it was under this vow of secrecy that I helped sneak Ashling away during the night. The huntsman led us once again to meet Ena and prepare for the birth."

"Didn't the Duke come after you?" Aoife asked.

"She left him a letter saying she was going to her parents' home to deliver the baby and avoid the bad luck of the previous births. He must have believed it since he did not have us followed right away."

Aoife scrunched up her brows.

"It makes me feel closer to Ronan to know all of this. He says nothing of his childhood."

Ronan sat with Aoife for long stretches of the day, their heads tipped together, but she never brought up the stories she had heard about his mother. The only time he had spoken of his past was just before the lightning struck the tree, and even then there had been tears in his eyes. He did not seem comfortable talking about it, so instead, she turned to Fiona for her information.

"I can still see the way Ena's eyes devoured Ashling's swollen shape when we arrived."

***

"So I see you've not spared the sweets," Ena said when she opened the door for Ashling. Her eyes swept Ashling's round face, the girth of her waist and her swollen ankles. She stepped back and made ample room for Ashling and Fiona to enter.

"These have been the longest months of my life, but they have also been the most important," Ashling replied, ignoring Ena's snipe. "If you'll allow me to skip the pleasantries, I must find my way to a chair."

"Please," Ena smiled and motioned toward the seat by the fire.

Fiona trudged across the floor, carrying a heavy traveling bag. The ride in the coach had been bumpy and arduous, but better than the alternative of riding on horseback. The huntsman refused to cross the tree line into the clearing, even if that meant saddling Fiona with Ashling's belongings.

Ena poured two cups of water from a pitcher painted over with a wispy strand of flowers. She returned and handed one to Ashling and the other to Fiona. Ena motioned to another seat and Fiona nodded and dropped down with a loud creak and gulped at the water. Ena stood regally, her skin as pearly white and her lips as ripe as they remembered.

"You asked me to be sure that your child made it into this world, and I have ensured that. Now let's see if it's time for him to join us."

Ena pulled a stool over and sat down before Ashling. She placed her hands on Ashling's knees and spread them wide, smiling slightly when Ashling gasped. She took the hem of Ashling's dress and pulled it all the way up over the massive expanse of her belly.

Ashling restrained her embarrassment. Ena adjusted the thick layers of fabric until they were out of her way. First her eyes and then her slender fingers traced the deep stretch marks that mapped the journey of Ashling's past nine months. Ashling looked toward the ceiling while Ena's fingers slipped into the grooves.

Her fingers danced for a moment longer and then she flattened her hands and Ashling felt the heat of her palms and the pressure of her fingertips as they ran over her womb like a crystal ball. Fiona walked over and held Ashling's hand while Ena closed her eyes and seemed to be listening to something inaudible to everyone else. The seconds ticked slowly by and a sob hovered at the edge of Ashling's breathing as all her hopes rested on the word of this cold siren.

Ena sucked in a halted breath and then opened her emerald eyes.

"It's time."

Ashling sobbed with joy while Ena moved the chairs from in front of the fire and dragged over a makeshift mattress of hay covered with a sheet. Ena arranged a pile of sheets and a deep metal basin of water beside the mattress with the pragmatic hands of a midwife. She instructed Ashling to change into something that wouldn't hamper the delivery.

After exchanging a frightened look with Fiona, Ashling rose and walked obediently over to the bags that Fiona had carried in. She dug through them and retrieved a slip with lace edging the collar and the cuffs. She looked around for a private place to change and then saw Ena raise an eyebrow at her misplaced modesty. Summoning up her courage, Ashling began to untie the

sash of her gown and tried to steel over her gaze as
Fiona lifted layers of clothing over her rounded body.
Ena pointed toward the mattress and Ashling walked
over and lay down, her aching body welcoming the soft
hay.

"This might be a bit uncomfortable," Ena said.

She reached in between Ashling's legs and her
fingers probed inside her body. Ena pulled out her hand
and something sloshed into the basin beside them. She
inserted her hand again and pushed and prodded until it
felt like she had pierced through the barrier of her womb.
Ashling bit back a cry.

"You have done your job," Ena said to Fiona.
"You applied the poultice well; it has fortified the womb
and kept another of your children from falling out too
soon."

Ashling tightened her hand around Fiona's, a
silent nod of gratitude for her unflagging support.

"Your loyalty to your master's wife supersedes
expectation," Ena gave Fiona a crooked grin. "Why have
you devoted yourself to fulfilling her every request no
matter what darkened corner of the woods she takes you
to?"

"Her charitable hand gives me the bread on my
table and the roof over my head," Fiona replied.
"Loyalty and compassion are the least of what I owe her
for all that she has done for me."

"And?"

"And I need not explain myself further to you."

"And just how far would you go to prove your
loyalty and compassion for this woman?"

"As far as it takes to protect her from the pain

that life has inflicted upon her."

"Interesting," Ena said. She turned back to Ashling. "Now that I've removed the poultice, your body will do what it does best: expel your child."

Ashling nodded, and Fiona knew to ready everything she had packed for the delivery. She opened the clasp at the top of the bag and lifted out a folded piece of deep blue velvet fabric. Fiona shook it gently and it billowed out through the air like a piece of ocean sparkling under a dazzling sun. A cascade of jewels sewn into the fabric glittered and reflected their light majestically across the walls of the cottage. Fiona stretched it out over the back of a chair and then pulled out a long-handled baby rattle. It clattered playfully in her hand as streams of pearls and jewels danced through the air. Fiona shook it a few times and smiled as she placed it on a small table next to the blanket.

"I want his birth to be as noble as it would have been, had I been able to deliver him at home," Ashling smiled. "I suppose it seems silly to you."

"We all have our secret wishes," Ena replied as Fiona finished pulling out the remaining items.

"Everything is so laden with jewels and finery," Ena said. "It might be hard to witness the beauty of your child with all of these gems sparkling about."

"Nothing could ever overshadow the beauty of this child, the first to live and breathe in my arms," Ashling said. "The jewels are not what's important, but the ritual they provide and the passing on of his father's title and wealth, which are all things he deserves."

"Things he deserves for being lucky enough to be born to such *regal* parents," Ena replied. "His birthright can never be taken from him?"

"Not by anyone," Ashling smiled and stroked her stomach affectionately.

"Rest, both of you," Ena said as she went to draw the curtains. "You must both be at your strongest for this delivery."

Chapter 21
Bedtime Stories

"Tell me what you want now, or I'll tell everyone about you and what you are trying to do!" Aoife shouted at the little man. Now that she was pregnant, she did not like meeting with him.

"No you won't," he replied, the agitation in his voice growing.

"I'm done with this. I won't have this deal following me indefinitely."

She hated that he took the liberty of appearing in her chamber.

"The end is nearing closer every day."

"You lie!" she shouted. "Your mouth is full of nothing but lies! And you are growing nervous because you know that Ronan and I are too close now for your deal with me to come between us. You know that if I tell him then all of this will be over!"

"It's not over until I say it's over!"

"Not if I finally tell him," Aoife said as she rose from her bed.

"Don't get yourself so upset," he said grabbing her arm. "It's not good for you and the baby."

"Stop pretending you care about me or my baby," she said, repulsed by his concern. She shook her arm loose. "I'm done with you. I'm going to tell Ronan everything."

She walked past him to the door.

"I'm warning you one last time," his voice was high pitched. "You are not to tell him about our deal."

"Nothing you can say will stop me anymore."

As she reached for the door her arms began to tingle and then her legs. A weariness descended upon her like an impossibly heavy albatross upon her neck. She leaned her palm against the door for balance. She turned toward him. His eyes were leveled squarely upon her.

"What are you doing to me?"

"Only what you've made me do," he said.

"So you will kill me now because I refuse to do your bidding?"

"No," he said. "Just put you to bed where you must stay until the time is right."

"The time for – "

But words were lost to her, as was her balance. She swayed and fell into his arms. He was shorter than Aoife and awkward in his movements, but stronger than she imagined as he lifted her and carried her to her bed. She wanted to call out for help or fight his touch, but a strange paralysis had taken over her body. He laid her down and stared into her eyes.

"Go to sleep, my child," he said, smiling at her victoriously. "Stop fighting me. Learn patience. Learn obedience to the will of fate and this cruel world."

He brushed his hand over her eyes, closing them and submerging her under a watery tide of sleep. She lost her connection to everything around her, everything but her child. She felt the cord inside her that linked them. Fearing that she would slip away from everything forever, she found herself drawing strength from the life that she felt flowing through the cord. It was as if it was Aoife who now existed in amniotic dream fluid.

Minutes passed. Hours past. Days. Months. Still she slumbered, a half conscious sleeping beauty. There were times when she could hear warbled voices coming to her. Ronan's terrified pleas for her to wake. The touch of her mother's hand. Her father's worried sighs. Tara's tears. Fiona's nurturing assurances. Even Maeve found her way into Aoife's chambers to visit. The doctors' whispers. She was able at times to sit up and see their faces through the fog the little man had laid upon her. She sipped. She ate. She swallowed her meals. But she could do little else.

Each time she slipped completely beneath the blanket of sleep, she went back to the last moments before the little man had appeared in her room and sent her away into this sleep. She replayed the story Fiona had been telling her before she left to replenish the tea and the little man showed up. The story of Ronan's birth.

***

Fiona leapt off the bed when Ashling's scream pierced the night air. Her hand reached up to her heart to steady her breathing and her nerves. When Ena tore the sheets off of Ashling, they all saw the mattress drenched with water. Another piercing cry filled the air and Fiona covered her ears.

"It appears that without my poultice, your body can't hold this child for more than a few hours," Ena muttered from beneath her hooded cloak. Her voice was raspy and oddly shrill. "Ready yourselves now."

Ena laughed. As she threw her head back, the hood of her cloak slipped off and the firelight revealed the grimy toothed smile of an old, wrinkled, and wiry-haired woman. Her skin hung in heavy folds, and her hair stood out on all sides in a motley mess.

Both women would have run out the door, had not another stabbing pain sent a shriek from Ashling's lips.

"Don't fear ladies," Ena smiled. "It's still me; this is the shape I am forced to take by night. But these hands hold the same power that they do by day. You wouldn't let the unfortunate hand that life has dealt me change the appreciation and loyalty you felt for me just hours ago, would you?"

"Stay back!" Fiona yelled as Ena leaned in closer.

"No!" Ashling cried in between pains. "I trust you. You have brought me this far. I can see beyond earthly masks."

Ashling screamed out as another pain seized her body.

"Interesting choice of words," Ena replied cryptically.

Ena pulled back the wet nightgown, exposing Ashling's legs. She leaned in close, put her hands over Ashling's stomach, and began to whisper something between a prayer and a song. Fiona leaned closer, thinking it might be an order she did not want to miss. She tried to listen, but the words did not sound like any Fiona had ever heard. Ena's eyes were closed and her gnarled hands frozen. There was something dark in the way she chanted that terrified Fiona. When Fiona asked what she was doing and she failed to respond, Fiona yelled. She yelled louder and louder, but nothing could pull Ena back from the dark place that she had gone.

Fiona held Ashling's hand and watched as the baby's head slowly made its way into the world. With his head face down, Fiona marveled at the dark brown curls of his hair, wet and pressed against his little head. Ena cried out sharply for Fiona to grab the gilded scissors they had brought for the delivery. Fiona obeyed and when she looked closer she saw the cord wrapped dangerously around the tiny neck. Ena yelled at Fiona to cut the cord, the fear in her voice razor sharp. Fiona hesitated, too frightened to slip the sharp scissors between the strangling cord and the delicate, translucent skin of his neck.

"Now!" Ena shrieked. "Or he'll die! He can't die! Do it!"

Fiona reached in and cut the cord that just moments ago had been the source of his life. Ena yelled for Ashling to push again and all at once the baby slipped out with a last gush of water, baptizing his entrance from one world into the next.

Chapter 22
Blame

"I want to see him," Aoife said. "I don't care what time it is or how long I've been in bed."

"I understand your impatience," Fiona said, "but the sun has not even risen and you've just finished your first real meal in months. Be gentle with your body, for you and for the baby's sake."

"If you will not bring him to me, then I will go to him."

She swung her feet over the side of the bed. She was still getting used to the massive swell of her belly, which had blossomed a great deal during her months of exile into darkness. Aoife knew she had slipped under the blanket of her illness for some time, but it was hard to believe Fiona when she said it had been over seven months. She stroked the circumference of her stomach like it belonged to someone else. For the moment, the little man had lifted his punishment and Aoife could see, think, and feel the world around her. She was not about to lie in bed a moment longer.

The way Fiona was talking in evasive circles about Ronan, Aoife knew something was wrong. Her vague memories of him beside her bed were too confused for her to even remember how long it had been since she had seen him. Mixed up with those memories was the constant presence of Tara. How strange it must have been for her to be the healthy one sitting vigil at Aoife's bedside. Aoife had to be careful; these hazy memories kept resurrecting themselves in a jumble since she woke up almost an hour ago. She knew Ronan would have been by her side right now, unless something had happened to him.

"In a few hours after you've rested," Fiona said, "I'm sure he'll be up and anxious to see you."

Fiona smiled hopefully, but Aoife shook her head.

"You have told me that I have been asleep for seven months. I will not lay here a moment longer without my husband."

She leaned on her hands, hiding how dizzy and weak she felt.

Fiona acknowledged defeat and called to Aemon, one of Ronan's oversized servants. He came in and swept Aoife up in his arms gently and carried her out into the hallway. They made a sharp turn toward the room beside Aoife's.

"Where are we going?" Aoife asked.

"He hasn't slept in his chamber since you took to your bed," Fiona replied. "He wants to be as near to you as possible."

One of the doctors carried a candle and walked ahead of them to open the door to light the way. The darkness was so eerily similar to that of her dreams that she feared she had slipped back into the little man's clutches. The candle illuminated an unkempt bed.

"Over by the fire," Fiona whispered. "That's where he sleeps most often."

Aoife looked at the dying embers, which lit up the couch and the edge of a blanket. Aemon brought her over, and only when the doctor carefully moved the edge of the blanket did Aoife realize Ronan was the lump underneath. When the candlelight stretched closer, Aoife gasped at the bloated mask of his features, his greasy hair, and unkempt clothes. At Aoife's request, Aemon seated her down, just inches from Ronan's head. She wanted to touch him, but he looked so sickly that she no more wanted to wake him than she would a fevering child. Beside him on a small table were two oversized bottles of mead, both of them empty. She recognized the stench of alcohol that oozed from every saturated pore of his body. It took a regular routine of drink to produce the odor and the bloating that reminded her all too much of her father.

"How long has this been going on?" Aoife whispered.

"Several months," Fiona whispered. She knelt down beside Ronan. "He's been so worried about you. In the beginning he paced your room until he nearly wore out the rug. He called in every doctor and every priest he could find. There was no talisman he didn't hang from the canopy above your bed. He slept beside you every night. And then — "

Fiona brushed his matted hair off his forehead. Her touch was so gentle it was like she was alone with him for a moment.

"And then what?" Aoife asked.

Ronan rolled over and startled everyone in the room, but he was not truly conscious. He touched Aoife's leg and grumbled something unintelligible before nuzzling his head in her lap and slipping back to sleep.

"And then the nightmares started again," Fiona said.

"Again?"

Fiona turned her gaze from Ronan to Aoife.

"When he was a child of about seven, he was plagued by relentless nightmares. I had been living deep in the woods when the late Duke summoned me back to the manor. The Duchess had died, and for months he had been fighting nightmares that his father feared were threatening his sanity. He was a shivering, lost child when I came back to the manor. He didn't fight my attentions or shudder away from my arms. From the start, he so took to me and me alone that I became indispensable to him. He begged for me to sleep in his chamber, as it was only then that he could sleep. I could not refuse, and so I moved back to the manor and became Ronan's servant. But eventually, a boy wants to be a man and a man who can't find a night's peace is no man at all. So he ran away and found rest in other lands and other arms."

This story sounded too familiar to be a coincidence. Aoife felt the tentacles of the little man's anger reaching far back in time. She sensed that he was a part of the bad memories that haunted Ronan. Just how long had he been tormenting Ronan? And why?

"But he's found no rest these past months," Fiona peered down at her hands, shaking her head.

Even in this low light, she could see new lines had grown around Fiona's eyes.

"The deeper you sank into your illness the deeper he sank into despair, mumbling prayers by your bedside and cursing the air. He believes he's responsible for your illness and all that has befallen the household. He cries out in his sleep against forces he feels are perched to harm both you and the child."

Fiona looked directly at Aoife as the dam of her emotions broke open.

"He thinks it's his fault, but I don't know how to tell him that the fault is mine. The Duchess and I are the cause of all the darkness in his life and now yours."

Aoife's body froze.

"What do you mean?"

She leaned in as if the walls were listening.

"The little man – "

Aoife felt her heart beating and waited for the room to collapse around her at the mention of him.

"The little man is my very angry son."

Chapter 23
Revelations

"Tell me again about the things you treasure most in life," Aoife asked as she ran her fingers through his hair.

"It's always the same answer," he said as he kissed her belly. "You."

She laughed as he tickled her ribs and nuzzled her stomach. Although everyone wanted her in bed for her final days of confinement, Aoife negotiated a seat by the fire. Ronan was by her side, always. Her renewed health kept his nightmares away, and, thus, the mead as well. Within just a few weeks, he looked like himself again.

"You always say that," she replied, tugging his hair.

"And yet you keep asking the same question every day."

"That's because I want to know the whole answer, not just the one you say to make me happy."

She kept hoping she could coax the riddle out of

him, but he thought she was playing the part of a coy woman only wanting to hear him profess his love for her.

"But it is true," he said and sat up. "I don't think you understand how strange it is for me to feel loved completely by someone."

Aoife remembered the way Fiona had rocked back and forth when she recounted how impossible it became to love and care for both the little man and Ronan. She said they had never been fond of each other, even in the few encounters they had as toddlers. But when the Duke asked Fiona to move from the cottage in the woods where she had lived with her son into the manor to care for Ronan, the relationship between the two boys became untenable. Each boy had held firm to either side of her heart and pulled and yanked for more until they left her broken.

"Are you saying that your mother and father didn't love you?"

"My father was a good man and he was proud of me, but he was distant and always seemed to look at me with a question in his eyes," he said. "And with my mother, her embraces always felt distant, too. I never truly understood it until – "

He stood and walked a few steps away from her.

It sounded like a lonely childhood, which might have explained why Ronan was so cruel to the little man when they were young. He would not have enjoyed sharing Fiona, the woman who acted as his mother, any more than her own son, the little man, would have. She toyed with the cloudy ring on her finger, wishing she could tell him that she knew about the little man and try to understand what happened between them. But after the tree limb and the sleep he had sent her into, Aoife would not risk mentioning him. Not even when Fiona asked Aoife if she knew the little man, her son, did she confess the whole story. All she told Fiona was that all those months ago when she was locked in the barn and then the tower, she had eventually cried herself to sleep. When she awoke each time, the gold had appeared. She told Fiona that she had not wanted to question her good fortune. Aoife wanted to tell Fiona the truth and ask her help, but it wasn't safe. Not for anyone, especially Ronan.

"The day my mother died, I took a ride out through the fields. She said she needed rest and wanted me to get fresh air. She worried I was too young to spend so much time in her sick room. Arguing with my mother never worked, even when she was ill, so I kissed her clammy forehead and left. I was relieved when the rain cut my trip short and rushed back to her room," his voice cracked. "Even though I was still a child, I knew the end was near and I couldn't imagine losing her. I just wanted to be by her side as much as I could. I ran up the stairs and burst through her chamber door and then – "

Aoife rose, crossed the floor and stood behind Ronan, wrapping her arms around him.

"Fiona was standing by her bed as usual. And he was there, too; her dwarfed son."

Aoife felt the air prickle around her. This was the first time Ronan had mentioned him. How was she to react? What would the little man do?

"He was a horror of a creature who tormented me relentlessly."

189

Aoife wrapped her arms around him tighter and kissed his shoulder. Her heart was pounding with curiosity and a fear.

"When I returned to her room, I found him sitting on my mother's deathbed, sharing an embrace with her. Her arms, weakened from months of illness, were wrapped around him, far tighter than they had ever held me. The way I felt when I saw them together is so indescribable. I began to cry, but no one noticed me at all until I ran over and tore him away from her."

Aoife imagined him as a rain soaked little boy who wanted his dying mother all to himself. She closed her eyes and caressed his arm.

"I was so confused and angry I pushed and shoved him out of the room. My mother sat up, crying and begging me to stop. Fiona dragged us both out of the room. While she returned to calm my mother who was in the midst of a coughing fit, I saw my mother's ring – the one that I gave you – in his hand. The ring that now looks as clouded over as his evil eyes." He turned his head toward Aoife as if about to ask her about the ring and then stopped. "I threw him to the ground and dug my nails into his palm to wrestle it away from him. He was trying to steal my mother's love and now her belongings. I kept seeing her arms wrapped around him, and all I wanted to do was hurt him. He actually said that *I* was the thief and threw himself on me, trying to take the ring back when Fiona came out and pulled us apart. She was chastising him with her back to me, so I held the ring high for him to see and then placed it in my pocket. He looked like he was going to charge me, but Fiona held him back. I turned and walked into my mother's room. I was ready to slam the door behind me when I saw her lifeless arm dangling over the side of the bed. She was gone. She had left me, and her last gesture of affection, the sincerest expression of love I ever saw her give, had been to him."

Aoife turned him toward her and pulled him close. Nuzzling her head under his chin, she tried to send him all the love he had never felt from his mother. The little man and Ronan clearly despised each other as boys. But why was the little man still so full of hatred for Ronan all these years later?

"And that is why I love you so much," he whispered into her hair. "You've looked into my eyes in a way my father and mother never did, and you love me anyway. You've seen the darkness in me, and it hasn't scared you away. So when I picture our child, I think of all the love you will give him or her, all the love I never knew."

He took her hands in his and kissed each of them tenderly.

Looking into her eyes he continued, "Your love for our child makes me love you more. And now I must amend my answer to the question about my most valuable treasure that you asked me by the fire a few minutes ago, and a day ago, and two days ago, and a week ago, and so many more times than that. For this gift you have given me, this child who grows so strong inside you, has truly become my greatest treasure."

Aoife shrieked, her insides screaming out as if she had been stabbed with a broad sword. She crumbled and Ronan caught her in his arms and carried her over to the bed. He cried out for Fiona. Aoife tried to speak, but the room was spinning and her grasp on the world was slipping. She could not afford to lose a single moment to protect her family now that the truth was so horribly clear. This was it. The little man's plan was finally clear. Horribly, unthinkably clear.

"He's going to – "

Her womb seized, knocking the wind out of her. Aoife could feel the little man's grip around her belly. His laughter filled her ears and drowned out every other sound. Fiona appeared and ran to Aoife's side, flinching as though she, too, were privy the sound of the little man's laughter.

The doctors and midwives were called and with every attempt Aoife made to shout the truth, the little man twisted the muscles of her body until she could not speak. Midwives whispered that the labor was strange and fast coming. Ronan ignored tradition and refused to leave her side.

Hours later, the baby slipped from her womb. The midwife held up their baby girl and called Ronan to cut the cord. Aoife was gathering her strength to finally speak now that the searing pain was loosening its grip on her. He was about to cut the cord connecting their daughter to her – the cord that nourished and protected her from the outside world and from the little man. Without that connection, he would steal her away.

As he cut the cord, Aoife cried out, her voice hers again.

"He's going to take the baby! The little man is coming for her."

All eyes turned to Aoife, and a rush of wind filled the room. The candles and lamps blew out and there was a scuffle of noise as everyone struggled in the darkness. Aoife pleaded for her daughter. When the midwife's assistant relit her lamp, Aoife sighed with relief at the sight of her crying baby tucked safely in Ronan's arms. He ran to Aoife's side, and they both searched the darkened room for the little man. A few more candles were relit as the midwives tended to Aoife and began removing the soiled linens, barely paying any mind to her words, the words that must have sounded like the mad ravings of many women during birth.

"He's coming to take her," Aoife said, her voice raspy. "When you made me spin the gold, I made a deal with him, but I didn't know... I swear I didn't know."

Ronan searched her eyes, realizing the danger looming around their daughter. Before he could say anything, the little man stepped out of the shadows, a triumphant grin perched on his lips. The midwife and doctors were so preoccupied with the candles and the chaos of the moment, they did not yet notice the oddly shaped man who lingered at the edge of the light. But Aoife and Ronan caught sight of him immediately and so, too, did Fiona.

Ronan handed the baby to Aoife and stood up drawing his sword and saying, "I won't let you take my wife or child."

"Don't worry about your wife," he sneered. "I've had enough of her."

"Leave our child alone," Aoife said. Any sympathy she had felt for him had died in the wake of the threat he posed to her daughter. "She's done nothing to deserve this."

"No, but your sweet husband took something from me a long time ago, something very dear to me. And now I'm going to take something very special from him."

"I'm not the thief," Ronan argued. "I'm done letting you steal my happiness. I'll have you killed before I'll let you take my daughter!"

"You don't really think a sword can stop me," the little man laughed. "I thought you knew me better."

He took a step toward them and the baby cried louder as Aoife pulled her close. The doctors and midwives huddled fearfully in the corner.

"Such a nice little family gathering," he said. "And mother it's been ages since we last met."

"That's not my doing," she replied.

As the little man approached, Ronan widened his stance, ready for battle, but just as Ronan was about to strike, Fiona stepped in between the two men.

"No," she said to the little man in a stern tone. "I won't let you take this baby. It will do nothing to ease your pain, and it will destroy *her* more than her father, who is the one you wish to hurt most."

"He stole something from me once before, and you took his side," the little man yelled. "Do you really intend to put him before me again?"

"This is about protecting an innocent child," she replied. "Which is all I've ever tried to do."

"You're trying to protect another innocent child? You haven't done a very good job of that now have you?"

He laughed and threw his head back. The room echoed with his cackle.

194

"Please," Aoife said. "I am the one who made this deal with you. So I ask you now, why would you want to take my child? Although I've hurt you deeply, is the hurt so bad that you would kidnap my infant? What could you possibly want with my newborn baby?"

The little man looked down at the child, so tiny and helpless in her mother's arms. The sight of her seemed to instantly soften him, and he stood silent, gazing upon her without any concern for the sword still pointed toward him. And when she saw the tear glistening at the corner of his eye, Aoife knew what he wanted.

"This isn't the way to secure a person's love," she said. "You can't just steal her away from her life and expect that she will grow up to love you."

"But why not? The only thing that comes between me and the world is this face, or everyone's knowledge that this face is hideous. So all I have to do is remove everyone else," he said.

"Then can we please amend our agreement so that we might have a few months with our child?" she said with desperation in her voice.

She needed to delay this. She needed time to make a plan.

"Why would I give you months to bend her toward you," he replied. "She will come with me. The world will have no ability to turn her against me."

"Then give me a week," Aoife countered. "Just enough time to have known my daughter before she is lost to her mother forever."

The little man stepped back and his eyes shimmered. She felt a wave of hope.

"Please, give me one week with her."

He looked down at his hands as if they were unclean and then back at the child who cried out for her mother's milk. He stepped back and closed his eyes.

"Three days," he whispered and turned away. "I'll give you three days with her and nothing more." He looked at Fiona. "You're right, Aoife. Every child deserves to know its mother. It's too bad life isn't always fair."

Chapter 24
So Much Depends Upon a Name

Aoife cuddled her daughter, feeling the warmth of her little hands. She memorized the curve of her cheek and the pout of her lips. She should have been thinking of a plan, but every moment with her daughter passed all too quickly, and since there might be so few, Aoife could not help but linger in the scent of her skin and the sound of her breathing.

The room was silent, except for the sighs of Fiona sleeping in the chair beside the fire. The doctors receded hours ago with a strict warning from Ronan not to share the story of the little man's appearance or demands. No one was allowed to share the news of the baby either. Aoife knew that her family would happily descend upon the manor and shower her with gifts, none of which they were ready for yet. When it was all over, Aoife knew her family would be hurt, especially Tara, but Aoife wanted to savor every moment with her daughter. She had convinced Ronan to also leave the guards outside the room, as the little man had guaranteed three days of safety. Ronan had gone to meet with his men to find a way to outwit the little man. Aoife nodded as he left but knew his attempts were as futile as sprinkling holy water on a blazing inferno. The little man's powers were such that he could kill them and take the baby if he wished.

Despite everything, Ronan refused to blame Aoife for the deal she made with the little man. He barely listened to her explanations, noting only that it was the little man's hatred for him that brought this curse upon their child. He blamed himself for having placed the bet in the first place.

Her daughter had just finished nursing and was drifting off to sleep. As she rocked and hummed soothingly over her little girl's head, Aoife felt the familiar lilt in the air as the little man materialized in the darkness. There was no anger in him, only longing. He was not here to take her daughter, yet. She knew that if she wanted to convince him to let her keep her daughter, she needed to do more than make amends for the hurt she had done to him. She needed to ameliorate the hurt the whole world had done to him. Her time alone with her daughter would have to wait, if she wanted to have more than three days with her.

After a moment's hesitation, a red, worn boot stepped out of the darkness. It looked lonely and tired with its other half still invisible. After a long moment, the little man emerged from the darkness, his eyes locked on the baby, whose head peaked out from under her blanket.

He made his way to Aoife's bedside, reached

inside his vest and pulled something out with a clatter. He held a golden rattle dripping with pearls and jewels of every color of the rainbow. At the end of each string of pearls was an oversized jewel whose iridescent glow was magnified by the candlelight. The prisms it cast about the room reminded Aoife of the jewels hanging from the ceiling of his cottage.

"Did you make this for her," Aoife asked in awe.

"No," he said without looking away from the baby. "It was a gift from my mother."

Aoife furrowed her brow and looked to Fiona, who sat quietly in her chair, wiping a tear. Aoife's heart beat faster as she gazed at the rattle and then the jewel encrusted sheers by her bed, which had severed her connection to her daughter. And then there was the sword that she had brought him with all the jewels, all family heirlooms passed down from the late Duke and Duchess. Aoife's heart pounded.

"You called my husband a thief," Aoife began.

"Because he is and always will be," he said without losing a moment's joy staring at Aoife's daughter. "Right, *mother*?"

Fiona pulled out a handkerchief and wiped her eyes.

"It's more than the ring on my finger you feel he's stolen from you," Aoife said.

"I've a long list of things and," he hesitated, "people he's taken from me. I would love to see him strung up in public for the imposter he is." His voice carried the eerie melody of a lullaby.

Aoife held her slumbering daughter closer.

"Maybe you would understand better if I showed

you how it all began."

He took Aoife's hand and swirled the rattle above it. The gems flickered with a sparkle from within. Their light hit upon Aoife's ring, and it began to glow. Swirling out of the ring's dark cloud came a foggy haze that grew and expanded until Aoife became frightened of losing herself and her baby in the fog.

"It's only a distant memory, which, when it's over, will dissolve like an ebbing dream," the little man explained.

The fog filled the room with a disorienting blindness and then began to recede as quickly as it came. Aoife hovered as a bodiless entity in a familiar room, but she could feel the little man and Fiona with her as clearly as if she could see them. While the light grew around her, she squeezed what should have been her arms and felt the press of her baby.

"She is sleeping safely in your arms and blissfully unaware of any of this," he said.

Aoife relaxed her hold and tried to adjust her sight to the hazy light and shapes emerging before her like a warped reflection at the bottom of a dark well.

A fire burned in a hearth. The sound of a distant cry grew stronger as the clarity of the scene crystallized into images and sounds Aoife understood. The cry of labor pains pierced the air above a mattress before the fire. Two women were huddled together, waiting anxiously beside the laboring woman, who had to be Ashling. As she moved closer to the scene, a woman pushed her hair from her face.

"Oh my God," Aoife gulped. That's you, Fiona. And you're very – pregnant. "

***

Ashling cried out and Ena caught the baby's slippery body in her wrinkly hands. She shouldered Fiona out of the way, which was not difficult to do given Fiona's late stage of pregnancy. Ena held him by the feet to empty his lungs and listen for the cry of life announcing his grand entrance. Fiona struggled to slip around her, but Ena's movements were fast and unpredictable. She laid his wet body in a blanket nearby and wrapped him up.

She stood up, surprisingly spry for the creaking age of her old bones and started muttering to herself. The guttural sound of her voice pulsed into a soft chant. Its sound frightened Fiona and she edged closer to take the child, but Ena turned toward the fire, immune to Fiona's efforts. As Ena's chants became louder, Fiona moved beside Ashling and they both looked up, cringing in fear as the firelight pulsed in unison with the cadence of her voice. Its strange light reached out like gnarled fingers around the room. Fiona hugged Ashling, fearing they might be swept up in the center of an ever turning gyre from which there was no escape.

A strange breeze pulsed through the room, sending Ena's wiry, gray hair in all directions. Suddenly, her hair began to bleed a lustrous ebony hue from the roots, working its way through every strand and curling them into sultry tendrils until it reached the ends. With her back still to them, she lifted one hand high in front of the fire, seeming to draw something from the flames. Ashling gave a cry of fright when Ena's wrinkled skin

and swollen knuckles shrunk and tightened into the
delicate hand of a young woman unaccustomed to work
and safe from the grip of old age. Ena stretched her hand
higher yet and laughed as though she had conquered the
world. She turned toward Ashling and Fiona and her
dress swirled and fanned out around her. Her wrinkled
skin had disappeared under the girlish, pink hue of her
cheeks and smooth, alabaster skin. She was restored to
her younger self.

"Give me my baby," Ashling cried.

Fiona rose and stepped nervously toward the
newly transformed Ena. She tried to grab the child from
her, but Ena pulled him back. Her laughter filled the
room, and she turned toward Ashling with a wickedly
proud grin.

"Our bargain here is complete," she said. "Against
the wishes of your body, God and nature, I've delivered
your son into this world. Here's the son who was never
supposed to be."

She handed him over to Ashling and watched as
she peeled back the heavy folds of the blanket. Her
happy eyes widened in horror, and she gave a sharp cry.
The room blurred into a bubbling cauldron of pain as the
blanket fell open revealing her child, his eyes were too
big for his face and his mouth tipped down on one side.
His joints were swollen and his limbs shriveled.
Somehow, atop these fragile appendages, his skin
sagged as if meant for a fat, robust baby, not this
shrunken misshapen body. It looked like a little boy
playing in his father's clothes. Only this child was
playing no games; he was barely moving.

Ashling held her child like something alien to her,

something definitely not of her making. Instead of cradling and cuddling her son, she extended her arms and the contorted bundle away from her. She looked to Ena, who only smiled and rubbed her hands in delight. Ashling turned to Fiona and stretched the infant out to her, pleading with her to take it away or fix it. Fiona stood paralyzed, unable to make any of this pain stop. She covered her ears as if she could erase the sound of Ashling's wailing.

Fiona looked from Ena's maiden figure, bright and beautiful as ever despite the dark shadows of night, to the wrinkled, broken form of Ashling's baby who was too weak to cry. Her tears became a cry that rose in pitch until she thought she would lose her mind. Ashling seemed to follow Fiona's thoughts, for she gaped wide eyed at Ena's nymph-like beauty with a new, heightened sense of horror.

"Why hold the child so far from you?" Ena asked. "I thought nothing would detract from your love for this child. I thought he was endowed with all the fittings of a Duke, so long as he survived into this world. That's what you said, isn't it?"

"No," Ashling whispered. "This can't be. This can't be my child. How can I ever –"

"Ever bring him home to your doting husband?" Ena finished. "Won't he love him no matter what? Can't you see passed his 'earthly mask?'"

Her laughter was cruel. Ashling broke into a sob. Fiona grabbed Ena by the arm roughly and shook her with a fury that surprised them both.

"Fix this!" Fiona shouted. "You can't leave this child so broken. Do something!"

"But I have," Ena said very calmly. "For reasons that seem all too clear now, this child was never meant to be; he wasn't supposed to live. I gave her womb and his body the strength to survive. I gave her exactly what she wanted. Although I don't know how long that little thing's got to live now."

Fiona turned to Ashling and the baby, covering her mouth with one hand and clutching her swollen belly with the other.

"Ah," Ena narrowed her gaze upon Fiona. "Have your actions made this burden too heavy for you?"

"You know nothing about what I feel," Fiona hissed at her.

"But what if I do?" Ena whispered into Fiona's ear loud enough for Ashling to hear. Each syllable raked like a rusty dagger across her skin. "What if I know all about the guilt that clings to your every breath?" She circled around to the other side of Fiona and continued. "What if I know that every night as you brush her hair you think of things far more tangled? With every gentle stroke of the brush you want to undo – "

"Shut your mouth," Fiona interrupted through clenched teeth.

"Fiona," Ashling whimpered. "Let her evil words fall on deaf ears. Come and take this – child – from my arms."

Fiona blinked and fought back the surge of violence coursing through her veins and moved to Ashling's side. She slipped her arms around the child and lifted his tiny body to her own, wrapping the blanket gently around him. His movements were so slow, his cry barely audible. She slipped her finger in his mouth to offer him what little soothing she could.

"It's all your fault," Ena said. "Is that what you think as you hold him close. His labored breathing and twisted limbs are all your fault."

"Leave us be," Ashling whined. "You've done enough already. You've won. There's no need to gloat and twist the knife."

"Oh, but it's not I who will twist the knife deeper into your back," Ena smiled. "I'll leave that to your loyal servant."

"Enough," Fiona yelled.

She stepped toward Ena, her eyes overflowing with hatred.

"The birth of your perfectly healthy baby boy is imminent and hardly a secret," Ena replied. "I'm sure that your gracious and ever grateful Duchess wouldn't begrudge you your moment of happiness at his birth or the lifetime of joy you will have watching him grow into a strong and healthy man with capable hands and gorgeous eyes."

"My sadness is not her fault," Ashling said, her words tumbling out between sobs. "I would never deprive her of her joy because of my tragedy. She's not to blame for my misfortune."

Ena placed her hands on her hips and raised a brow at Ashling.

"And what if she is largely to blame for the misfortune unfolding all around you. What if the very reason she stands here overflowing with life is because she lay with your doting husband and let him – "

"Quiet!" Fiona interrupted.

With one arm clutching the infant, she lunged

toward Ena, but tripped over a stool. Ena sidestepped and made no move to catch Fiona's imbalanced body as she tumbled to the floor. Fiona cradled the baby with one arm and cupped his head with the other as she fell. She landed on her side, her hip and belly sustaining the hardest of the fall. She gave a sharp cry, and the child's feeble whimper rose.

"Fiona?" Ashling said, her eyes pinched in pain. "It can't be true."

Ashling inched over to the edge of the mattress and touched Fiona's head with a desperate look in her eyes.

"You told me of your baby's father, the farmhand who was thrown from his horse. The one we buried."

"Such a good mix of truth and lies," Ena laughed. "She may have lain with him, but that was long before she conceived this son. That was very chivalrous for him to die and grant you such a believable story."

Fiona could barely breathe.

"You've held my hand and stroked my hair and washed my aching back all these months. You've caught my every tear, eased my every fear and followed me to the ends of the earth to save this baby. You wouldn't. He couldn't have possibly – "

"It's not like she says," Fiona sobbed.

She could barely move or right herself since her hip and every muscle in her body throbbed with pain. Despite it all, she still clutched the poor, whimpering child, who no one attempted to take from her.

"Then tell her what it was like when he took you into his chamber and stripped you of your clothes and admired your ripe curves," Ena said.

"No," Ashling cried. "Please say she's lying." She shook her head, pleading with Fiona frantically.

"She can't deny it," Ena said. "She's too honest to commit a lie in words, but lying by omission was not quite as difficult, was it."

Fiona let out a shriek that rattled the room. Ena knelt by her side as Ashling cowered away.

"Which was more painful," Ena asked. "The fall upon the floor or the fall from grace?"

Fiona rolled the infant onto the mattress and the blanket fell off of him, revealing his crooked limbs and feeble movements. She grabbed her back as another fit of pain gripped her body.

"It would seem these brothers are a bit overly anxious to meet. Move over Duchess. Here comes the Duke's other son. The healthy one."

***

Fiona's cries dissolved into the dark fog that once again enveloped Aoife. It swirled like a growing tornado until it sucked with it all the pain and sadness of the long ago night into a funnel that grew and grew until it looked like it would swallow the entire world into its vortex. Just when the sound became deafening, it began to contract in a powerful whirl until it collapsed upon itself and into Aoife's ring.

Her body jerked as if she had physically stumbled out of the dizzying tornado. On the other side of the bed Fiona gripped the arms of her chair, equally disoriented.

"So now you know all that he stole from me," he said. "The bastard son of a servant sits at the honored seat at *my* table, in *my* manor, residing over *my* lands and *my* people."

He pounded his chest indignantly with each claim.

"It can't be true," said Aoife.

She looked to Fiona for another explanation, but Fiona was bent over pouring her guilty sorrow into her hands.

"Fiona, you said the little man was your son!"

"He is my son," she replied, "in every way that matters."

"Except that little detail about you not having bore me," he sneered.

"I raised you as my own," she said. "I nursed you, clothed you – "

"And lied to me until the day my real mother died."

"And what about Ronan?" Aoife interrupted. "Does he know you are his real mother?"

"No," Fiona shook her head. "Ashling revealed the truth to him," she gestured to the little man, "her real son, just before she died, under the condition that neither of us tell Ronan."

"Wouldn't want to upset the poor bastard with the truth," he said. "But me, the rightful heir and son, she saw nothing wrong with letting me know how unwanted I was. I could have told him. I thought about it. But he would never have believed me without mother alive to confirm it. But he's about to get what he deserves."

The little man walked over to Fiona and watched her rocking figure.

"Come on," he said. "Why don't you tell her how the rest of the night unfolded or do we need to go back and see it for ourselves."

"Go ahead!" he shouted. "Tell her how my mother refused to hold me or even look at me! Tell her how she listened to my hungry cries and covered her ears. Tell her how I would have starved to death that very night if left up to my mother!"

"I couldn't let that happen," she cried and shook her head. She looked up into his eyes. "I fed my son and I heard you crying for milk, for love, and I – " the words stuck in her throat.

"You told my mother to feed me and she turned away and ignored you, didn't she! And when you picked me up and fed me yourself to shut me up – "

"I did it because I loved you!" Fiona interrupted. "I loved you from that moment as much as I loved my own son and I knew I would do everything in my power to protect both of you."

"And you showed your love by letting your bastard son take my place in my home?"

Aoife's daughter whimpered in her sleep, and Aoife held her closer, wishing that neither of them had to hear any of this.

"We didn't think you had the strength to live more than a few days! And if you did we feared your father's reaction if he discovered that his son, the one set to inherit all his estate was…It was for your protection!"

"And that of everyone else!" he said. "My mother spoke little of her concern for me that next morning. It was her own shame at birthing me and her scorn for your disloyal, whoring ways that has led us here."

He paced back and forth with a sadistic lightness in his movements.

"Let's see," he tapped his lip, his barely containable rage seeping out from behind his staged mirth. "I think the way she put it was 'you disloyal wretch. You should count yourself lucky that I won't have your heart sliced through for what you've done. You should be grateful that all I'm taking from you is your bastard son. I don't want to see you anywhere near my home again!' I think that was it."

He panted softly, spent from reliving the heavy memories he had carried upon his stooped shoulders for so long. He looked at Fiona who sighed and reached out her hands like a mother to a child with a scraped knee. His harshness lasted but a moment before wilting. He knelt down before her.

"I can't deny her words that morning," Fiona said. "They wounded me deeply and have lived in my memory ever since. But if you've the power to revisit that awful night, then surely you've seen the next night and every night after until she called for her coach to take us home? She didn't banish us from her side; she kept you close. And after we returned home, she let us stay in the cottage at the edge of the manor and she watched you grow into a little boy. When the fighting between you and Ronan made our closeness impossible, we moved deeper into the woods, into the cottage where you were born. Ena was long gone by then."

His mouth trembled as did the tears in his eyes. He leaned his head into her lap and wrapped his arms around her waist. Fiona kissed his head and caressed his cheek.

"I've seen the way she loved me over those days! She held me and hugged me for two whole days. But then how could she leave me behind?"

"I don't try to read everything in her heart," Fiona whispered. "But I do know that once the shock wore off, she held you like a loving mother. And I know that we both feared what would happen if we introduced you as the Duke's son. Wound a man's pride and there's no telling what he's capable of doing. It killed me to give her my own son, but I never regretted keeping you safe and loving you."

He wept and held tighter to Fiona.

"And during your few days together, she rocked you and sang to you for hours on end, singing a song she wrote out of the notes of her own heart. Sometimes when those nights come back to me in dreams, I almost get close enough to hear the words."

He looked up and swallowed.

"When I sink myself into those nights," he whimpered, "I try so hard to hear the song, but I've never been able to make out a single word. She whispered it so softly it was more of a hum."

"She told me once that it was your song, her song for you. We really didn't think you had the strength to survive, so she said that the song and your name were her parting gifts to you."

"My name?" he whispered. "I had a name?"

"Yes, of course," she said. "Your name was written into every line of that lullaby. I asked her the name she whispered into your ear, but she became private. She talked about majestic ships that made their eternal beds among the sandy shores of the far away sea. She said like them, her son would go to his eternal rest with the name she had given him. She never thought you would live long enough to be called by a name of your own. I, too, thought Ena's curse meant an early death for you and I vowed to make your days the best I could. After everything I had done, I owed you and your mother that much. When your mother left you in my arms, you became my dearest, little man."

"And forever after have I been known as the nameless, worthless little man."

Fiona's smile faltered as her name of endearment for him transformed into a stain. The night air hung heavy with sadness and loss. Nothing could be said to assuage a lifetime of suffering, not by Fiona, Aoife, or even God. Just then, Aoife's daughter cried out, and all eyes turned to her. Aoife pulled off the jeweled blanket and placed a lighter, satin blanket awkwardly over her shoulder to feed her. With so few days promised to her, Aoife refused to send her daughter out to a wet nurse.

The little man eyed the jeweled blanket lying in a heap on the bed. He touched the edges of his stolen inheritance delicately, as if it was a holy relic, an artifact from those often revisited memories in which Ashling wrapped him and sung to him like a real mother. What was it like, Aoife wondered, to be able to revisit over and over again memories so beautiful and yet so cutting? Aoife watched his head tilt and his eyes crinkle as her daughter's hand reached up from underneath the blanket and touched Aoife's collarbone. He looked so much more human. She wanted to beg him to spare her daughter, but she knew that sniveling and groveling would only make him despise her. She swallowed hard, stifling the tremble in her voice.

"After seeing how much suffering the separation

from your own family has caused you, why you would inflict that same pain on another child?"

He flinched.

"It's not the same," he muttered more to himself than Aoife. "This is completely different. I won't raise her in a world that makes her feel unloved and unwanted. She'll have all my love and devotion and she will want for nothing."

"Except answers about her parents," Aoife replied. "She will suffer just like you have."

"No she won't. She will only know what I tell her, which will be that I am her father and her mother died."

"You know that lie will never suffice," Aoife said. She kept her voice calm to avoid losing his ear completely. "Whether she thinks I'm dead or alive, she'll want to know her mother. You know that better than anyone. And then you will be reminded of what you have denied her."

"No!" he raised his voice. He stood and paced the room. Despite his protest, she could tell he was mulling it over.

"If you leave her with me, you could spoil her and love her and give her anything you want," Aoife spoke quickly, hoping to capture his attention before he disagreed completely. "You are her uncle and if you end this feud you can forge an honest connection with her."

"You act as though I caused the feud!" He hung on the post of the bed, glaring at her. "And you act as if my brother and I could all sit down for a meal together and talk about the upcoming harvest! Do you think I'm a fool?"

"Of course not," she replied. "I've been the center

of your attention for much of my life and there is nothing more wonderful I could hope to pass onto my daughter than your affection. And you must know that I have tremendous sway over Ronan. If I declare peace between you and your brother, then it will be so."

Aoife sat tall in her bed, ignoring the exhaustion and throbbing pain racking her body. He might have the power to spin straw into gold, but Aoife hoped her wits were enough to spin an argument strong enough to keep her infant in her arms. His boots clipped on the cold floor as he walked in a circle. He was considering her proffer, or at the very least he was not refusing it.

Aoife's confidence swelled, but before he could respond, Ronan came in and caught sight of the little man standing near the bed. His weary eyes snapped to attention and he drew his sword.

"What are you doing here? You promised three days!" he shouted.

Aoife gritted her teeth, irritated that he still had not realized his brute strength was no match for the little man. Fiona ran in between the two of them again, shoving Ronan back with one hand and the little man with the other.

"Stop it," she shouted, "both of you. "I'll not have you fighting like this in front of the baby."

All at once Aoife reimagined the years in which Fiona was more of a mother to Ronan than a servant and a mother in every sense that counted to the little man. How did she manage to raise them both with all this animosity between them?

"Put your sword away, Ronan," she said. "This is no place for bloodshed."

"But he's come to steal – "

"I don't want to hear it," Fiona interrupted. "Put the sword and threats aside, and do what's right for this baby."

Aoife sat dumbfounded. She had worried over her every word with both these men, and then with a firm voice and the crack of a mother's whip, Fiona silenced both their tongues. The little man finally broke off his cold stare and turned to the baby. He walked toward her, and Aoife's heart beat faster. He leaned over, and Aoife moved the blanket away from her daughter's head so he could see her. He smiled and softened as he gazed upon her. Fiona moved to the bed, absorbing the infectious glow that lit up the little man's face. The child's hand stretched up into the air. He laughed and pressed his hands together with unsuppressed glee. Aoife nodded to him, and he looked surprised. She nodded again and he slowly reached out his gnarled hand toward the infant's pink fingers. He hesitated when he neared them, and Aoife nodded reassuringly again. If her daughter's presence could soften his heart, Aoife wondered what kind of healing was implicit in her touch. He stretched his fingers further until her fingers wrapped around his. His smile lit up with a golden warmth.

This deal was not just about revenge against his brother, it was about bonding someone to him forever who would never reject him or run from him.

"You aren't afraid of me, little one," he whispered. "And what will you name her?" he asked without looking up at Aoife.

"With all that's happened, we have barely had time to speak of it. I'm not sure yet," Aoife replied.

"A name is an important thing," he smiled sadly. "It will tell her where she belongs, that she was meant to be, that you love her. For her sake, don't delay," he said, his gaze still locked upon the child.

Aoife shivered as a snarl escaped his lips. He reeled himself around in a move so swift and fierce that the room seemed to swirl with him. He turned and stepped aside as Ronan tried to plunge his sword into his brother's back. Aoife shrieked and pulled the child closer as Fiona shielded them both from Ronan's failed attack.

"No!" Fiona cried. "Put the sword down!"

They both ignored her. Ronan turned toward his brother, who was caught up in a fit of laughter. Furious at the little man and his own incompetence, Ronan ran toward him. The little man neither stopped laughing nor moved. It seemed Ronan would drive the sword right through his gut. Fiona yelled at Ronan to stop, and there was the sound of a scuffle that gave way to a blood-curdling scream.

Deep in the corner of the room, far from her bedside and the candle's light, Aoife could see the vague outline of the little man's body on top of someone. His hands gripped the sword plunged into a contorted body. A thick gush of blood streamed out from the shadows. Aoife could feel the well of her own tears rising as her husband's life bled out onto the floor.

The little man let go of the sword he had somehow commandeered and jumped up, his hands shaking and drenched in blood. There was a strange movement from the shadows and then an arm unfolded and a crimson stained hand lay limp, in the midst of the stream of blood making its way toward Aoife. But it was not her husband's hand.

"No!" Ronan shouted.

He came out from under Fiona's body, which had protected him from his own sword. He had never felt loved by the Duchess, the woman he thought was his mother. And now, Fiona lay dying in his arms, and he had no idea she was his real mother.

"Oh God," Ronan shouted again. "Please don't die! Don't leave me!"

The little man stared at his bloodstained hands hovering out before him. Aoife jumped out of bed with the child in her arms and felt the world sway around her. She held the bedpost for a moment until her balance returned and then ran to Fiona's side, the stabbing burning pains in her body inconsequential. Ronan sat against the wall cradling Fiona in his arms. Aoife knelt down beside them, her eyes locked on the bloody rose blooming around the sword that pierced her chest. Fiona looked like she had already departed this world when she suddenly coughed and sputtered. They all leapt with surprise and then, after a slow blink of her eyes, Fiona turned her head up to Aoife.

"I knew when I saw that gold sparkling all around you in the barn that you were the one who could bring peace between these boys."

"You are lying here in your own blood. How can you say that?"

"Because it's true," Fiona whispered. "You are strong and brave. You see through the darkness where no one else has the courage to look. You will set right the wrongs committed long ago."

Aoife trembled. She was not strong. She was not brave. She had been brash and lucky, but there were lies, curses, blood, and now death.

Fiona touched Ronan's cheek and looked at the little man.

"All these years I've loved you both as best as I knew how," Fiona whispered in broken syllables. "But it wasn't enough to fix everything Ashling and I did."

Ronan wept and the little man crumbled to his knees and watched as the life emptied from her eyes.

"Please," she pressed, "Let this be enough. Be good to each other – for your mothers' sakes."

Her last words slipped out in a sigh. Her eyes glazed over, and her uneven gasps silenced. Ronan shuddered as he pulled her tighter in his arms and rocked her. The little man leaned in and kissed her hand one last goodbye and then rose from the ground. He watched as the woman who had raised him as her own lay dead from his hand in the arms of her one, true son.

Aoife sobbed, wanting Ronan to know exactly who Fiona was to him, his true mother. But she could hardly tell him now.

She turned to the little man, whose expression was almost as empty as Fiona's. He backed away slowly. Sensing his retreat, Ronan looked up with a hatred that made Aoife shiver.

"You've haunted me my whole life, stolen my final moments with my mother, tormented my wife, threatened my child, and now you've killed the woman who raised me!" He hugged Fiona's limp body tighter for emphasis. "You don't deserve to live."

"You are more right than you realize," the little

man said. "I am the man who never should have been born. I am the man whose eventual gravestone will be as empty and inconsequential as the life he lived."

"What can we do so that all this can end now like Fiona wished?" Aoife cried.

The little man seemed to be thinking this over as he eyed the blood on his hands.

"It has always come down to one thing for me," he said, his eyes far away. "Find me my place – if I have one in this world. Night is upon us, and this day is closed. I will give you three days more. You have three chances each day to find my name. My place."

"Three days? Three chances each day? What do you mean?" She shook her head. His body began to dissolve into the moonlight that slipped through the window behind him and through him. "Don't go yet! I don't understand!"

"Find it for me."

His voice was growing as faint as his body.

"Find what?"

"My name."

Chapter 25: Day 1

Dusty Secrets

No one slept that night. There were funeral preparations to make and the little man's name to uncover. The next morning Fiona's funeral was dignified, but short. As Ronan pressed his hand to the simple, wooden casket and whispered a private farewell, Aoife shuddered. Although he did not know Fiona was his real mother, she had been more of a mother to him than the Duchess ever had. How much worse, she thought, would this moment have been if he had known what he was letting go of when he watched her body lowered into the grave? Aoife's own secret knowledge felt like a betrayal, but she could not bring all the truth to light just yet, or maybe ever.

When he announced his plan at the close of Fiona's burial to search the woods with his men for anyone who might know the little man and his name,

Aoife nodded her head, knowing it would be much easier to perform her own search with Ronan and his men far away.

She turned the key in the lock and listened as the disused gears shifted until, with a final cough, the door lurched open. It was still early in the morning, not even a full twenty-four hours since she had given birth and watched Fiona's blood spill across the floor, but Aoife had no time to worry about exhaustion, her wobbly legs, or leaving her sleeping baby in the nurse's care. She had precious little time to discover the little man's name. He had given her only three days and three chances each day to guess his name. Nine guesses. That was all to save her daughter.

She looked down the hall in both directions, and then pushed the door open. The heavy shades were drawn and the musty smell of stale air filled her nose. Through the slant of light that made its way inside, Aoife could see the sparkle of dust swirling through the air.

She leaned against the door as she nudged it closed behind her and let her eyes adjust to the darkness. Aoife lifted her candle before her and slowly made her way across the floor to one of the windows. She placed her candle down on a small bedside table and caught sight of an ornately stitched design on the bed cover. Its twists and turns and the color pattern were even more delicate and complicated than her mother's work. She gripped the velvet, purple curtain and yanked it back to let in the light. A poof of dust sent her coughing while she found the tie and secured the curtain. Only then, in the light from half a window, did Aoife turn back toward the late Duchess's long abandoned room.

Fifteen years of dust could not detract from the beauty of this chamber. It was the size of Aoife's and decorated with a lavish style that would have garnered her mother's nod of approval. Although yellowing with the years, the lavender bedspread complimented the heavy royal purple drapes. The carved feet peeking out from under the covers on the tables and chairs hinted at a taste for finery far beyond Aoife's comprehension. Who was this woman who traded her son for another's, Aoife wondered as she looked about her.

She tied back the other curtain to let in more light and dusted off her hands, trying to decide where to begin. Where would Ashling keep her secrets? She walked by the bed, the story of the Duchess' deathbed confession replaying itself. Her need to purge her conscience had left Fiona the impossible task of mending the broken hearts of two young boys. It seemed so selfish to have waited until the last moments of her life to offer up the truth when she would not be forced to face the consequences. Aoife wondered if it might have been better if she had kept her secret.

Beside the bed was Ashling's dressing table. Aoife removed the cover on the chair and sat down. When she pulled the sheet off the table, she held her breath at the sight of her sleepless eyes and runaway hair in the mirror. The glass was massive and framed by shells from the far away sea. Pearls, large and small, filled the gaps between shells.

It was unsettling the way the opalescent glow of every pearl reflected back Aoife's image. She imagined Ashling perfecting her appearance each day while these pearls reflected back her secrets a hundred times over. She ran her fingers over them, having never seen anything so opulent before. One of the pearls came lose and clattered down onto the table. She picked it up and pressed its coolness in her palm. This rare and mysterious treasure pried from a stubborn, seaweed covered oyster miles and miles away seemed to promise that Aoife would find her answer hidden somewhere in this dusty vault of secrets.

She put the pearl in her pocket for good luck and began to rummage through the boxes before her. She lifted lids and searched through drawers. She looked for hidden compartments and false bottoms in the vanity without luck. Only dusty jewels and aged lotions remained. A few strands of hair in a brush made Aoife imagine Fiona untangling Ashling's hair as she did Aoife's just yesterday. She brushed away her sorrow and pressed onward, promising to properly mourn Fiona after she saved her daughter.

She gave up on the dressing table and moved onto the wardrobe, bureau, bedside tables, writing desk, and even beneath chair cushions. But nothing, not even the smallest clue, presented itself. She doubled over, trembling with fatigue and pain. She worried this task might be too much for her, just a day after having a baby, but her daughter needed her. She breathed deeply, summoning up more strength.

Aoife was about to rise to her feet when she saw a chest amidst the pile of sheets she had tossed at the foot of the bed. Of course! How had she missed that! She knelt down gingerly and saw the lock, which gave her hope that there was something worth hiding inside.

Aoife gouged the lock open with a pair of sheers from the Duchess' drawer. She lifted the top and dove her hands inside. There were heavy brocade capes in all different colors neatly folded side by side, one on top of the other. She tossed them all about. Why would anyone lock up capes? There had to be something buried in the chest worth hiding. She slid her hand around the wooden bottom, searching for a stash of letters, a hidden compartment, anything. She poked her fingers into every corner, but she found nothing. Nothing. Aoife ran her fingers through her hair ready to scream.

She sat back down at the dressing table and took the pearl out of her pocket. Sheets riddled the floor and chairs and tables stood at odds. The walls were pocked with ghostly imprints where paintings had been removed and drawers hung open like the mouths of the dead. And yet, she had found nothing that even hinted that the Duchess had a secret son, let alone loved and named him. She slammed her fist on the dressing table and cursed Ashling. She had been crazy to think that she could bring this ghost of a woman back to life and pry the truth from her shriveled heart.

Exasperated, Aoife stood up and pulled the sheet off the chair, revealing an emerald green gown made of watered silk. Whenever Aoife paused in her day for a rest or a nap, Fiona always laid her gowns over her dressing table chair just like this one. Did it follow that this was the gown she wore just before she died in her bed the way Ronan described? Aoife ran her fingers over the fabric, watching the way the shine undulated. Dejected by failure, she was folding it over when red and purple stitching on the inside caught her eye. She turned the bodice over, revealing an embroidered monogram. Tiny, delicate stitches feathered out in intricate and interwoven spirals done by a seasoned and devoted hand. She had seen these on the inside of Ashling's under slips. She had thought it odd, but nothing more. But as she looked closer, there appeared to be initials embroidered into the center of the design. Aoife remembered that her mother had often hidden words and names in her designs that only a careful eye could catch. Aoife tilted the fabric toward the window for better light. She made out an "A". Aoife shifted into the light more and saw what looked like three letters in total.

ABB.

It took a careful eye to make out the letters hidden in the webbing. ABB. This was not the family monogram. A, for Ashling. Perhaps *B* for Bradyn, the late Duke. And the other B. It was not Ronan. Could it possibly stand for the little man's name? Could Ashling have named him after his true father and embroidered it here? Could she have carried close to her heart the names of her true family? Aoife felt herself grow dizzy at the thought that she may have just solved the mystery. But why would she stitch it here in this dress?

She went back to the wardrobe closet and grabbed a rich peacock blue colored gown with pink accents. She yanked it off the hanger and turned the bodice inside out. There it was. ABB stitched into the left side over the heart. She tossed it on the floor and grabbed the next gown, a sea foam green. She flipped it inside out and there it was again. ABB. She searched the next three, and there it was on every one of them. ABB. ABB. ABB. She opened a drawer and pulled out one of the handkerchiefs she had glanced earlier. There was no monogram. She turned it over and around. Then in the trim around the edges she spotted the pattern of tiny stitches. ABB.

This could not be a coincidence. She turned back and picked up the emerald green gown that Ashling had worn on her last day of life, pleading silently to the Duchess for more. She felt something small and hard in the lining just below the monogram. She traced the lump until she spied a small pocket stitched into the fabric. She pinched open the top of the pocket and a dark ruby, cut into a large heart with an eye to impress, slipped out. She lifted it up to the light to admire it. She kissed the ruby with hope and then slipped it back into the dress pocket.

She held a handkerchief in her hand and felt a wave of dizziness sweep over her. She grabbed the bedpost, and then gasped at the bedspread she had uncovered earlier. Larger than Aoife and embroidered in bold colors for all who looked close enough into the Celtic webbing, were the letters ABB in the middle of the coverlet. She turned toward the room and there it was, woven into a throw pillow, and then another, and then a seat back and on the inside of a cape on the floor.

Now that she had teased out the secret in Ashling's needlework, it stood everywhere. She caught her breath, hoping that the rest of the letters would reveal themselves soon, hiding somewhere in plain sight for all to see.

Chapter 26
Theatrics

She poked at the flames, trying to warm the room for her daughter while awaiting the little man's visit. Aoife had nestled her sleeping daughter into a basket beside the fire. It was a last minute decision to bring her here. The time was ticking away so quickly, and she could not be sure how long the little man would make her wait. She would take as many moments as she could get with her daughter.

Ronan was far away, searching for names and sending back messengers with lists of the oddest names Aoife had ever heard of. He had not argued when she asked that he stay away the evening of the first day, when the little man was expected to return. The stain of Fiona's blood was still fresh on the manor floor, proof that their presence together was dangerous.

She chose Ashling's room for their meeting. She had recited the late Duke's name, wondering if she could be lucky enough to find that the Duchess had named her first born after his father, but it had not elicited the slightest reaction from the ring on her finger. It had pulsed and squeezed so angrily when she had defied him that she could only hope that saying the right name would elicit some conversely positive response. But perhaps that was ludicrous. Could the magic in the ring know Ashling's secret? Either way, she had opened the census registry, searching page after page for a name that might belong to the little man. His own name, of course, was not recorded there, but it did contain a bank of names, any of which might be the same as his. Aoife read them out loud yet again, waiting for a reaction from the ring, but feeling nothing.

Three days and three chances each day to discover his name. That was all. She cursed under her breath, wondering what kind of a name Ashling would have given a sickly son she refused to keep and assumed would die. Would she have given this lost soul a family name, a noble name as a final gesture of her love? Aoife called out names faster as she paced back and forth, waiting for a sign that never came.

A breeze rushed through the room, ruffling the curtains on the windows and around the bed.

"I see you have a penchant for theatrics, Aoife," the little man said.

She shivered at his icy tone. This whole quest sprung from his yearning for his mother. Aoife had hoped being near his mother's things might make the omnipresence of his initials enough of a sign of her love for him to end his search even if Aoife could not produce a name. But he stood among her things ambivalent. She watched the way he threw his shoulders back. The concave of his chest opened up and his spine stretched taller and straighter than she thought possible. Although he still leaned at an awkward angle, he looked several inches taller. He was hardly as small as Aoife had originally thought.

"You said you wanted to find your place in this world," Aoife said, "to know your name, the name your real mother gave you. There seems to be no better place to look for the answer than her room. I hoped these quarters might bring you peace."

He took a few steps around the room, avoiding eye contact. His movements were abrupt and strange. It was as if walking upright was more painful than his usual stooped hunch. He walked over to the dressing table and peered down at Ashling's things like a peasant at the market who held his money close, revealing not the slightest bit of interest or vulnerability, which would only serve to drive the price higher.

"After her death I spent quite a bit of time here," he said turning toward the fire. As he held his hand above it, the flames stretched higher and cast off a wave of heat Aoife felt across the room. "Using my magic to slip in and out and peek through her things became a habit. In those early years I hungered for anything that would help me understand her or feel close to her. I thought there would be something that would explain it all. A letter of apology. A diary of guilt. But all I ever found were sparkly trinkets and fancy clothes, hardly the markers of a suffering conscience. Nothing here ever made any of the pain go away. Perhaps that's why all she had to offer me on her deathbed was a ring – that damned ring my brother stole from me moments later and placed upon your silly finger. She thought my forgiveness and her redemption could be bought."

Aoife stepped closer to him, feeling the disappointment running through his voice. The pain this room caused him made him seem more human.

"You find my name and speak it aloud," he said, "and the ring, which has bound you to our bargain and was on my mother's finger when she whispered my name so many years ago, will release us both. Maybe it will prove itself able to grant us both redemption."

He rested his arm on the dusty mantle and leaned his head against his arm. The slight shudder he tried to hide broke Aoife's heart. This was not the man intent on stealing her child; this was the man whose life, its very meaning, had been stolen from him. She stood beside him and took his hand in hers.

"I guess you know how it feels to be bartered away," he said sadly. He looked down at her fingers entwined with his and his chest swelled. He took a deep breath.

There was nothing to say. His pain was too big and too monstrous for words and perhaps even actions to cure. She stepped closer, lifted her hands to his face and stroked his wet cheeks. He was still a lost little boy looking for his mother's arms to hold him and make him feel safe. She leaned in, and he closed his eyes. She felt him tremble, and she hesitated for a moment before she kissed his forehead tenderly, waiting for the release she hoped would follow. But instead, he pushed her away.

"You'll never love me enough to give me your whole heart."

"So if I can't give you my whole heart and live solely for you, then you believe I cannot love you at all?"

"Experience has proven that when I have to share someone's affection, I always lose. And your kiss just proved it true again."

He backed away and seemed to be refortifying the barricade around his heart. He wiped his eyes while Aoife tried to recover the moment that had just slipped away.

"I thought *you* were different, but I was wrong, so wrong," he said, more to himself than her. "Your strength and tenacity made me think you might be the one person with a power greater than mine. A kind of magic which just might be able to rescue my name and prove that I have a place in the world. That I am more than a punishment for my mother's deal with that evil woman. That I was loved."

"Me? Powerful? Magical?" Aoife shook her head. "I'm none of those things. I've let down Fiona, and now I've disappointed you, too. I'm no mythical creature."

"Mythical, no. You are flesh and blood and far more real than any of the gilded stories of childhood fantasy," he said. "Magical, yes. Everywhere you go you bring a light inside you that is nothing short of magical. It satiates the thirsty souls of all you meet. No trickery. No beguiling spells. What you have is something greater, something I hoped could save me in a way my magic has not. I can bend the trees and even time, but I can't divulge what's hidden in the quiet whispers of the past. I can't see deep enough. But you – you look into the places of the human heart where few have the will, the power, or the insight to go, and you see – you see it all."

He stepped closer to her.

"You see it all and you never blink. You never flinch. And you never turn away – not even from me." He fell to his knees before her. "Tell me you have looked through this room, through my mother's things and seen what no one else could. Tell me you've found the truth hidden under the sheets, under the dust, and under the stony walls of my mother's heart."

Aoife felt the world spinning around her. She had none of the powers he described. She sank to her knees, and a soft sob slipped over her lips. He searched her eyes, looking for any sign of hope. A tear fell down his cheek, and Aoife produced a handkerchief from her pocket.

"It is your mother's," Aoife said. "It's one of many she carried with her. It, like all the rest, is embroidered with the initials of your names."

She traced the border with her fingertips and a bolt of electricity surged through his spine. He sat down, devouring the letters with his eyes.

"ABB," Aoife said, pointing to each letter. She read the letters over and over again as she traced the pattern. His hungry eyes followed hers, swallowing it up and looking for more. She saw his appetite growing and hoped she had enough to fill him up.

"She carried your name with her wherever she went. Look here," Aoife turned Ashling's cape over and showed him the monogram.

"ABB is not your family's monogram or your mother or father's ancestors'," Aoife said. "But she sewed these letters into the family crest and the fabric of her life."

Aoife nodded as they both rose to their feet. She turned toward the two chairs beside the fire and pointed to each letter in their design as she read ABB. She pointed to the pillows and did the same. She turned toward the bureau and pulled out slip after slip, handkerchief after handkerchief, his eyes missing not one stitch. Aoife picked up the emerald green gown on the back of the chair and turned it over, telling him that from the first gown in her closet to the last dress she wore, she carried his name upon her heart.

"Even to the last breath she drew," Aoife said as she brought him to the bed with the dress still clutched in his hands, "her deep love and sadness for her sins against her son were etched upon her heart."

He looked wide eyed at the initials burned into the coverlet under which she slept every night and under which she drew her last breath after offering him a final embrace. He was speechless, but Aoife knew he was waiting for something more.

"And also next to her heart," Aoife continued, "she kept a sign of her love for you."

He trembled as she reached for the pocket of the gown he held in his hands. She pinched the bottom of the pocket and the ruby slipped out, its blood red gleam glowing against her ivory palm. He froze for a second and then gasped.

"This ruby is cut like a heart, the heart of the son she loved but could never hold again."

He took the ruby in his hand and frowned. He was about to say something and then held back. He shook his head in disbelief and looked from the dress, to the ruby, to the bed, and around the room. The presence of these letters was overwhelming, but was it enough to prove his mother's love and his place in her heart and this world?

"And so," he nodded, the dress and ruby shaking in his hands, "My name?"

His voice trailed off. The ensuing silence told him all he needed to know.

"You do like theatrics," his voice warbled. "You have nothing for me, so you gave me this charade. You brought me here and seduced me with your lies so that I might believe these meaningless letters were for me!"

"That's not true," Aoife cried. She reached out for his arm, but he jumped back like she was diseased. "These are the initials of your mother, your father, and you! I haven't been able to uncover your name, but you wanted to know you had a place in this world and here you are – stitched right over your mother's heart."

He looked down at the dress and threw it upon the floor.

"These letters don't mean anything. Her dresses and jewels and furniture, that's what mattered to her."

"No!" Aoife cried. "You've seen too much through those memories to think that true."

"Well three letters don't prove either of us right! So let's get back to our bargain. You've got three chances to give me my name!"

Aoife shook her head at the absurdity of the game.

"Say my name!"

Aoife sighed and pulled out the sheet of paper where she had listed any name, no matter how obscure, that started with B. His eyes flickered from hers to the sheet in her hand.

"Read them!"

His voice was a threat, not a request. Aoife swallowed hard.

"Bradyn."

He bellowed with laughter.

"You really think my mother would have named her crippled, dying son after his father? You really are desperate. Desperately wrong! Come on, try again."

"Brinley."

He glanced at her unaffected ring smugly.

"Well thank God that wasn't it. Too pretty. Give me another one!"

Aoife knew it was futile. She just wanted the charade over for the day.

"Baldwyn."

He leaned over her ring with his hands behind his back, laughing until he ran out of air and it was nothing but a wheeze. He looked up and filled his lungs, returning to his former, dark self. He stepped over to the basket where the baby slept under the jeweled blanket. Aoife felt the worn edges of her heart pick up speed. Two more days, she reminded herself. Her baby was safe for two more days.

"Hello little girl," he cooed. "Don't you worry, sweet one. I'll whisk you away from here soon enough and then you'll never have to live in this big, old, dreary house with these people ever again. I'll make sure the fire is always warm enough, and your little world is always right. I don't need the fickle love of a wife. A daughter's love is forever. Your mommy is proof of that."

Aoife did not even bother to respond.

"Two more days. Six more guesses. That's all you get."

He stepped backwards, and his laughter faded away as he vanished into the air and swished out the window.

Chapter 27: Day 2

Hope

"She's beautiful," Bronagh cooed over the bassinet. "And such a sound sleeper, too."

"She's almost as gorgeous as her mother," Finnegan leaned down and kissed Aoife. "If she's got half her mother's smarts, she'll bring you joy and profits in no time. But you better get back to work."

"Now don't talk like that," Bronagh chided him.

"Well she's given him a daughter," he shrugged. "I have enough of them to know what the Duke's thinking. He needs a son."

His belly shook with laughter, despite Bronagh's glare. Now that Aoife was a mother, her father's poor choices seemed even more inconceivable to her. How could he turn his back on his family and spend all his money on cards, mead, and women?

"I don't think a son could have protected you or

237

our estate any better than I did," Aoife said.

"I shudder to think what would have become of us all if you had a son by your side," Tara said, meeting Aoife's eyes.

"I'm sure you're right," he laughed. "A son might have become my compatriot instead of my shepherd. But daughters eventually leave you – sometimes all too soon."

He leaned over and kissed her again with a sniffle. His rosy cheeks blushed a little deeper as he wiped his eyes. His sentimentality made it difficult to stay angry with him, and she leaned into his embrace. Word had spread about the baby's birth and her family had descended upon them with only mild chiding about being the last to know. The excitement of the first grandchild with a Duke for a father seemed to overshadow any slight they may have felt. Thankfully, they knew nothing of the reason for the secrecy.

Her mother chattered on with the nurse about the baby, making no secret of her surprise that she slept in Aoife's room. This was hardly tradition, as the child was supposed to stay with the wet nurse until she was weaned. Bronagh paced the room and ran her fingers over the furniture, probably looking for signs of dust. But not even her mother's critical eye could bother Aoife now.

Aoife took the baby from the nurse's arms and snuggled her close. She missed Fiona terribly. She could only imagine the way she would have doted on her grandchild, singing lullabies and clucking her tongue when she cried. Aoife also felt that she would have known how to fix all this. With her motherly advice and warm embraces, she would have helped all of them. Last night Aoife had failed with the little man, but Fiona would have reminded her that this morning was a new day. She missed Maeve, too, and wished she could have made time for a visit with her. She probably would have had some helpful advice now that Aoife could tell her what was going on.

She would endure her family's visit a little longer. Their excitement over the baby filled the room with euphoria. Aoife had finally done something that everyone sincerely loved and appreciated without question. Tara had entered the room and stolen the child into her arms before anyone else, rocking her and singing like no one else was in the room. Aoife's heart swelled at the sight of Tara, unencumbered by illness. Her walks through the forest and the village and the regular meals she was now able to enjoy since her lungs had cleared had allowed her to grow and blossom into a beautiful girl of sixteen. She looked at her family and her daughter; in that single moment everything was perfect. She wished she could stop time and the future that threatened to take her daughter away from her.

Tara called out baby names from the sofa, teasing her sister for her indecisiveness and blissfully unaware of the crisis Aoife and Ronan faced which had made choosing the baby's name secondary. They had talked about several names before she was born and he had mentioned Ashling's more than once, but Aoife knew too much secret knowledge about her to want to pass on her legacy. Thus, they had never really narrowed it to one name.

"It would seem you might be too late," Bronagh

chimed in. "The baby's name might already be embroidered in this beautiful monogram."

Aoife looked up, surprised to see her mother running her fingers over the lush fabric of the Duchess' cape.

"That's not meant for you to see," cried Aoife.

The cape had been left out by mistake. She did not want to her mother asking difficult questions. She tried to calm her voice.

"I mean, that's not for the baby."

"Then whose is it?" Bronagh asked.

Aoife thought quickly and realized it was safest to resort to a piece of the truth.

"It belonged to the late Duchess."

"But this can't be hers," Bronagh shook her head. "The initials are all wrong. Who is RSS?"

"What?" Aoife replied. "The initials are ABB, her name, the late Duke's and – "

"Oh no, Aoife," Bronagh smiled. "You never were very careful with your stitches. Look here." She leaned over Aoife and traced her fingers over the ornately rounded letters RSS. "You see. The letters are woven so intricately into the monogram design that it would be easy to mistake them, but it is very clearly RSS."

Aoife's heart leapt. She pulled out one of Ashling's handkerchiefs from her pocket and handed it silently to her mother. She tilted her head and spread the fabric out in her hand as she sat down on the bed beside Aoife. She turned it round and then nodded.

She pointed at the trim and said, "RSS. The 'R' could be Ronan, the final 'S' for Stanishire, but the middle S doesn't fit with his name. Unless it's not his name. Who is RSS and why is this name embroidered into the late Duchess' cape?"

Aoife hugged her mother around the neck and Bronagh nearly tumbled off the bed. The first 'R' for Ronan. The final "S" for Stanishire. And the middle 'S' for the little man's name. When Aoife released her, Bronagh leaned back and searched her daughter's eyes.

"Or do these belong to someone else?" Bronagh asked. She kissed Aoife's head, and then searched her eyes. "Most men are not as constant as we'd like," she said, brushing her fingers over Aoife's arm. "But try not to expect it and you might be able to protect your heart better than I have."

Aoife tilted her head, confused by the turn in the conversation. Then she pieced together the mysterious initials in the cape, the handkerchief, their embrace, and realized Bronagh must have thought that the cape and the handkerchief belonged to another woman, Ronan's mistress. Bronagh's own experiences could see no other explanation. She wanted to correct her mother, but a part of her wanted to linger in her mother's sudden show of empathy, an emotion her mother had never exerted before. Bronagh blinked back tears and rose to leave. Just before she exited, she turned back.

"Many wives find more comfort from their priest than their husbands," she said. "Something to consider."

Aoife nodded, thanking her mother, not for her assumptions or advice, but for her attempt to understand and help, no matter how misguided. For the first time in a long time, Aoife felt her mother's love. Aoife had spent so many years despising her mother's stooped shoulders and embroidered tapestries. They never brought Aoife the solace and comfort that they brought her mother. They never solved any of their problems either. All they had given their family was a house filled with tapestries and pillows whose colorful, cheery designs and pictures mocked the struggling reality her family actually lived. But all those hours may have finally proven worthwhile, since her mother may have given Aoife the means to free her own daughter.

"RSS," Aoife whispered.

Her ring grew warm and Aoife lifted it up before her eyes. The gold gave off a rosy hue and then loosened ever so slightly.

Chapter 28
From Priests on High to Hags Down Low

Aoife climbed the front steps of the chapel slowly, her body still weak from childbirth. Her new servants, Nessa and Molly, who had replaced Fiona, helped her up the stairs and opened the doors as she stepped inside. Aoife made the sign of the cross, reminding her of the prayers she had said over Fiona's coffin just yesterday morning. She and Ronan should have been reciting prayers for the dead and mourning her loss, but there was no time for the rituals that Fiona deserved. As the doors closed behind her, the clatter of the horses and the shouting of the market vendors hushed. Molly and Nessa dismissed the confessors waiting for Father John, dropping a few coins in the box for their sins, but Aoife hardly noticed as she leaned against the church pew to hold herself steady.

During the terribly bumpy carriage ride here, she

had thanked her mother silently for suggesting she confide in a priest. Though she had no intention of confiding in the man, she did recall that he had served as the late Duchess' private confidant.

As she walked up the aisle assisted by Nessa and Molly, her dress brushed over the stone floor. Off to the left was a statue of Mary holding the lifeless body of her son. Her marble eyes radiated an enormous and unearthly pain. Now as she thought about her daughter back at the manor sleeping heavily after her feeding, the daughter she might lose if she failed in her task, she understood the sorrow of losing a child. She prayed silently to this mother to protect Aoife from meeting a loss that might as well mean death.

She turned and entered the confessional.

"Bless me father for I have sinned," Aoife said through the screen. "My last confession was a long time ago, but what I need from you now is your own confession."

"Pardon?" whispered Father John as he leaned in toward the screen.

"It's Aoife, the Duchess and the woman whose hand controls the purse strings that pay for the wood that heats this church and the food on your table."

She had no time to warm him with small talk or compassionate pleas.

"My good lady," he replied nervously. "It is an honor that you have come to confide in me and – "

"And you will give me the information I need."

The force of her voice left no doubt as to the power behind it. Fear seemed the most efficient weapon. Father John leaned back and folded his hands.

"Well, I will do my best to tell you what you want to know."

"I need to know the name of the late Duchess' son, her real son," Aoife said.

She watched his reaction through the screen for the slightest sign of recognition. He flinched and stumbled over an incomprehensible set of monosyllabic sounds.

"Tell me what she told you about the malformed child that she traded away."

"I'm not sure I know what you mean – "

"Yes you do," Aoife said, trying to remain calm. "I already know that the Duchess's real son was a malformed little boy who never would have inherited his father's titles. What I need to know now is his name and anything she told you about him. The fate of this church and the gravy on your meat depends upon how forthcoming you are."

He took a handkerchief from his pocket and wiped his brow. He pulled back the curtain of the confessional and scanned the chapel for stray ears. Aoife sat quietly. Satisfied, he pulled the curtain back and pinched the bridge of his nose.

"I don't know as much as you might think," he replied with trembling hands. "The late Duchess was a very private woman. I knew guilt ran deep in her about the young Duke. Of another son, I knew nothing. I didn't even know one existed. I swear it!"

"That's impossible!" Aoife said through clenched teeth. "You provided private counsel to the Duchess for nearly two decades through every miscarriage and were present with her up until her death. And you tell me she never confessed or asked absolution for consorting with a witch or trading away her firstborn son?"

"She confessed to having brought a curse on her child, but I assumed she was speaking of your husband. He looked healthy to me, which was why I never understood her supposed sins. But are you speaking of her servant's son? The dwarfed one? Wasn't he sent away when he was young?"

"So you do know something," Aoife said. "He was her son, the one whose name I need."

He shook his head with confusion.

"I knew very little about him, as he was only the misshapen child of her servant. Whenever I questioned her further about the guilt she spoke of, she broke into sobs and begged for more prayers of penance."

"I don't believe that's all she said!"

"I swear it," he pleaded. "In fact she refused even my prayers of absolution because she said she was undeserving of them. She said there were things that could never be undone, things that would go to the grave with her."

Aoife could hear the fear in his voice. The threat to his comfortable quarters had made him forget all too quickly the sanctified privacy of the confessional. If he knew more, he would not have held back.

"So she took it to the grave with her," Aoife replied. "These walls are covered with payment for her guilty conscience, yet the nature of her sins and the torment they caused her were of no concern to you so long as her gold kept making its way into your coffers."

Aoife rose from her kneeler and stepped out of the confessional. She had knocked at God's door and received nothing more than her own echo in return. She pulled back the curtain and stared at Father John.

"I might lose my daughter because you didn't ask more of her," she said. "When you are needed most, you can't even provide a simple name."

"She was a very complicated woman," he said. "And I'm just a tired, old priest. I wish she had given me the name you are looking for. I do as I'm told and – "

"You care nothing for the truth or doing what's right so long as you are compensated; rest assured you will be justly compensated for the choices you have made."

She threw a handful of coins against the floor, their clatter echoing throughout the church.

"Treasure these coins as they may be among the last you see from me or my husband," Aoife's voice was cold. "Many people have suffered in their own private prison's because of that woman's lies and now – "

"Wait," he said. It looked like some distant memory was surfacing from the murky waters of his mind.

Aoife steadied herself.

"The Duchess refused to tell me much in the way of what plagued her," he said. "But there might be one person who knows more about this curse than I do."

***

The passageway down to the dungeon below the manor was narrow and windowless. Torches mounted on the walls did little to light her way. The walls were damp, and here and there the wetness had coagulated until it formed trickles of water on the stone walls. The pungent odor of mildew and stagnant air made it difficult to breathe.

When she reached the landing and turned, she saw that just a few more wooden steps led to the main floor of the dungeon. She walked down into the cavern, which opened up like an animal's underground den.

There was a large hearth rigged for everything from cooking to smelting. Not too far away was a long table, flanked by two benches, and littered with cups and plates of scraps. Hanging all around the room were heavy chains and rusty, pointed torture devices whose exact uses Aoife could only guess. She visited Maeve's brothel and heard the thoughts of men better not shared with decent company. But none of it prepared her for this pit in the earth, the darkest depths man was capable of sinking. Behind bars, men and women covered in filth with rashes and wounds lay on soiled patches of hay. Some begged for water, while others shivered silently with only sparse straw for warmth. The length of their tangled hair offered ample evidence that none of these prisoners were recent offenders.

Ronan could not have possibly been responsible for allowing these conditions, since he had spent most of his adult life away from home and had only recently returned. But now that he was home, she would have to make sure that he saw this. She shied away from the bars, but the pleas of the prisoners became louder and more desperate as they recognized the power that must have accompanied her velvet cloak and the jewels around her neck. No crime seemed to fit this punishment.

"Stop your whining!" a voice shouted from by the fire.

Aoife turned and saw a guard seated in a chair in the shadows. His feet were up and his back was to her and the prisoners. He gnawed on a piece of meat, his ambivalence, a necessary requirement for the job, hardly less forgivable. She had not noticed him, as the back of his head blended in with the iron torture devices. He, too, was equally unaware of Aoife.

"They might whine less if they could warm their feet by the fire or share a plate with you," Aoife said, her voice clipped and calm.

He jumped and turned, stammering at the sight of Aoife in her finery. Based on his imposing size, he was no man to cross. His skin was as pale as the prisoners and the grit under his fingernails made Aoife wonder how deep into the soul the grime of such a place could seep.

"I'm here to find a prisoner who would have been brought here many years ago when the late Duchess was still alive and my husband was a small child."

"I'm afraid I wasn't here then, my Lady," he replied nervously. He was searching for a set of manners that eluded him.

"But surely you take notice of the prisoners as you feed them," Aoife raised a brow. "Although I'm not sure exactly when she was brought here, she was quite beautiful at the time. Despite the passage of time and the layer of filth, she should still be – "

Loud maniacal laughter broke out somewhere far away. Aoife shuddered and looked between two cells, where a dark, barely visible hallway stretched.

"There is a woman down in the last cell there, my Lady," he said, "And she has been here many more years than me, but she is far from fair."

The pitch of the laughter heightened. In its distant ring Aoife heard something eerily similar to the cackle from the vision the little man revealed to her. She walked toward the voice, but the guard stepped in front with his hands up to stop her.

"This prisoner has been kept in the furthest cell for years. I tell you she can drive a person mad," he whispered. "I wouldn't want to see her twist you up in one of her games."

"Then she may very well be the woman I'm looking for."

She marched over to the hallway and was about to grab a torch from the wall when the guard lifted it for her. He stepped in front and nodded for her to follow. The laughter had ebbed into unintelligible mutterings.

When they reached the end of the hall, he placed the torch outside the cell beside the one whose flame had almost expired. He banged on the bars with a wooden club.

"You've a visitor," he yelled. "Come forward and show yourself to the Duchess."

He stepped back, alert and ready for anything. Aoife walked closer to the bars than he dared. In the far corner a dark figure sat stooped over, rocking incessantly. Her rough, burlap blanket was too small to cover her bare, bony legs and feet.

"Show yourself!" the guard shouted again.

The speed of her babble quickened, but the woman continued rocking as though she had heard nothing.

"Don't bother," Aoife said. "This creature can't be the one who tricked a Duchess and cursed her son. She's nothing but a mad scrap of a woman."

All at once the rocking ceased and she straightened up beneath the blanket.

"Maybe all that's left of me is a mad scrap of a woman," she replied in a raspy voice. "But I once owned powers greater than anything you have ever known, greater than the Duchess' little dwarf you mentioned."

"What is your name," Aoife demanded, her heart pounding.

Could there be anyone else besides Ena who knew the little man was her son?

In one swift move the hag rose to her feet, swished her blanket round and revealed a hideous face that made Aoife leap back in horror. The woman charged forward and threw herself against the bars. She looked a hundred years old, with skin that had wrinkled like a piece of fruit weathered by the sun. Her teeth were as yellow as the guard's. Her gray, wiry hair shot out in every direction like lightning bolts. She slapped the bars with her hands, revealing arthritic knuckles and curled fingernails.

"Not what you expected," the woman laughed. "Not the wondrous beauty the stories of Ena foretold?"

"What's happened to you?" Aoife asked. "What has left you as discolored on the outside as you are on the inside?"

"Nothing comes for free, Duchess," she said. "A plate of what goes for food down here and a cold drink of water first."

"Done," Aoife replied. "Guard, go and fetch her a plate."

"Don't forget the cold drink!" the woman smiled at him.

Aoife kept her urgency hidden beneath a mask of calm.

Ena spoke, focusing her attention back on Aoife. "You are beautiful, but not so much to have made the bastard upstairs swoon. You're not soft, coy, or enchanting – the things a man with everything looks for." She pressed the wrinkled flesh of her face against the bars until her lips protruded between them. "What is it about you that won his heart?"

Aoife fought the tremble of her lip. She did not like the way this old woman looked through her eyes and into her soul.

"There are some women who are better appreciated for traits that cannot be seen by the eye," Aoife replied.

The guard returned. As he neared, Ena lost interest in Aoife and grabbed the plate through a slit cut into the bars. Her greedy hands shook as though she feared he might try to steal it back and eat it himself.

"The drink, give me the drink!" she shouted.

He passed her the drink and she put the plate down on the grimy floor and huddled over it, shoving the sticky sludge into her mouth with her fingers. She used a piece of crust to slop up the remnants. She grabbed the cup and poured the water down her throat until drips rolled down her chin. Aoife suppressed the urge to look away in disgust. Ena put her plate and cup down and licked her fingers. She had one of them in her mouth when she remembered her company.

"So tell me how you came to be here," Aoife asked.

"Well, it's a rather boring story," she said and put her hands on her hips. "A might bit anti-climactic after all the years I spent casting spells, weaving webs, and thinking that the curse of my nighttime transformation into the hag you see now was the worst thing that could befall a girl." Her eyes drifted away for a moment. "I could talk for hours about the lusty men I've duped and the worrisome women I've made my living off of."

"Those are not the stories I seek," Aoife interrupted.

"That's right," the woman said, pulling herself reluctantly back to the present. "We'll save them for another day," she laughed. "We'll chat and laugh like a couple of washerwomen by the river. As to how I ended up here, a woman so enchanting that they had to lock me in a dungeon away from weak-kneed men, you can thank your predecessor. Once she found out about all the trouble I was causing across the countryside stealing away every man in sight like a shipwrecked siren on her lands, she decided I had to be contained. My beauty had to be hidden from the world because one look at me and your husband was mine, all mine."

She pressed her breasts up against the bars as if the sight of her body still held its power of persuasion and then flicked her eyes at the guard.

"This fellow here knows my powers," she raised her brows at him. "He can hardly keep his hands off me."

"That's not true," he shuddered and shook his

head. "I swear it! I never– "

Aoife put up a hand to stop him.

"I've no interest. Go back to the fire and let us be. What I am interested in is why this woman can't explain how she went from seductress to hag. I won't waste my time with an imposter."

The guard skulked off, probably relieved to be sent away. Aoife stepped back, waiting.

"It is embarrassing for a great woman like myself to admit it, but it was my own powers that did this to me, little Duchess," Ena said. "I never met anyone with powers as great as mine. But with that power came my nocturnal curse, a visage quite similar to the one you see before you. I thought I'd bartered it away when I used my power to shore up the Duchess' sorry excuse for a womb. My curse was supposed to evaporate and rain down on that infant I managed to help her bring into this world."

"So you passed your curse onto an innocent child?" Aoife said.

"Passed it on, maybe," she shrugged her shoulders. "Or brought forth the already tangled mess of limbs that nature knew couldn't and shouldn't have survived. I never was totally concerned with the details of the spell. But I should have been, since details are what I'd always used to lay my traps for others. I should have known better than to let myself fall prey to my own thorny details."

She squinted her eyes and her hands curled slowly into fists, empty shells of their long lost powers.

"Details seem to have ensnared both of us," Aoife said. "What detail has held you captive here?"

"The detail that cured one problem, left me with a few others," she laughed, more to herself than Aoife. "When I fortified that womb and sent out a spell to aid the survival of that measly, broken baby, I apparently sent with my protection ... *all* my magic. The tingle in my fingers and the spells that rose to my lips all dried up, faded and died the night I brought him into this world. Or as I came to learn much later, they drained from my fingers and seeped through his skin; he drank them up like a forsaken wanderer in the wilderness. I cast a spell to protect his broken body into this world, just like his mother asked, never realizing that it would take every drop of my powers to keep him alive."

She turned away from Aoife so only her profile was visible. Her chest sank and her fingertips came together as if she were reliving this story for the hundredth time. If she had not done such monstrous things, her defeated expression might have looked almost tragic. But her spell had sunk its fangs through the flesh of two generations, all the way to Aoife's daughter.

"So losing your powers made it easy for the late Duchess to lock you up in this cell," Aoife said. "But I had no idea these walls could steal away beauty as entirely as they could one's freedom."

"Now that, too," she raised up a calcified finger, "is where the details - not this prison - tricked me again. The old Duchess may have had her men find me out. Lord knows that was not difficult with my beauty and the men falling at my feet. And she managed to capture and imprison me, because my powers were lost to me, including the power that protected me from old age.

Within months of that child's birth I began to see the truth in every mirror. The tiny lines around my eyes. The slight droop under the chin. A wiry gray hair here and there. I knew within those first few months I was doomed. I had been tricked by my own spell, so I decided to live it up for as long as I could, making merry with every man I could find until all my beauty was lost. After the late Duchess had me locked up, she would come down here just to admire the rapid fading of my beauty."

Aoife imagined the late Duchess dressed in her finest gown with her hair neatly braided taking regular trips to this pit of hell for the sole purpose of driving the dagger deeper into Ena's back. It was not the men Ena was seducing that drove Ashling to imprison her. It was Ashling's need to keep the story of the boys' birth secret and, no doubt, a mother's revenge. She pictured the Duchess sipping wine from a golden goblet while denying even a proper blanket to Ena. Aoife wondered if she would have done the same if Ena had crippled her daughter. She could not deny the way her mother's instinct to protect her child was feeding a darkness in her that had been uncoiling inside her since she laid eyes on Ena. And if she could not get the little man's name from this tattered woman and save her daughter, just how far might the loss of her daughter push her?

"So are we to become friends as well," Ena chirped. "It's been so many years since I've had any visitors that I've actually come to miss that barren old hag."

"I'm not here to offer you friendship," Aoife turned back to Ena. "I'm here for the answer to a question. I have found out your story, and now I need only one detail to complete the picture."

"Damnable details," Ena said as she shook her head.

"The Duchess' true son – I need to know the name his mother gave him before she turned him over to her servant, Fiona."

She eyed Aoife over and licked her chapped lips.

"Why so interested in the name of that little wretch?" she narrowed her eyes and pried the lid on Aoife's soul. "Ah. You've met that twisted baby – who must be a man by now – and … "

Ena saw a thread of the story unfolding before her. She grinned and something dark leaked out of the gaps in her smile. She might have lost her magic, but Aoife could feel the power of Ena's devious mind.

"You lured the dwarf in with your pretty face. You made him think you loved him."

Aoife wrung her hands.

"You made him think you loved him and then you married his brother, the better looking, rich bastard who stole his life."

Ena grabbed the bars again and leaned her face close. She tilted her head to the side, searching Aoife's eyes. Aoife felt a fury trembling within her as Ena mocked her plight.

"You and I have quite a bit in common!" Ena laughed. "Hiding under your fancy dress, you've got a sultriness that men will do anything for. Oh, I remember when I had that same power! I knew there was something I liked about you. Your wits and wares served you well until you met that dwarf. You lured him in and bartered with him. But he got you with the details, didn't he? So tell me, why do you need the name? What's at stake?"

Her grizzly laughter shot a chill up Aoife's spine.

"You're in no position to make accusations or requests," Aoife said trying to sound unmoved by her words. "You either know the name or you don't."

"Oh how I miss the days of my youth when I bedded all those men in the evening only to roll over and kiss them with these cankered lips by moonlight," Ena said completely unmoved by Aoife's ultimatum. "The look on their faces was almost worth the curse. So tell me, did you bed the little man? Did you go that far? And just what did you say that spoiled the whole affair and sent him over the edge?"

"You know nothing of me or what's brought me into this story. I have found out everything I know without you," Aoife said, fighting to keep calm. "But what I need to know is the name the Duchess gave her one, true son."

Aoife stood before Ena, closer than she had dared yet. Only a few inches separated them. They held each other's gaze, but Ena finally blinked slowly and with patronizing thoughtfulness. She tapped her lip and stepped back from the bars.

"You know," Ena began, "it was a long time ago. I'd have to put some effort into thinking back that long. It might be easier to think if I had a warm bath and a soft robe."

"I think it might be easier for you to think with a hot iron bearing down over your shackled body," Aoife countered.

258

She reddened, shocked by her own threat. But she owned her words and the force behind them.

"Oh," Ena said with mock fright in her voice. "I'm so afraid." She dropped her hands to her sides and her expression sizzled with hatred. "You are a cold one."

"Tell me what I want or the guard will get it out of you," Aoife shouted.

"Then let the fun begin." Ena doubled over with laughter and Aoife backed away, terrified of what must follow. Aoife could not back down from her threat. How had she been so stupid and arrogant to have thought that she could battle with the wits of Ena?

She had always felt like a pawn in everyone else's game. She used to be the punch line in her father's jokes. Her mother's personal pincushion. Then a trinket won over a hand of cards. The damsel in distress rescued by a magical man. Her powerlessness was humiliating and by itself would have been enough to crush her spirit. But the dark, angry thoughts of revenge that had been slowly unfurling inside her fed on her humiliation and powerlessness and grew exponentially as Ena laughed. Her maternal vengeance devoured everything else inside her.

"Lay her out on the rack and shackle her down!" Aoife shouted to the guard, her eyes never leaving Ena. "Poke her. Prod her. Use whatever means necessary to get what I need."

Ena continued her torrent of laughter, without betraying an ounce of fear or hesitation.

Had Aoife really called for the torture of another human being? The cord that her mother whipped her with paled in comparison to the tools of torture the guard was probably laying out. She could stop it with a word, a command uttered away from this woman and into the ear of the guard as Aoife departed the dungeon. She felt the throb of her hands, as if the stain of Ena's blood was already there. Aoife turned and stormed down the dark hallway, trying to shake the guilt creeping over her skin.

"Don't you have the courage to do the dirty work yourself?" Ena shouted. "Or are you only good at the dirty work in bed! Sisters is what we are, sweet Duchess!"

Every word and every ounce of laughter tore through Aoife until she thought she would dissolve into a scream. She reached the main chamber where the guard was making preparations. On the long table where he had gobbled up mead and meat from dirty cups and plates, now lay chains and shackles. They had unfolded like mythical tentacles from their hiding place beneath the meal table.

She could stop the torture and save her soul before she became more monstrous than any of the people who had ever harmed her. Just then she felt the swell of her breasts, her body reminding her that somewhere upstairs her daughter was hungry. Their connection was little more than a day away from being severed because of this woman, a woman who deserved no mercy.

She stepped close to the guard who stood suddenly alert, waiting for the next order. The 'R' in Ashling's design must have been for Ronan. The 'S's' had to be for the little man and Stanishire. She swallowed and then rose up on her toes as she leaned into his ear.

"The woman, Ena," Aoife whispered. She

hesitated and he flushed under her breath. "I need a boy's name from her that begins with an S. You are not to tell her of this hint. Nor are you to fail to employ whatever means necessary to rip this name out of her."

Chapter 29
A Mother's Love

Aoife paced her room, holding her daughter close. She was not sure she would ever forget the sight of Ena laid out on a slab, manacled from head to foot. Ena had told the guard she was prepared to die with the name locked in her soul unless Aoife returned to the dungeon. Aoife had barely been able to look at Ena's body, the trail of burn marks on her skin a map of human degradation. Whenever Aoife had entered Maeve's, she always used the kitchen entrance, managing to walk the edges of the darkness without ever stepping into it. Looking upon Ena, Aoife feared she had become as dark and evil as the Duchess, Ena, and the little man.

She shook her head at the memory and pressed the list of names in her pocket, the ones she had ready just in case Ena's confession proved as deceitful as every other deal she had made. She kissed her daughter's head, praying Ena had spoken the truth. The letters matched, but Aoife was too frightened to hope.

Just as the corners of the room fell into liquid darkness, she felt the air whisper past her ear and the little man appeared in the shadows. He stepped out with his hands behind his back. His eyes darted between the ground and Aoife. His gaze was distant and almost sad.

"You look tired, Aoife," he said. "You look like you've lost something."

"Don't taunt me with your threats," Aoife hissed.

He walked a few steps closer and then looked into her eyes as if he knew the truth of all she'd done to Ena.

"What lengths would you go to in order to keep your daughter?"

"I'll do whatever it takes," Aoife said.

"I see," he said, looking a little afraid of her.

Having Ena and now the little man look at her like she was the villain was terrifying. Things had turned completely upside down.

"The lengths I have gone to today have given me three possible names."

"Oh, so you're not sure then," he looked at her out of the corner of his eye. "You need all three guesses, not just one."

He put his hands behind his back and nodded for her to begin. She pulled the paper out of her pocket.

"Seireadan."

He looked about him and waited for some sign from the ring or the air around them, but nothing happened.

"My name now starts with an S? I guess my initials were not the ones stitched right over my loving mother's heart?"

"It was a simple matter of misreading the letters," Aoife said with irritation. "You can thank my mother for clarifying my mistake."

"I'll be sure to thank her the next time we meet."

"Shey."

Nothing happened.

"Just one more guess," he said and stepped closer.

Aoife closed her eyes and prayed with all her might that before Ena took her last breath, crucified on the piece of wood where Aoife put her, she had done one thing to right this situation – even if only to save her own soul.

She opened her eyes and whispered, "Seafra."

His eyebrows lifted and he tipped backwards waiting for something, any sign that she had got it right. But her ring did not glow. The skies did not rain down. Nothing. Nothing happened. His head slumped along with his shoulders and Aoife shook her head. She knew it. She should never have told the guard the initial. Ena had probably tricked him into giving up the hint, and she had used her last moments on this earth to do what she had done her entire life – trick people. Aoife would never know if Ena truly knew the name. And now there was no one else from those long ago days to turn to.

Aoife walked to the window hugging her child. She had failed. Again. She was so absorbed in her worries she did not notice the quiet that permeated the room. There were no jokes or revelry in her failure.

"So was it worth it?" he asked.

"Was what worth it?"

"The lengths you went to."

His omnipresence meant he could be anywhere

and everywhere, including the dungeon where she found Ena. Aoife turned and saw in his gaze everything she had done to Ena reflected back at her.

"You've gone so far to keep your child, further, perhaps, than even I might have gone."

She burst into tears. He knew everything. Had she really become more evil than he was?

"You have changed since I sent you on this quest," he said. "Do I frighten you so much so that you would risk becoming a part of the evil that you have miraculously avoided all these years? Is that the effect I have had upon you?"

"This is not about whether I am good or evil," she replied. "This is about a mother's love, and I confess I have yet to find out how far a mother will go to protect her child."

"I suppose that is the very question that started all of this," he said. "Where it will end is as unknown to me as it is to you. I hope you are ready to live with the aftermath of the choices you are making."

"And is that not terribly hypocritical!" Aoife nearly shouted.

"I am who I am and always have been," he replied. "I know who you were, but the question now is who are you becoming."

"What are you – "

"You found her," he stammered. "You found the very woman who brought me into this world, and you have discovered many details of my story that I never knew until now. All these years she has lived right here beneath our feet and in our midst and I, despite all my power – the power that I now know came from her, never knew of her presence, never sensed it. I never thought to sink beneath the earth for answers. Without a magic wand, you've put so many pieces together in so few days. You've brought me closer to who I am than ever before. But perhaps bringing me closer to who I am is taking you too far away from who you are."

"Then let's end this tonight," Aoife pleaded. "Let go of this quest and you can learn to exist in my daughter's life as her uncle."

"No," he shook his head. "You've brought me too close to stop now. By this time tomorrow I will have secured a place in this world, either as your daughter's father, or as a son whose mother cared enough to name him."

"Please, no," Aoife cried. "Please don't do this to me. I don't know how to solve this mystery!"

"You may be right," he said as he stepped backward into the shadows. "But if there is anyone who can solve this, it is the audacious, fearless, Aoife."

He backed away into the darkness and dissolved before Aoife could argue any further. She sat down on her bed and looked out at the white glow of the moon. Her ruthlessness had done her no good. But what was she to try next?

Chapter 30: Day 3

All Along

Out of ideas, Aoife had returned to Ashling's room and turned over tables, chairs, and even ripped open the mattress with a dagger searching for any clue, but there was nothing. Dozens of letters about the weather, Ronan, the late Duke, and instructions for a seamstress were strewn about the floor where Aoife had tossed them during her search. They gave up their shallow secrets without a fight, their waxy seals broken long ago, but not one of them confessed anything helpful. The noontime sun was threatening, but Aoife was no closer to discovering the little man's name. Weak, tired and wishing she could just hold her daughter instead of nestling her away in the corner of this room in the bassinet, she tossed another letter upon the ground and began to cry.

"For heaven's sake, what is going on here?"

Aoife gasped at the sight of Ronan in the doorway. She looked at the destruction around her and tried to start a sentence, but did not know where to begin. Instead, she stepped over the pile of letters, sheets, overturned tables and chairs, and threw her arms around him.

"What's wrong?" his voice was confused, but full of suspicion. "What's driven you to tear my mother's chamber apart?"

"The truth," the words tumbled out.

With only hours left to save their daughter, she could no longer afford to protect him from the truth that Fiona, not Ashling, was his mother. She needed help, and her husband might be the only one still living who knew the Duchess well enough to find her darkest secret.

"The truth about you, your mother, Fiona, the little —"

"What are you talking about?" he interrupted.

He stepped back as Aoife stepped toward him. It was a horrible way for Ronan to find out, but with so little time left, Aoife did not have the luxury of moving slowly.

"You remember when you told me about how you were determined to show our child a kind of love you never felt from your mother?" He flinched. "There's a reason you always felt distance between you. There's a reason she had difficulty being close to you – and it's not your fault. The Duchess, the woman you have known as your mother, is not –"

"Aoife," he shouted.

He yelled at her as though she was an insolent

child. She shuddered, and he seemed equally surprised by his outburst. He collected himself a bit and placed his hands on her shoulders.

"You've just had a baby under the most frightening of circumstances, and you're living with the terror that she will be taken from us. The strain has clearly been too much, and I want you to let me take care of this while you go back to your room to rest."

"No! I won't! I can't!" she called out, regretting the hurt she was about to inflict upon him. "And you have to hear what I'm telling you! Fiona is – "

"Stop it!" he shouted and covered his ears. "I won't listen to your crazy ideas!"

She grabbed his hands and tried to pry them from his ears as she shouted that Fiona was his mother. He yelled over her that she was crazy and tried to drown out her words until he finally broke free and shouted, "I know!"

"What?" Aoife looked at him, astonished.

"The day she died," he began, "the day I saw my mother hugging and holding him on her deathbed, I knew. I finally knew why she never held me close. I was ten, but I understood all at once why I always felt less loved than I should have as her first and only son – because I was neither her first nor her only son. Her ring, the one she tried to give to him, proved it."

Aoife ran her fingers through his hair and he wrapped his arms around her waist.

"I knew that day that he was hers. We were the same age, meaning that at best he was the forgotten twin and at worst I was an imposter. Something in me knew the answer, but I wasn't prepared for all that it meant. It wasn't until the nightmares came and Fiona started to sleep in my chamber and comfort me that I began to understand who my real mother was."

He looked out the window. Aoife ran her fingers through his hair again.

"The way Fiona looked at me," he said. "The way she hugged me. There was a tenderness and a love for me I had never known from the woman I called my mother. I saw the way my father looked at her and how she avoided him. It should have pushed me over the edge, but I was only a boy, and I had found a mother to love me – my mother. So I hugged her back with all my might knowing the truth, the truth that could never be spoken out loud."

"And you never said anything to Fiona?"

"To speak the truth would have made it real. It would have changed everything about my life as I knew it."

Aoife wrapped her arms around him tighter. She finally saw him completely.

"I'm so sorry I've done this to you, Aoife. Now that you know all about the worst parts of me – the lies and betrayals that created me – what will you do? Will you leave me? Will you ever look at me with love in your eyes again?"

"I've looked into enough hearts to know that darkness resides inside us all, even me," she answered as she stroked his cheek. She could admit the truth, but not all the details. "If you could look past my affinity for drunkards and prostitutes and all else that I'm capable of and see beauty in my heart, I think I can look past the lies of your mothers that brought you to me. But now, I need your help."

He looked around the room at the mess Aoife had made of his mother's belongings. She showed him the embroidery and the ruby and explained her mother's insight and the priest's unspoken complicity. She left out her meeting with Ena.

"And I thought I was the secretive one," he laughed. "I guess I really have met my match."

Their daughter's sudden cry interrupted her story and they both turned toward the basinet. Ronan scooped her up in his arms where she looked so tiny and fragile. Aoife stood at his elbow as he soothed her cries. He leaned close and hummed a gentle tune in her ear. She squawked a few more times, but then began to calm under the spell of his gentle voice.

Suddenly, Aoife's ring began to warm. She lifted it in front of her and it began to glow like it had the day before. Ronan continued to hum, unaware of the ring's reaction. Its grip loosened ever so slightly and her hands trembled. He nuzzled close to their daughter, gazing at her as she returned to the blissful dreams he had lost long ago. As the lullaby ebbed and faded, so too did the glow and vibrations of the ring. Aoife grabbed it and tried to pry it off, and although it was looser, it would not come off her finger.

"That melody," she said as she grabbed Ronan. "What is it?"

"The one I was humming?" he replied. "I don't know, I was just – "

"It was something your mother sang to you when you were little?"

"Well no, not exactly. Why are you panicking

over a – "

"Sing it!"

"I can't... I mean it doesn't have any words it's just something my mother used to hum whenever she was lost in thought."

"Well then hum it!"

He frowned, but hummed while he rocked their daughter. Aoife held her hand out in front of her, watching the ring. When it began to glow and vibrate once again and he realized his song was causing it, he hummed louder until there was no more tune left.

"Try to remember the words, any of them. This has to be the lullaby she sang to him, the one that has his name in it!"

He hummed a few more notes and then broke off.

"She hummed this melody constantly, but she never sung any words."

They both looked down at the ring, whose glow faded away along with the hours of the day.

Chapter 31
Out of Time

The morning fog had long since lifted, but a murky sense of dread still hovered over Aoife's family. They needed someone who knew more about the ways guilty people hid their secrets. They needed Maeve. And so, grabbing the Duchess' cape and the baby, Aoife and Ronan had rushed to Maeve's kitchen, where she listened and nodded as Aoife explained the entire story up until their present danger. Maeve leaned back from the table and rubbed her temples.

"I thought there was little left that could shock me," Maeve finally said. "But I'm not sure what you think I can do. I'm a purveyor of vice, not a magician or a miracle worker. I doubt I could change this little man's mind even with my best girls."

"No, but you know about people and the secrets they keep," Aoife said. "Please help us think of where else to look or who else to turn to," she looked down at her daughter. "Please, please don't let me lose her."

"And you can't outrun him or hide the child away?"

"No," Aoife shook her head. "His powers are too strong and his presence is everywhere. I think he would destroy us all before he would let us keep her from him."

Aoife looked at Maeve with desperation. Maeve rose to her feet and paced the room with her arms folded. She asked Ronan to hum the lullaby for her. He looked from Maeve to Aoife, feeling a bit embarrassed and then leaned over the baby and hummed. The ring trembled and glowed and Aoife held it up for them to see. Maeve stopped pacing and leaned in closer, watching as the glow faded along with the last notes of the melody.

"I've never witnessed such magic or sorcery," Maeve said.

She shook her head and pulled her shawl tighter around her shoulders, her fingers toying with the fringe while her mind sifted through the facts.

"Most secrets of this magnitude refuse to stay completely hidden in the heart. The embroidery on the cape you're wearing and every gown of hers is proof of that. No, this woman made the truth a part of her everyday life. I think it's likely she expressed the whole truth to someone or in someway. If we could discover either that person with a hidden relationship to her, or the canvas upon which she whispered her secret, then we'd have a chance – "

"That's it!" Aoife's eyes sparkled with revelation.

***

The journey by carriage to the little man's cottage was a long one. Ronan had ordered a crew of men to travel ahead of them to where the road became impassible by carriage and cut a path. Otherwise, Aoife could never have ridden by horse the final miles.

The little man was born there, named there, and spent the only days he knew as his mother's son there. Ena had deserted the cottage when she believed her curse had been lifted right after the babies were born. Aoife believed a trace of his name had to be there somewhere. Aoife rubbed her head as the sun began to fall, wondering if it was really possible that the little man had missed the truth. But there was nowhere else to search. She looked to the skies trying to discern the sun's hiding place behind the thickening clouds.

"Don't worry," Ronan said. "We've hours until sundown."

When they rounded a curve, the path ended abruptly at the meadow surrounding the cottage. Aoife recognized the picturesque cottage with the steep pitched roof, bright flowers, and the spiral of the smoke stretching up to the sky.

Ronan stepped out of the coach and helped Aoife and the baby out. Her feet met the ground gently and he guided her over to a fallen log. Ronan took the baby while she rested her arm around his shoulder and watched their daughter stretch her fists to the sky. Her back was aching and her body weak, begging to return to bed where a woman who just had a baby should have been. But if she did not solve this riddle in the next hour or so, she would lose her daughter and never find any rest again.

She took their daughter to feed her. She and Ronan sat with their heads tipped together, watching the sleepy lull of her eyes as she nursed. The threat ahead slipped away when her little hand reached up to touch her mother's skin. Fiona said her final moment with the Duchess at the edge of the woods, the exact place where Aoife and her family now sat, was the last time she ever saw the Duchess happy. Aoife felt her daughter's heart beating against her, and her own heart pounded as Aoife wondered if this might be her last moment of happiness, too.

Her fear was growing and threatening to paralyze her, but she could not let that happen. She adjusted her dress and rose, embracing the anger rising within her. She knew this emotion and how to control it and use it. Unlike the former Duchess, she would not cross this threshold unsuspecting and ill prepared. She was ready to face the little man.

"You will remain here with the carriage," Aoife said decisively as she slipped the baby back into the sling that held her close to Aoife's body.

This could not look like an ambush and she could not risk Ronan angering the little man. He opened his mouth to argue, but she put up a hand that was final. If he truly believed in her, then it was his turn to step back.

The wind howled and the long grass shivered as it rose and fell with the storm threatening overhead. Thick droplets of rain began to pummel the bright flowers along the path to the cottage. Aoife kissed her daughter's head and pulled the cloak around their bodies. She embraced Ronan one last time before walking with her daughter down the stony path to the cottage, her cape rippling behind her.

She pounded on the front door, any shred of reticence voided by the storm overhead that had started pouring down. There was no answer, so Aoife pounded again and again. She looked through the large window next to his easel and saw the fire sputtering, but no one in the cottage. She opened the door and ran in, slamming the door on the rain behind her. She straightened up and walked slowly into the middle of the room, letting her eyes adjust to the darkness.

The gems and crystals hanging from the ceiling with all the images and experiences encased in them, tinkled softly and scattered their light as the wind eked weakly through unseen cracks in the house. She remembered how he had begged her to stay and witness their sparkle in the sunrise. Aoife lit a candle by the fireside and then several more around the cottage, illuminating many of the paintings around the room. A smaller one near his bed caught her attention. In her last visit here she had known nothing of the secrets of his birth and had not appreciated the loss that must have filled every stroke of the brush as he painted the mother peering over her child's cradle. The corners of her mouth tipped up in a gentle smile, and Aoife could almost hear the lullaby on her lips. The child in this painting was fat and round with hands outstretched. Was he rewriting the story of his birth with every stroke?

Aoife's daughter whimpered. She went to the chair beside the fire and draped her wet cape over the side and dropped the satchel with her infant's things. She sat down and slipped the baby out of the sling, relieved that it was not a soiled diaper or food that had awakened her. Aoife nuzzled and kissed her face. At the foot of the chair was a cradle, ornately carved and painted with whimsical flowers and fairies. She recoiled from the sight of it with blankets folded inside and ready to receive her child.

Just beyond it on a table sat an oversized hourglass with dark red sand slipping away inside. Soon the little man would be here, extending his gnarly hands to take her child. By her best guess, she had perhaps an hour left, maybe only a half.

With the baby in her arms, she knew she would have a hard time tearing this place apart the way she had done in the Duchess' room. Fighting her fears, she placed the child in the cradle and kissed her nose, vowing that this would be the only time she would ever lay there. She turned and tried to decide where to look first.

She started with the drawers and the small, carved boxes beside his bed, searching for mementos of the Duchess, things she might have left behind when he was born or that he might have lifted from her room after her death. There were extra stockings, breeches and shirts and even a dog-eared book of poetry, but nothing resembling anything from his mother. She turned over chairs, poured out the insides of the cupboard and sifted through drawers to no avail. The cottage was small and his belongings scarce, so within far fewer minutes than she had spent in the Duchess' room, Aoife had exhausted all of her options.

She turned back to her daughter who squeaked by the fire and felt the weight of her own failure in her empty arms. She walked over and was soothing her when she noticed a golden box glimmering in the firelight on a table near the hearth. How had she missed it? Aoife snatched it up and opened the top, revealing the jeweled rattle he had waved above her daughter on the day of her birth. She lifted it out of the box and listened to the clatter of jeweled strands. It was heavy and she tried to imagine the little man's toddler hands gripping the evidence of his stolen legacy and swinging it through the air. She turned it over several times. She noticed something was missing just as a crack of thunder rattled the windows.

"So you've delivered her right to me," the little man announced. He stood silhouetted by the window. "It was so thoughtful of you to save me the trip."

He looked at the disarray of his home and the rattle in her hand.

"It looks to me like your mother forgot to teach you manners," he continued. "And I must say I'm not too happy with the way you've rummaged through my things while I was out."

His shoes clipped across the floor with deliberate control until he reached her side. His irritation grew into anger, despite Aoife's stammered apologies. He snatched the rattle from Aoife, frightening her with his gruffness. His hair stood up, electrified by the storm, and his eyes bulged as if their stare was powerful enough to turn anything in their path to stone.

"I've found something of yours," she whispered, finding the strength to speak.

"I can see that," he said.

"I mean I've found something you've lost."

He turned and looked at her, a sliver of hope

shining behind his terrifying grimace. She pulled the heart shaped ruby out of her pocket and unrolled her fingers. He peered down at the ruby, a deep red against her palm. He squinted at it and laughed, rattling the house to the rafters with the dark reverberations emanating from his soul.

"You showed me this two nights ago and there's no proof that this stone or the emblem had anything to do with me!"

Aoife shook her head and took his hand in hers. She lifted up his hand with the rattle and turned it a notch. Then she raised her other hand and moved the ruby ever closer to the place on the handle where the broken pattern in the rainbow of gems revealed the ruby's long lost home. The ring on Aoife's finger began to glow with a cool, blue light, and the gems on the rattle glinted with a mysterious sparkle. But just before the ruby made contact, the little man yanked the rattle away.

"Why are you fighting the truth?" Aoife asked. "The stone, the initials, and their place over her heart," she implored. "You are smart enough to know why she would have bothered to sew this into every gown, slip and cape she owned."

"That stone doesn't represent her love for me," he shouted. "It represents her heart of stone that allowed her to leave me in the hands of a promiscuous wench! And there is nothing you or anyone can show me to prove otherwise!"

"So you gave me this quest to find your name and prove your mother's love for you, all the while believing it didn't exist? It doesn't matter what proof of her love I offer since you refuse to see it!"

"I don't refuse to see it. It's simply not there! She didn't even name me!"

"None of this matters," Aoife reminded him. "According to your deal, if I produce your name, then your mother's love will have been proven, and I will keep my daughter. That is what you said!"

"Then go ahead," he shouted. He turned and grabbed the timekeeper and pointed to the few remaining granules of sand. "I'll keep to my end of the bargain if you keep yours!"

He laughed and threw his head back like he was possessed by something darker than the hurt inside him.

Aoife picked up her daughter, who had started to cry. Lightning flashed through the room and the thunder roared quickly on its heels. She shuddered and something dropped from her hand to the floor. It was one of the blankets the little man had put in the cradle and that she must have accidentally grabbed when she lifted her daughter. It was faded blue and speckled with the stains of toddler hands and time.

"Give me that," he shouted.

Aoife turned toward the light. Clearly emblazoned across the center was the emblem with his letters RSS. She turned to him, astonished.

"This is from your mother," she exclaimed. "She must have embroidered this for you in the days before she left here."

"The few short days before she traded me in," he shouted. "I assumed the blanket came from Fiona until the day I held my real mother's dying body in my arms and then saw the design from my blanket as large as possible across her bedspread."

"Then you had to know how much she cared for you."

"I didn't know there were letters hidden in the design or that they were for me until you – "

The sentence refused to come to an end, the implications too big.

"But you surely understand now after all I've shown you from her dresses to the ruby that she loved you. Fiona's story about her naming you must be true."

"I know nothing of the sort," he shot back. "What I do know is that in just a few minutes I will take something from my brother, something as important to him as my real mother once was to me. I will have the chance to love someone who will always love me back!"

Aoife cursed the Duchess, and her damn emblem. The least she could have done was left more than a few letters behind.

"Time's almost up!" he cackled and danced around the hourglass. He began to hum the lullaby in a cheery voice. "You may know the tune, and think you know the truth, but you will never find the name that was never mine!"

She ignored him and slipped her daughter into the sling. Her fingers and eyes roamed over the stitching. Lightning lit up the room as bright as noontime and the thunder cracked right above them again. The blanket shook in her quaking hands, but her eyes were locked on the detailed stitching. And then Aoife saw it. A stitch at odds with the design. The color, the angle, the size, none of it matched the emblem Aoife had been studying for days. She pulled the fabric closer and spotted another stray stitch several inches away, and then another. What were these red stitches doing here? She thought back to her mother's lessons and tried to determine what kind of a stitch they were when she realized they were the backside of a stitch. The backside meant that there was another side, another pattern!

She turned over the blanket but there was nothing there, not a single thread. She froze for a moment, terrified by the trickle of sand. Then she felt the two pieces of fabric sewn together to make the blanket. She grabbed the satin trim that bound the two pieces together and ripped. The baby began to whimper from the tossling, but Aoife had no time to soothe her fears.

The little man screamed out a chain of curses and insults and tried to reclaim the blanket. Aoife pushed him away and ripped the other sides of the blanket open until she saw it, right there in front of her eyes. It was a separate piece of fabric, upon which a rhyme or set of words had been embroidered and then secured to the blanket with a few anchor stitches.

"It's here! It's right here!" she cried out.

He could see the evidence over her shoulder. He covered his eyes with his hands and shook his head.

"No!" he shouted. "This can't be! She didn't love me!"

"But she did and here's the proof," Aoife shouted over the wind outside, which howled like an angry animal bearing down upon them.

She leaned closer to the firelight and began to read the words.

"Like a ruby buried at the bottom of a mine
Or mossy covered treasure on the ocean floor

My sweet child hides behind this veil of rumpled flesh
Your mommy had conjured for you."

"No!" he shouted.

The window beside his easel shattered; the broken glass showered into the cottage in tiny fragments that sparkled like diamonds in the lightning's halo. The curtains blew in with the wind. The baby cried out in its sling, and she held her closer as she shouted the truth aloud.

"Too still is your skin
Too shallow your breath
To ever sustain your little body and soul
Within a world as cold as this."

The words of the lullaby poured out the Duchess' secrets. The little man kept shaking his head and screaming into the wind, trying to sew his ears up against the truth. He stumbled away from Aoife and fell upon the floor, but she followed his steps.

"Too rumpled and too still is your skin.
Others won't mine deep enough to find
The magical sparkle of your ruby red heart."

Another window nearby popped and shattered. A shard as deadly as a dagger flew through the air and sliced Aoife's arm. She screamed and grabbed at her gaping flesh, almost dropping the blanket. The little man rose to his feet and seemed barely aware of Aoife's wound. He flung open the door and ran outside. Despite the pain of her arm, the howling storm, and the infant at her chest, Aoife followed after him. She paused in the doorway, his figure lost for a moment beyond the curtain of pelting rain. Aoife put up her hand and caught sight of him stumbling through the meadow.

She ran a few steps toward him, but froze when a lightning bolt struck nearby. Knowing that time was almost gone, she ran forward against her fears. When she reached him, he was lying on his back, shaking in a fit of delirium. She knelt over him and tried to bring him back to his senses so he could hear the rest of his mother's lullaby.

"But no matter how rumpled and still is your skin,
You'll always remain my flesh, my son – all mine."

His head dropped back on the ground and from his trembling body broke tears and lamentation more tragic and fearsome than the wind roaring around them. Lightning flashed again, and the thunder shook the earth. Aoife gripped his tunic and leaned in to be sure he heard her voice calling over the howl of wind.

"But no matter how rumpled and still is your skin,
You'll always remain my flesh, my son – all mine.
My rumpled, still-skinned son,
My dear Rumpelstiltskin."

He looked into Aoife's eyes, shaking his head back and forth. His hands rose slowly and he touched her face. They slipped down to the child clinging to Aoife and wrapped in his torn blanket, the proof he had carried with him all along that he was loved. He patted her head, her wails an echo of the long ago wails he had sent up after his mother deserted him.

"You were loved," Aoife whispered.

A bolt of lightning struck the other side of the meadow, and Aoife felt the hair on her scalp tingle from its nearness. In its wake, she could make out the shape of Ronan running across the field toward them.

"Come, Rumpelstiltskin," she shouted, pulling at his arm. His body seized at the sound of his name. "We have to get inside and out of the storm."

Unaffected by the danger all around them, he shook his head. Aoife pleaded again and yanked his arm. Ronan reached them and was shouting that they had to get out of the field.

"Rumpelstiltskin!"

He sat up and rubbed his head and eyes as if waking from a deep sleep. Another lightning bolt hit just as close and sent the ground shaking and her hair upright again. The storm was right over them. Aoife pulled Rumpelstiltskin's arm, but he remained immovable. Ronan's attempts were just as futile, and he finally turned to Aoife and yelled that they had to go for their daughter's sake. She could argue with him no longer and dropped Rumpelstiltskin's hand. She ran a few feet and stopped, pleading again for him to follow. The thunder rolled through the sky, and the child in her arms wailed until she could bear it no longer. She turned and ran toward the shelter of the cottage, her head tucked down against the rain.

As they stepped over the threshold of the cottage she turned and saw him standing in the middle of the field, his eyes turned up to the sky. His expression was unreadable, but his arms rose upward in slow motion.

She screamed through the storm, "Rumpelstiltskin!"

The syllables of his name had scarcely passed her lips when a bolt of lightning struck the spot where he stood, lighting up the entire world with its white-hot light. His body convulsed in one quick movement as it was enveloped by the light. For a second he appeared to shatter into a million pieces of sparkling light and then dissolve into the lightning. Ronan pulled Aoife and their wailing child closer as all their hearts pounded with the drumbeat of death.

Almost immediately, the rattling skies began to ebb as the storm moved away toward the distant mountains, signaling an abrupt end to its cosmic show. Aoife rushed to lay the baby in the cradle and then ran back out toward the place in the field where the grass still smoldered, with Ronan quick on her heels.

The grass of the clearing had flattened from the force of the lightning. But rather than having blown outward like a halo from the blast, it bowed inward, as if paying homage to the hole in the earth at the center. The smoking pit in the ground frothed like an angry caldron, hiding what lay beneath its cryptic surface. Aoife ran over the grass, the smell of smoke and ash filling her nose with dread. She reached the ruptured edge of the crater, coughing as she leaned over. Ronan took her hand, afraid it might suck her down below the surface.

"Rumpelstiltskin!" she called out, the last syllables nearly lost in her throat.

The smoke and ash swirled into long fingers and

then slithered out and evaporated into the sky above. Aoife stared into the abyss. She stepped forward and slid down the edge and into the empty cavity. Ronan shouted after her as he made his way down behind her. Mud stained her dress and streaked her cheek. Her hair still stood on end from the charged current lingering in the air.

She stepped slowly toward the place where the heavens had met the earth and swallowed up Rumpelstiltskin. But there was nothing left of his body. He had appeared for her so many times and displayed so many spectacular feats of magic, yet she knew instinctively that he would never reappear again. But she could feel his presence and his light beaming down from the stars above – beyond the dark cap of sky that separates us from all that lays above and beyond our knowing. Her guardian angel had spent his whole life searching for a place where he belonged. Only now that he had left this world had he finally found his home – in the stars twinkling above, perhaps where he was always intended to shine.

She placed her hands reverently at the center of the scorch mark and felt a heat growing and emanating from her ring. It pulsed faster and hotter than it ever had; she gritted her teeth against the burn. Ronan gripped her shoulder as he watched. The ring flashed with a light as white as lightning and the world was shadowless for the briefest moment. Then suddenly all was dark and still.

There was a small clanking sound as the ring slipped from Aoife's finger. It lay at the center of the scorch mark, a wisp of smoldering heat swirling up from the middle as it made its way back to heaven. Ronan picked the ring up and turned it over in his hand. It was dangerously hot, but the dark murky stone had transformed back into a light topaz color. Aoife took it and peered at it.

An engraving inside the ring caught her eye. She tipped it toward the starlight shining in between the receding clouds and saw the first of a long line of letters starting with the letter R. She rubbed the rest of the engraving. Having read the script inside the blanket, Aoife knew the name spelled out inside the ring that Ashling had worn everyday of her life, the ring she had tried to give Rumpelstiltskin the day she died, the ring stolen back by Ronan, the one magically sealed upon Aoife's hand for the past year. Sorrow washed over Aoife as Ronan took it, his hand tightening around the ring and the truth that he had stolen from his brother. The ring that spoke of their mother's twisted love for her rumpled, still-skinned child. The gift which, if given so many years ago as the Duchess intended, might have prevented the storm that had raged for more than a decade and caused so much destruction and death.

Aoife took the ring from Ronan and placed it back at the center of the crater. She felt inside her pocket and pulled out the ruby heart the Duchess carried with her. It gleamed in the moonlight. She laid it at the center of the ring, framing its beauty. Her hand rested upon them. For so much of her childhood she had craned her neck with her father looking at the stars in the sky, never realizing how close to earth some of them had fallen.

Her tears fell upon the soil as Ronan scooped some of it up in his hands and covered the ring and ruby in the closest thing to a burial he could offer his brother.

Aoife patted the soil and tucked it around these treasures, putting them to bed forever.

Chapter 32
Ever After

Aoife jumped from her sleep, jarred by the hollering from the cradle beside her. The two new teeth Emelyne was cutting tore to shreds any chance she or Aoife had of getting more than an hour's sleep for the past three nights. Aoife dipped her finger into the tonic the nurse had given her and reached over the side of the cradle and into Emelyne's mouth. She clamped down hard on Aoife's finger, and sucked at the sweet tonic. Aoife rested her head against her pillow and felt her eyes close, hoping it would not be long before Emelyne's did the same.

Within seconds, Aoife felt her daughter's body relax. She clutched Aoife's finger in one of her pudgy hands, and Aoife sighed, welcoming the sleep that overtook her exhausted body.

Had she the energy to open her eyes, Aoife might have noted the alertness in Emelyne's eyes as she

watched the flicker of the candle against the walls and
the curtained, velvet canopy above her cradle. She might
have wondered how the breeze was affecting the candle,
which had burned low inside the glass chimney around
it. She might have sung to Emelyne, seeking desperately
to lull her back to sleep. But as she was already lost in
her own dreams, Aoife neither saw nor felt the swish of
the breeze across her cheek that sent the tassels fringing
Emelyne's canopy fluttering above her head.

Aoife had drifted too far into her dream of the
misty waterfall and the rippling water that rocked her
safely to notice the gentle spiraling of air that tickled
Emelyne's nose and coaxed a smile out of her. In
quicker and tighter circles it whirled, throwing the
candle's glow around the room until in a flash of light
there appeared around the tall neck of the glass chimney
a string of clear, sparkling crystals. The candlelight
danced off the crystals in a dazzling display. Emelyne's
smile widened, relieving some of the pressure on Aoife's
finger. Another small breeze blew around the candle,
lifting the string of crystals ever so slightly above the
rim of the chimney and then sending them round and
round in a slow, hypnotic circle. The candlelight pierced
the crystals, reflecting light all around the room.

Had Aoife awakened, she might have seen the
kaleidoscope of crystal stars making their slow journey
across the ceiling and Emelyne's canopy. She might
have sensed the invisible hand of a guardian angel
lighting up the night for her daughter, showering her
with all the unharnessed, disembodied love he could
never have shared with her from the confines of his
twisted body. But Aoife slept on, dreaming dreams less

miraculous and less magnificent than the light and love of the universe that shines upon us and through us without fail, without end, forever and ever.

About Bonnie Marie Hennessy

Bonnie grew up a shy, quiet girl who the teachers always seated next to the noisy boys because they knew she was too afraid to talk to anyone. She always had a lot she wanted to say but was too afraid to share it for fear she might die of embarrassment if people actually noticed her. Somewhere along the line, perhaps after she surprised her eighth grade class by standing up to a teacher who was belittling a fellow student, she realized that she had a voice and she didn't burst into flames when her classmates stared at her in surprise. Not long after that, she began spinning tales, some of which got her into trouble with her mom. Whether persuading her father to take her to the candy store as a little girl or convincing her parents to let her move from Los Angeles to Manhattan to pursue a career at eighteen as a ballet dancer with only $200 in her pocket, Bonnie has had a lot of practice weaving good stories.

Now she spends her time reading and making up stories for her two children at night. By day she is an English teacher who never puts the quiet girls next to the noisy boys and works hard to persuade her students that stories, whether they are the ones she teaches in class or the ones she tells to keep them from daydreaming, are better escapes than computers, phones, and social media.

Connect with Me:

Thank you for following my imagination all the way until the last period! If you enjoyed it and would like others to give it a read, I would love for you to leave me a review at your favorite retailer.

Also, stay tuned for my forthcoming novel, inspired by a bedtime story I used to tell my daughter about a mysterious boy hidden away in a tower. When a girl discovers, the mystery of his banishment unfolds.

For more about *Twisted*, my upcoming book, and to register for updates and giveaways, visit my website

www.BonnieMHennessy.com

You can also friend me on Facebook
www.facebook.com/Twisted-The-Book

Follow me on Twitter @BonnieMHennessy

And Instagram @BonnieMHennessy

Acknowledgments

I would first like to acknowledge the love and patience of my husband, Jimmy, which made this entire endeavor possible. I also can't forget to thank him for all the laundry, dusting and mopping he did while I was playing with magic.

And what kind of a mother would I be if I didn't thank my children, who found many creative ways to entertain themselves while I wrote, although some of those ideas may have included more mud, leaves, and mysterious potions than I would have liked.

And to my daughter, to whom I reread the story of Rumpelstiltskin from my own childhood fairy tale book, thank you for begging me for one more story. That tiny paragraph was the seed that lead to all of this.

Along the way I have had assistance from the most honest, thorough, and patient editor, Heather Lazare, whose input is part of the reason my readers stayed with me until the end to read this page. Thank you, Heather!

Lastly, thank you to my cover designer, Andreea Vraciu, who created a hauntingly beautiful design that captured the strength of my heroine and gave her a face after all these years of writing about her.

Printed by Amazon Italia Logistica S.r.l.
Torrazza Piemonte (TO), Italy

13576726R00176